"THE TASK IS FINISHED"
—*Colonel Starbottle's Client*

"ARGONAUT EDITION" OF
THE WORKS OF BRET HARTE

COLONEL STARBOTTLE'S CLIENT

FLIP

FOUND AT BLAZING STAR

BY

BRET HARTE

ILLUSTRATED

P. F. COLLIER & SON
NEW YORK

*Published under special arrangement with
the Houghton Mifflin Company*

COPYRIGHT 1892
BY BRET HARTE

COPYRIGHT 1882
BY HOUGHTON, MIFFLIN & COMPANY
All rights reserved

CONTENTS.

	PAGE
COLONEL STARBOTTLE'S CLIENT	1
THE POSTMISTRESS OF LAUREL RUN	75
A NIGHT AT "HAYS"	108
JOHNSON'S "OLD WOMAN"	148
THE NEW ASSISTANT AT PINE CLEARING SCHOOL	175
IN A PIONEER RESTAURANT	215
A TREASURE OF THE GALLEON	243
OUT OF A PIONEER'S TRUNK	255
THE GHOSTS OF STUKELEY CASTLE	268

A—Bret Harte

COLONEL STARBOTTLE'S CLIENT.

CHAPTER I.

It may be remembered that it was the habit of that gallant "war-horse" of the Calaveras democracy, Colonel Starbottle, at the close of a political campaign, to return to his original profession of the Law. Perhaps it could not be called a peaceful retirement. The same fiery-tongued eloquence and full-breasted chivalry which had in turns thrilled and overawed freemen at the polls were no less fervid and embattled before a jury. Yet the Colonel was counsel for two or three pastoral Ditch companies and certain bucolic corporations, and although he managed to import into the simplest question of contract more or less abuse of opposing counsel, and occasionally mingled precedents of law with antecedents of his adversary, his legal victories were seldom complicated by bloodshed. He was only once shot at by a free-handed judge, and twice assaulted by an over-sensitive litigant. Nevertheless, it was thought merely prudent, while preparing the papers in the well known case of "The Arcadian Shepherds' Association of Tuolumne *versus* the Kedron Vine and Fig Tree Growers of Calaveras," that the Colonel should seek with a shotgun the seclusion of his partner's law office in the sylvan outskirts of Rough and Ready for that complete rest and serious preoccupation which Marysville could not afford.

It was an exceptionally hot day. The painted shingles of the plain wooden one-storied building in which the Colonel sat were warped and blistering in the direct rays of the fierce, untempered sun. The tin sign bearing the dazzling legend, "Starbottle and Bungstarter, Attorneys and Counselors," glowed with an insufferable light; the two pine-trees still left in the clearing around the house, ineffective as shade, seemed only to have absorbed the day-long heat through every scorched and crisp twig and fibre, to radiate it again with the pungent smell of a slowly smouldering fire; the air was motionless yet vibrating in the sunlight; on distant shallows the half-dried river was flashing and intolerable.

Seated in a wooden armchair before a table covered with books and papers, yet with that apparently haughty attitude towards it affected by gentlemen of abdominal fullness, Colonel Starbottle supported himself with one hand grasping the arm of his chair and the other vigorously plying a huge palm-leaf fan. He was perspiring freely. He had taken off his characteristic blue frock-coat, waistcoat, cravat, and collar, and, stripped only to his ruffled shirt and white drill trousers, presented the appearance from the opposite side of the table of having hastily risen to work in his nightgown. A glass with a thin sediment of sugar and lemon-peel remaining in it stood near his elbow. Suddenly a black shadow fell on the staring, uncarpeted hall. It was that of a stranger who had just entered from the noiseless dust of the deserted road. The Colonel cast a rapid glance at his sword-cane, which lay on the table.

But the stranger, although sallow and morose-looking, was evidently of pacific intent. He paused on the threshold in a kind of surly embarrassment.

"I reckon this is Colonel Starbottle," he said at last, glancing gloomily round him, as if the interview was not entirely of his own seeking. "Well, I've seen you often enough, though you don't know me. My name's Jo Corbin. I guess," he added, still discontentedly, "I have to consult you about something."

"Corbin?" repeated the Colonel in his jauntiest manner. "Ah! Any relation to old Maje Corbin of Nashville, sir?"

"No," said the stranger briefly. "I'm from Shelbyville."

"The Major," continued the Colonel, half closing his eyes as if to follow the Major into the dreamy past, "the old Major, sir, a matter of five or six years ago, was one of my most intimate political friends, — in fact, sir, my most intimate friend. Take a chyar!"

But the stranger had already taken one, and during the Colonel's reminiscence had leaned forward, with his eyes on the ground, discontentedly swinging his soft hat between his legs. "Did you know Tom Frisbee, of Yolo?" he asked abruptly.

"Er — no."

"Nor even heard anything about Frisbee, nor what happened to him?" continued the man, with aggrieved melancholy.

In point of fact the Colonel did not think that he had.

"Nor anything about his being killed over at Fresno?" said the stranger, with a desponding implication that the interview after all was a failure.

"If — er — if you could — er — give me a hint or two," suggested the Colonel blandly.

"There was n't much," said the stranger, "if you don't remember." He paused, then rising, he gloomily dragged his chair slowly beside the table, and taking up a paper-weight examined it with heavy dissatisfaction. "You see," he went on slowly, "I killed him — it was a quo'll. He was my pardner, but I reckon he must have drove me hard. Yes, sir," he added with aggrieved reflection, "I reckon he drove me hard."

The Colonel smiled courteously, slightly expanding his chest under the homicidal relation, as if, having taken it in and made it a part of himself, he was ready, if necessary, to become personally responsible for it. Then lifting his empty glass to the light, he looked at it with half closed eyes, in polite imitation of his companion's examination of the paper-weight, and set it down again. A casual spectator from the window might have imagined that the two were engaged in an amicable inventory of the furniture.

"And the — er — actual circumstances?" asked the Colonel.

"Oh, it was fair enough fight. *They'll* tell you that. And so would *he*, I reckon — if he could. He was ugly and bedev'lin', but I did n't care to quo'll, and give him the go-by all the time. He kept on, followed me out of the shanty, drew, and fired twice. I" — he stopped and regarded his hat a moment as if it was a corroborating witness — "I — I closed with him — I had to — it was my only chance, and that ended it — and with his own revolver. I never drew mine."

"I see," said the Colonel, nodding, "clearly justifiable and honorable as regards the code. And you wish me to defend you?"

The stranger's gloomy expression of astonishment now turned to blank hopelessness.

"I knew you did n't understand," he said, despairingly. "Why, all *that* was *two years ago*. It's all settled and done and gone. The jury found for me at the inquest. It ain't *that* I want to see you about. It's something arising out of it."

"Ah," said the Colonel, affably, " a vendetta, perhaps. Some friend or relation of his taken up the quarrel?"

The stranger looked abstractedly at Starbottle. "You think a relation might; or would feel in that sort of way?"

"Why, blank it all, sir," said the Colonel, "nothing is more common. Why, in '52 one of my oldest friends, Doctor Byrne, of St. Jo, the seventh in a line from old General Byrne, of St. Louis, was killed, sir, by Pinkey Riggs, seventh in a line from Senator Riggs, of Kentucky. Original cause, sir, something about a d—d roasting ear, or a blank persimmon in 1832; forty-seven men wiped out in twenty years. Fact, sir."

"It ain't that," said the stranger, moving hesitatingly in his chair. "If it was anything of that sort I wouldn't mind, — it might bring matters to a wind-up, and I shouldn't have to come here and have this cursed talk with you."

It was so evident that this frank and unaffected expression of some obscure disgust with his own present position had no other implication, that the Colonel did not except to it. Yet the man did not go on. He stopped and seemed lost in sombre contemplation of his hat.

The Colonel leaned back in his chair, fanned himself elegantly, wiped his forehead with a large pongee handkerchief, and looking at his companion, whose shadowed abstraction seemed to render him impervious to the heat, said: —

"My dear Mr. Corbin, I perfectly understand you. Blank it all, sir, the temperature in this infernal hole is quite enough to render any confidential conversation between gentlemen upon delicate matters utterly impossible. It's almost as near Hades, sir, as they make it, — as I trust you and I, Mr. Corbin, will ever experience. I propose," continued the Colonel, with airy geniality, "some light change and refreshment. The bar-keeper of the Magnolia is — er — I may say, sir, *facile princeps* in the concoction of mint juleps, and there is a back room where I have occasionally conferred with political leaders at election time. It is but a step, sir — in fact, on Main Street — round the corner."

The stranger looked up and then rose mechanically as the Colonel resumed his coat and waistcoat, but not his collar and cravat, which lay limp and dejected among his papers. Then, sheltering himself beneath a large-brimmed Panama hat, and hooking his cane on his arm, he led the way, fan in hand, into the road, tiptoeing in his tight, polished boots through the red, impalpable dust with his usual jaunty manner, yet not without a profane suggestion of burning ploughshares. The stranger strode in silence by his side in the burning sun, impenetrable in his own morose shadow.

But the Magnolia was fragrant, like its namesake, with mint and herbal odors, cool with sprinkled floors, and sparkling with broken ice on its counters, like dewdrops on white, unfolded petals — and slightly soporific with the subdued murmur of droning loungers, who were heavy with its sweets. The gallant Colonel nodded with confidential affability to the spotless-shirted bar-keeper, and then taking Corbin by the arm fraternally conducted him into a small apartment in the rear of the bar-room. It was evidently used as the office of the proprietor, and contained a plain desk, table, and chairs. At the rear window, Nature, not entirely evicted, looked in with a few straggling buckeyes and a dusty myrtle, over the body of a lately-felled pine-tree, that flaunted from an upflung branch a still green spray as if it were a drooping banner lifted by a dead but rigid arm. From the adjoining room the faint, monotonous click of billiard balls, languidly played, came at intervals like the dry notes of cicale in the bushes.

The bar-keeper brought two glasses crowned with mint and diademed with broken ice. The Colonel took a long pull at his portion, and leaned back in his chair with a bland gulp of satisfaction and dreamily patient eyes. The stranger mechanically sipped the contents of his glass, and then, without having altered his reluctant expression, drew from his breast-pocket a number of old letters. Holding them displayed in his fingers like a difficult hand of cards, and with something of the air of a dispirited player, he began: —

"You see, about six months after this yer trouble I got this letter." He picked out a well worn, badly written missive, and put it into Colonel Starbottle's hands, rising at the same time and leaning over him as he read. "You see, she that writ it says as how she had n't heard from her son for a long time, but owing to his having spoken once about *me*, she was emboldened to write and ask me if I knew what had gone of him." He was pointing his finger at each line of the letter as he read it, or rather seemed to translate it from memory with a sad familiarity. "Now," he continued in parenthesis, "you see this kind o' got me. I knew he had got relatives in Kentucky. I knew that all this trouble had been put in the paper with his name and mine, but this here name of Martha Jeffcourt at the bottom did n't seem to jibe with it. Then I remembered that he had left a lot of letters in his trunk in the shanty, and I looked 'em over. And I found that his name *was* Tom Jeffcourt, and that he 'd been passin' under the name of Frisbee all this time."

"Perfectly natural and a frequent occurrence," interposed the Colonel cheerfully. "Only last year I met an old friend whom we 'll call Stidger, of New Orleans, at the Union Club, 'Frisco. 'How are you, Stidger?' I said; 'I have n't seen you since we used to meet — driving over the Shell Road in '53.' 'Excuse me, sir,' said he, 'my name is not Stidger, it 's Brown.' I looked him in the eye, sir, and saw him quiver.

'Then I must apologize to Stidger,' I said,
'for supposing him capable of changing his
name.' He came to me an hour after, all
in a tremble. 'For God's sake, Star,' he
said, — always called me Star, — 'don't go
back on me, but you know family affairs —
another woman, beautiful creature,' etc.,
etc., — yes, sir, perfectly common, but a
blank mistake. When a man once funks
his own name he'll turn tail on anything.
Sorry for this man, Friezecoat, or Turncoat,
or whatever's his d—d name; but it's so."

The suggestion did not, however, seem to
raise the stranger's spirits or alter his manner. "His name was Jeffcourt, and this
here was his mother," he went on drearily;
"and you see here she says" — pointing to the
letter again — "she's been expecting money
from him and it don't come, and she's
mighty hard up. And that gave me an
idea. I don't know," he went on, regarding
the Colonel with gloomy doubt, "as you'll
think it was much; I don't know as you
wouldn't call it a d—d fool idea, but I got
it all the same." He stopped, hesitated,
and went on. "You see this man, Frisbee
or Jeffcourt, was my pardner. We were
good friends up to the killing, and then he

drove me hard. I think I told you he drove me hard, — did n't I? Well, he did. But the idea I got was this. Considerin' I killed him after all, and so to speak disappointed them, I reckoned I'd take upon myself the care of that family and send 'em money every month."

The Colonel slightly straitened his clean-shaven mouth. "A kind of expiation or amercement by fine, known to the Mosaic, Roman, and old English law. Gad, sir, the Jews might have made you *marry* his widow or sister. An old custom, and I think superseded — sir, properly superseded — by the alternative of ordeal by battle in the mediæval times. I don't myself fancy these pecuniary fashions of settling wrongs, — but go on."

"I wrote her," continued Corbin, "that her son was dead, but that he and me had some interests together in a claim, and that I was very glad to know where to send her what would be his share every month. I thought it no use to tell her I killed him, — may be she might refuse to take it. I sent her a hundred dollars every month since. Sometimes it's been pretty hard sleddin' to do it, for I ain't rich; sometimes

I've had to borrow the money, but I reckoned that I was only paying for my share in this here business of his bein' dead, and I did it."

"And I understand you that this Jeffcourt really had no interest in your claim?"

Corbin looked at him in dull astonishment. "Not a cent, of course; I thought I told you that. But that weren't his fault, for he never had anything, and owed me money. In fact," he added gloomily, "it was because I hadn't any more to give him — havin' sold my watch for grub — that he quo'lled with me that day, and up and called me a 'sneakin' Yankee hound.' I told you he drove me hard."

The Colonel coughed slightly and resumed his jaunty manner. "And the — er — mother was, of course, grateful and satisfied?"

"Well, no, — not exactly." He stopped again and took up his letters once more, sorted and arranged them as if to play out his unfinished but hopeless hand, and drawing out another, laid it before the Colonel. "You see, this Mrs. Jeffcourt, after a time, reckoned she ought to have *more* money than I sent her, and wrote saying that she had always understood from her son (he that never wrote but once a year, remember) that this claim of ours (that she never knew of, you know) was paying much more than I sent her — and she wanted a return of accounts and papers, or she'd write to some lawyer, mighty quick. Well, I reckoned that all this was naturally in the line of my trouble, and I *did* manage to scrape together fifty dollars more for two months and sent it. But that didn't seem to satisfy her — as you see." He dealt Colonel Starbottle another letter from his baleful hand with an unchanged face. "When I got that, — well, I just up and told her the whole thing. I sent her the account of the fight from the newspapers, and told her as how her son was the Frisbee that was my pardner, and how he never had a cent in the world — but how I'd got that idea to help her, and was willing to carry it out as long as I could."

"Did you keep a copy of that letter?" asked the Colonel, straitening his mask-like mouth.

"No," said Corbin moodily. "What was the good? I know'd she'd got the letter, — and she did, — for that is what she wrote back." He laid another letter before the Colonel, who hastily read a few lines and then brought his fat white hand violently on the desk.

"Why, d—n it all, sir, this is *blackmail!* As infamous a case of threatening and *chantage* as I ever heard of."

"Well," said Corbin, dejectedly, "I don't know. You see she allows that I murdered Frisbee to get hold of his claim, and that I'm trying to buy her off, and that if I don't come down with twenty thousand dollars on the nail, and notes for the rest, she'll prosecute me. Well, mebbe the thing looks to her like that — mebbe you know I've got to shoulder that too. Perhaps it's all in the same line."

Colonel Starbottle for a moment regarded Corbin critically. In spite of his chivalrous attitude towards the homicidal faculty, the Colonel was not optimistic in regard to the baser pecuniary interests of his fellow-man. It was quite on the cards that his companion might have murdered his partner to get possession of the claim. It was true that Corbin had voluntarily assumed an unrecorded and hitherto unknown responsibility that had never been even suspected, and was virtually self-imposed. But that might have been the usual one unerring blunder of criminal sagacity and forethought. It was equally true that he did not look or act like a mean murderer; but that was nothing. However, there was no evidence of these reflections in the Colonel's face. Rather he suddenly beamed with an excess of politeness. "Would you — er — mind, Mr. Corbin, whilst I am going over those letters again, to — er — step across to my office — and — er — bring me the copy of 'Wood's Digest' that lies on my table? It will save some time."

The stranger rose, as if the service was part of his self-imposed trouble, and as equally hopeless with the rest, and taking his hat departed to execute the commission. As soon as he had left the building Colonel Starbottle opened the door and mysteriously beckoned the bar-keeper within.

"Do you remember anything of the killing of a man named Frisbee over in Fresno three years ago?"

The bar-keeper whistled meditatively. "Three years ago — Frisbee? — Fresno? — no? Yes — but that was only one of his names. He was Jack Walker over here.

Yes — and by Jove! that feller that was
here with you killed him. Darn my skin,
but I thought I recognized him."

"Yes, yes, I know all that," said the
Colonel, impatiently. "But did Frisbee
have any *property?* Did he have any
means of his own?"

"Property?" echoed the bar-keeper with
scornful incredulity. "Property? Means?
The only property and means he ever had
was the free lunches or drinks he took in at
somebody else's expense. Why, the only
chance he ever had of earning a square meal
was when that fellow that was with you just
now took him up and made him his partner.
And the only way *he* could get rid of him
was to kill him! And I did n't think he
had it in him. Rather a queer kind o' chap,
— good deal of hayseed about him. Showed
up at the inquest so glum and orkerd that
if the boys had n't made up their minds this
yer Frisbee *orter been* killed — it might
have gone hard with him."

"Mr. Corbin," said Colonel Starbottle,
with a pained but unmistakable *hauteur*
and a singular elevation of his shirt frill, as
if it had become of its own accord erectile,
"Mr. Corbin — er — er — is the distant rela-

tive of old Major Corbin, of Nashville — er — one of my oldest political friends. When Mr. Corbin — er — returns, you can conduct him to me. And, if you please, replenish the glasses."

When the bar-keeper respectfully showed Mr. Corbin and " Wood's Digest " into the room again, the Colonel was still beaming and apologetic.

"A thousand thanks, sir, but except to *show* you the law if you require it — hardly necessary. I have — er — glanced over the woman's letters again; it would be better, perhaps, if you had kept copies of your own — but still these tell the whole story and *your own*. The claim is preposterous! You have simply to drop the whole thing. Stop your remittances, stop your correspondence, — pay no heed to any further letters and wait results. You need fear nothing further, sir; I stake my professional reputation on it."

The gloom of the stranger seemed only to increase as the Colonel reached his triumphant conclusion.

"I reckoned you'd say that," he said slowly, "but it won't do. I shall go on paying as far as I can. It's my trouble and I'll see it through."

"But, my dear sir, consider," gasped the Colonel. "You are in the hands of an infamous harpy, who is using her son's blood to extract money from you. You have already paid a dozen times more than the life of that d—d sneak was worth; and more than that — the longer you keep on paying you are helping to give color to their claim and estopping your own defense. And Gad, sir, you're making a precedent for this sort of thing! you are offering a premium to widows and orphans. A gentleman won't be able to exchange shots with another without making himself liable for damages. I am willing to admit that your feelings — though, in my opinion — er — exaggerated — do you credit; but I am satisfied that they are utterly misunderstood — sir."

"Not by all of them," said Corbin darkly.

"Eh?" returned the Colonel quickly.

"There was another letter here which I did n't particularly point out to you," said Corbin, taking up the letters again, "for I reckoned it wasn n't evidence, so to speak, being from *his cousin*, — a girl, — and calculated you'd read it when I was out."

The Colonel coughed hastily. "I was in

fact — er — just about to glance over it when you came in."

"It was written," continued Corbin, selecting a letter more bethumbed than the others, "after the old woman had threatened me. This here young woman allows that she is sorry that her aunt has to take money of me on account of her cousin being killed, and she is still sorrier that she is so bitter against me. She says she had n't seen her cousin since he was a boy, and used to play with her, and that she finds it hard to believe that he should ever grow up to change his name and act so as to provoke anybody to lift a hand against him. She says she supposed it must be something in that dreadful California that alters people and makes everybody so reckless. I reckon her head's level there, ain't it?"

There was such a sudden and unexpected lightening of the man's face as he said it, such a momentary relief to his persistent gloom, that the Colonel, albeit inwardly dissenting from both letter and comment, smiled condescendingly.

"She's no slouch of a scribe neither," continued Corbin animatedly. "Read that."

He handed his companion the letter, pointing to a passage with his finger. The Colonel took it with, I fear, a somewhat lowered opinion of his client, and a new theory of the case. It was evident that this weak submission to the aunt's conspiracy was only the result of a greater weakness for the niece. Colonel Starbottle had a wholesome distrust of the sex as a business or political factor. He began to look over the letter, but was evidently slurring it with superficial politeness, when Corbin said: —

"Read it out loud."

The Colonel slightly lifted his shoulders, fortified himself with another sip of the julep, and, leaning back, oratorically began to read, — the stranger leaning over him and following line by line with shining eyes.

"'When I say I am sorry for you, it is because I think it must be dreadful for you to be going round with the blood of a fellow-creature on your hands. It must be awful for you in the stillness of the night season to hear the voice of the Lord saying, " Cain, where is thy brother?" and you saying, "Lord, I have slayed him dead." It must be awful for you when the pride of your wrath was surfitted, and his dum senseless corps was before you, not to know that it is written, " Vengeance is mine, I will repay," saith the Lord. . . . It was no use for you to say, " I never heard that before," remembering your teacher and parents. Yet verily I say unto you, " Though your sins be as scarlet, they shall be washed whiter than snow," saith the Lord — Isaiah i. 18 ; and " Heart hath no sorrow that Heaven cannot heal." — My hymn book, 1st Presbyterian Church, page 79. Mr. Corbin, I pity your feelins at the grave of my pore dear cousin, knowing he is before his Maker, and you can't bring him back.' Umph ! — er — er — very good — very good indeed," said the Colonel, hastily refolding the letter. "Very well meaning and — er " —

" Go on," said Corbin over his shoulder, " you have n't read all."

" Ah, true. I perceive I overlooked something. Um — um. ' May God forgive you, Mr. Corbin, as I do, and make aunty think better of you, for it was good what you tried to do for her and the fammely, and I 've always said it when she was raging round and wanting money of you. I don't believe you meant to do it anyway, owin' to your kindness of heart to the ophanless and the widow since you did it. Anser this letter, and don't mind what aunty says. So no more at present from — Yours very respectfully, SALLY DOWS.

"'P. S. — There's been some troubel in our township, and some fitin'. May the Lord change ther hearts and make them as a little child, for if you are still young you may grow up different. I have writ a short prayer for you to say every night. You can coppy it out and put it at the head of your bed. It is this: O Lord make me sorry for having killed Sarah Dows' cousin. Give me, O Lord, that peace that the world cannot give, and which fadeth not away; for my yoke is heavy, and my burden is harder than I can bear.'"

The Colonel's deliberate voice stopped. There was a silence in the room, and the air seemed stifling. The click of the billiard balls came distinctly through the partition from the other room. Then there was another click, a stamp on the floor, and a voice crying coarsely: "Curse it all — missed again!"

To the stranger's astonishment, the Colonel was on his feet in an instant, gasping with inarticulate rage. Flinging the door open, he confronted the startled bar-keeper empurpled and stertorous.

"Blank it all, sir, do you call this a saloon for gentlemen, or a corral for swearing cattle? Or do you mean to say that the conversation of two gentlemen upon delicate professional — and — er — domestic affairs — is to be broken upon by the blank profanity of low-bred hounds over their picayune gambling! Take them my kyard, sir," choked the Colonel, who was always Southern and dialectic in his excited as in his softest moments, "and tell them that Colonel Starbottle will nevah dyarken these doahs again."

Before the astonished bar-keeper could reply, the Colonel had dashed back into the room, clapped his hat on his head, and seized his book, letters, and cane. "Mr. Corbin," he said with gasping dignity, "I will take these papahs, and consult them again in my own office — where, if you will do me the honor, sir, to call at ten o'clock to-morrow, I will give you my opinion." He strode out of the saloon beside the half awe-stricken, half-amused, yet all discreetly silent loungers, followed by his wondering but gloomy client. At the door they parted, — the Colonel tiptoeing towards his office as if dancing with rage, the stranger darkly plodding through the stifling dust in the opposite direction, with what might have been a faint suggestion to his counselor, that the paths of the homicide did not lie beside the still cool waters.

CHAPTER II.

THE house of Captain Masterton Dows, at Pineville, Kentucky, was a fine specimen of Southern classical architecture, being an exact copy of Major Fauquier's house in Virginia, which was in turn only a slight variation from a well-known statesman's historical villa in Alabama, that everybody knew was designed from a famous Greek temple on the Piræus. Not but that it shared this resemblance with the County Court House and the Odd Fellows' Hall, but the addition of training jessamine and Cherokee rose to the columns of the portico, and over the colonnade leading to its offices, showed a certain domestic distinction. And the sky line of its incongruously high roof was pleasantly broken against adjacent green pines, butternut, and darker cypress.

A nearer approach showed the stuccoed gateposts — whose red brick core was revealed through the dropping plaster — opening in a wall of half-rough stone, half-wooden palisade, equally covered with shining moss and parasitical vines, which hid a tangled garden left to its own unkempt luxuriance. Yet there was a reminiscence of past formality and even pretentiousness in a wide box-bordered terrace and one or two stuccoed vases prematurely worn and time-stained; while several rare exotics had, however, thriven so unwisely and well in that stimulating soil as to lose their exclusive refinement and acquire a certain temporary vulgarity. A few, with the not uncommon enthusiasm of aliens, had adopted certain native peculiarities with a zeal that far exceeded any indigenous performance. But dominant through all was the continual suggestion of precocious fruition and premature decay that lingered like a sad perfume in the garden, but made itself persistent if less poetical in the house.

Here the fluted wooden columns of the portico and colonnade seemed to have taken upon themselves a sodden and unwholesome age unknown to stone and mortar. Moss and creeper clung to paint that time had neither dried nor mellowed, but left still glairy in its white consistency. There were rusty red blotches around inflamed nail-holes in the swollen wood, as of punctures in living flesh; along the entablature and cornices and in the dank gutters decay had taken the form of a mild deliquescence; and the pillars were spotted as if Nature had dropped over the too early ruin a few unclean tears. The house itself was lifted upon a broad wooden foundation painted to imitate marble with such hopeless mendacity that the architect at the last moment had added a green border, and the owner permitted a fallen board to remain off so as to allow a few privileged fowls to openly explore the interior. When Miss Sally Dows played the piano in the drawing-room she was at times accompanied by the uplifted voice of the sympathetic hounds who sought its quiet retreat in ill-health or low spirits, and from whom she was separated only by an imperfectly carpeted floor of yawning seams. The infant progeny of "Mammy Judy," an old nurse, made this a hiding-place from domestic justice, where they were eventually betrayed by subterranean giggling that had once or twice brought bashful confusion to the hearts of Miss Sally's admirers, and mischievous security to that finished coquette herself.

It was a pleasant September afternoon, on possibly one of these occasions, that Miss Sally, sitting before the piano, alternately striking a few notes with three pink fingers and glancing at her reflection in the polished rosewood surface of the lifted keyboard case, was heard to utter this languid protest: —

"Quit that kind of talk, Chet, unless you just admire to have every word of it repeated all over the county. Those little niggers of Mammy Judy's are lying round somewhere and are mighty 'cute, and sassy, I tell you. It's nothin' to *me*, sure, but Miss Hilda mightn't like to hear of it. So soon after your particular attention to her at last night's pawty too."

Here a fresh-looking young fellow of six-and-twenty, leaning uneasily over the piano from the opposite side, was heard to murmur that he did n't care what Miss Hilda heard, nor the whole world, for the matter of that. "But," he added, with a faint smile, "folks allow that you know how to *play up* sometimes, and put on the loud pedal, when you don't want Mammy's niggers to hear."

"Indeed," said the young lady demurely. "Like this?"

She put out a distracting little foot,

clothed in the white stocking and cool black prunella slipper then *de rigueur* in the State, and, pressing it on the pedal, began to drum vigorously on the keys. In vain the amorous Chet protested in a voice which the instrument drowned. Perceiving which the artful young lady opened her blue eyes mildly and said: —

"I reckon it *is* so; it *does* kind of prevent you hearing what you don't want to hear."

"You know well enough what I mean," said the youth gloomily. "And that ain't all that folks say. They allow that you're doin' a heap too much correspondence with that Californian rough that killed Tom Jeffcourt over there."

"Do they?" said the young lady, with a slight curl of her pretty lip. "Then perhaps they allow that if it wasn't for me he wouldn't be sending a hundred dollars a month to Aunt Martha?"

"Yes," said the fatuous youth; "but they allow he killed Tom for his money. And they do say it's mighty queer doin's in yo' writin' religious letters to him, and Tom your own cousin."

"Oh, they tell those lies *here*, do they?

But do they say anything about how, when the same lies were told over in California, the lawyer they've got over there, called Colonel Starbottle, — a Southern man too, — got up and just wrote to Aunt Martha that she'd better quit that afore she got prosecuted? They did n't tell you that, did they, Mister Chester Brooks?"

But here the unfortunate Brooks, after the fashion of all jealous lovers, deserted his allies for his fair enemy. "I don't cotton to what *they* say, Sally, but you *do* write to him, and I don't see what you've got to write about — you and him. Jule Jeffcourt says that when you got religion at Louisville during the revival, you felt you had a call to write and save sinners, and you did that as your trial and probation, but that since you backslided and are worldly again, and go to parties, you just keep it up for foolin' and flirtin'! *She* ain't goin' to weaken on the man that shot her brother, just because he's got a gold mine and — a mustache!"

"She takes his *money* all the same," said Miss Sally.

"*She* don't, — her mother does. *She* says if she was a man she'd have blood for blood!"

"My!" said Miss Sally, in affected consternation. "It's a wonder she don't apply to you to act for her."

"If it was *my* brother he killed, I'd challenge him quick enough," said Chet, flushing through his thin pink skin and light hair.

"Marry her, then, and that'll make you one of the family. I reckon Miss Hilda can bear it," rejoined the young lady pertly.

"Look here, Miss Sally," said the young fellow with a boyish despair that was not without a certain pathos in its implied inferiority, "I ain't gifted like you — I ain't on yo' level no how; I can't pass yo' on the road, and so I reckon I must take yo' dust as yo' make it. But there is one thing, Miss Sally, I want to tell you. You know what's going on in this country, — you've heard your father say what the opinion of the best men is, and what's likely to happen if the Yanks force that nigger worshiper, Lincoln, on the South. You know that we're drawing the line closer every day, and spottin' the men that ain't sound. Take care, Miss Sally, you ain't sellin' us cheap to some Northern Abolitionist who'd like to set Marm Judy's little niggers to something worse than eavesdropping down there, and mebbe teach 'em to kindle a fire underneath yo' own flo'."

He had become quite dialectic in his appeal, as if youthfully reverting to some accent of the nursery, or as if he were exhorting her in some recognized shibboleth of a section. Miss Sally rose and shut down the piano. Then leaning over it on her elbows, her rounded little chin slightly elevated with languid impertinence, and one saucy foot kicked backwards beyond the hem of her white cotton frock, she said: "And let me tell you, Mister Chester Brooks, that it's just such God-forsaken, infant phenomenons as you who want to run the whole country that make all this fuss, when you ain't no more fit to be trusted with matches than Judy's children. What do *you* know of Mr. Jo Corbin, when you don't even know that he's from Shelbyville, and as good a Suth'ner as you, and if he hasn't got niggers it's because they don't use them in his parts? Yo'r for all the world like one o' Mrs. Johnson's fancy bantams that ain't quit of the shell afore they square off at their own mother. My goodness! Sho! Sho-o-o!" And suiting the action to the word the young lady, still indolently, even in her simulation, swirled around, caught her skirts at the side with each hand, and lazily shaking them before her in the accepted feminine method of frightening chickens as she retreated backwards, dropped them suddenly in a profound curtsey and swept out of the parlor.

Nevertheless, as she entered the sitting-room she paused to listen, then, going to the window, peeped through the slits of the Venetian blind and saw her youthful admirer, more dejected in the consciousness of his wasted efforts and useless attire, mount his showy young horse, as aimlessly spirited as himself, and ride away. Miss Sally did not regret this; neither had she been entirely sincere in her defense of her mysterious correspondent. But, like many of her sex, she was trying to keep up by the active stimulus of opposition an interest that she had begun to think if left to itself might wane. She was conscious that her cousin Julia, although impertinent and illogical, was right in considering her first epistolary advances to Corbin as a youthful convert's religious zeal. But now that her girlish enthusiasm was spent, and the revival itself had proved as fleeting an excitement as the old "Tournament of Love and Beauty," which it had supplanted, she preferred to believe that she enjoyed the fascinating impropriety because it was the actual result of her religious freedom. Perhaps she had a vague idea that Corbin's conversion would expiate her present preference for dress and dancing. She had certainly never flirted with him; they had never exchanged photographs; there was not a passage in his letters that might not have been perused by her parents, — which, I fear, was probably one reason why she had never shown her correspondence; and beyond the fact that this letter-writing gave her a certain importance in her own eyes and those of her companions, it might really be stopped. She even thought of writing at once to him that her parents objected to its further continuance, but remembering that his usual monthly letter was now nearly due, she concluded to wait until it came.

It is to be feared that Miss Sally had little help in the way of family advice, and that the moral administration of the Dows household was as prematurely developed and as precociously exhausted as the estate and mansion themselves. Captain Dows' marriage with Josephine Jeffcourt, the daughter of a "poor white," had been considered a *mésalliance* by his family, and his own sister, Miranda Dows, had abandoned her brother's roof and refused to associate with the Jeffcourts, only returning to the house and an armed neutrality at the death of Mrs. Dows a few years later. She had taken charge of Miss Sally, sending her to school at Nashville until she was recalled by her father two years ago. It may be imagined that Miss Sally's correspondence with Jeffcourt's murderer had afforded her a mixed satisfaction; it was at first asserted that Miss Sally's forgiveness was really prompted by "Miss Mirandy," as a subtle sarcasm upon the family. When, however, that forgiveness seemed to become a source of revenue to the impoverished Jeffcourts, her Christian interference had declined.

For this reason, possibly, the young girl did not seek her aunt in the bedroom, the dining-room, or the business-room, where Miss Miranda frequently assisted Captain Dows in the fatuous and prejudiced mismanagement of the house and property, nor in any of the vacant guest-rooms, which, in their early wreck of latter-day mahogany and rosewood, seemed to have been unoccupied for ages, but went directly to her own room. This was in the "L," a lately added wing that had escaped the gloomy architectural tyranny of the main building, and gave Miss Sally light, ventilation, the freshness and spice of new pine boards and clean paper, and a separate entrance and windows on a cool veranda all to herself. Intended as a concession to the young lady's traveled taste, it was really a reversion to the finer simplicity of the pioneer.

New as the apartment appeared to be, it was old enough to contain the brief little records of her maidenhood: the childish samplers and pictures; the sporting epoch with its fox-heads, opossum and wild-cat skins, riding-whip, and the goshawk in a cage, which Miss Sally believed could be trained as a falcon; the religious interval of illustrated texts, "Rock of Ages," cardboard crosses, and the certificate of her membership with "The Daughters of Sion" at the head of her little bed, down to the last decadence of frivolity shown in the be-ribboned guitar in the corner, and the dance cards, favors, and rosettes, military buttons, dried bouquets, and other love gages on the mantelpiece.

The young girl opened a drawer of her table and took out a small packet of letters tied up with a green ribbon. As she did so she heard the sound of hoofs in the rear courtyard. This was presently followed by a step on the veranda, and she opened the door to her father with the letters still in her hand. There was neither the least embarrassment nor self-consciousness in her manner.

Captain Dows, superficially remarkable only for a certain odd combination of high military stock and turned-over planter's collar, was slightly exalted by a sympathetic mingling of politics and mint julep at Pineville Court House. "I was passing by the post-office at the Cross Roads last week, dear," he began, cheerfully, "and I thought of you, and reckoned it was about time that my Pussy got one of her letters from her rich Californian friend — and sure enough there was one. I clean forgot to give it to you then, and only remembered it passing there to-day. I didn't get to see if there was any gold-dust in it," he continued, with great archness, and a fatherly pinch of her cheek; "though I suspect that isn't the kind of currency he sends to you."

"It *is* from Mr. Corbin," said Miss Sally, taking it with a languid kind of doubt; "and only now, paw, I was just thinking that I'd sort of drop writing any more; it makes a good deal of buzzing amongst the neighbors, and I don't see much honey nor comb in it."

"Eh," said the Captain, apparently more astonished than delighted at his daughter's prudence. "Well, child, suit yourself! It's mighty mean, though, for I was just thinking of telling you that Judge Read is an old friend of this Colonel Starbottle, who is your friend's friend and lawyer, and he says that Colonel Starbottle is *with us*, and working for the cause out there, and has got a list of all the So'thern men in California that are sound and solid for the South. Read says he shouldn't wonder if he'd make California wheel into line too."

"I don't see what that's got to do with Mr. Corbin," said the young girl, impatiently, flicking the still unopened letter against the packet in her hand.

"Well," said the Captain, with cheerful vagueness, "I thought it might interest you, — that's all," and lounged judicially away.

"Paw thinks," said Miss Sally, still

standing in the doorway, ostentatiously addressing her pet goshawk, but with one eye following her retreating parent, "Paw thinks that everybody is as keen bent on politics as he is. There's where paw slips up, Jim."

Reëntering the room, scratching her little nose thoughtfully with the edge of Mr. Corbin's letter, she went to the mantelpiece and picked up a small ivory-handled dagger, the gift of Joyce Masterton, aged eighteen, presented with certain verses addressed to a "Daughter of the South," and cut open the envelope. The first glance was at her own name, and then at the signature. There was no change in the formality; it was "Dear Miss Sarah," and "Yours respectfully, Jo Corbin," as usual. She was still secure. But her pretty brows contracted slightly as she read as follows: —

"I've always allowed I should feel easier in my mind if I could ever get to see Mrs. Jeffcourt, and that may be she might feel easier in hers if I stood before her, face to face. Even if she didn't forgive me at once, it might do her good to get off what she had on her mind against me. But as there wasn't any chance of her coming to me, and it was out of the question my coming to her and still keeping up enough work in the mines to send her the regular money, it couldn't be done. But at last I've got a partner to run the machine when I'm away. I shall be at Shelbyville by the time this reaches you, where I shall stay a day or two to give you time to break the news to Mrs. Jeffcourt, and then come on. You will do this for me in your Christian kindness, Miss Dows — won't you? and if you could soften her mind so as to make it less hard for me I shall be grateful.

"P. S. — I forgot to say I have had *him* exhumed — you know who I mean — and am bringing him with me in a patent metallic burial casket, — the best that could be got in 'Frisco, and will see that he is properly buried in your own graveyard. It seemed to me that it would be the best thing I could do, and might work upon her feelings — as it has on mine. Don't you?

"J. C."

Miss Sally felt the tendrils of her fair hair stir with consternation. The letter had arrived a week ago; perhaps he was in

Pineville at that very moment! She must go at once to the Jeffcourts, — it was only a mile distant. Perhaps she might be still in time; but even then it was a terribly short notice for such a meeting. Yet she stopped to select her newest hat from the closet, and to tie it with the largest of bows under her pretty chin; and then skipped from the veranda into a green lane that ran beside the garden boundary. There, hidden by a hedge, she dropped into a long, swinging trot, that even in her haste still kept the languid deliberation characteristic of her people, until she had reached the road. Two or three hounds in the garden started joyously to follow her, but she drove them back with a portentous frown, and an ill-aimed stone, and a suppressed voice. Yet in that backward glance she could see that her little Eumenides — Mammy Judy's children — were peering at her from below the wooden floor of the portico, which they were grasping with outstretched arms and bowed shoulders, as if they were black caryatides supporting — as indeed their race had done for many a year — the pre-doomed and decaying mansion of their master.

CHAPTER III.

HAPPILY Miss Sally thought more of her present mission than of the past errors of her people. The faster she walked the more vividly she pictured the possible complications of this meeting. She knew the dull, mean nature of her aunt, and the utter hopelessness of all appeal to anything but her selfish cupidity, and saw in this fatuous essay of Corbin only an aggravation of her worst instincts. Even the dead body of her son would not only whet her appetite for pecuniary vengeance, but give it plausibility in the eyes of their emotional but ignorant neighbors. She had still less to hope from Julia Jeffcourt's more honest and human indignation but equally bigoted and prejudiced intelligence. It is true they were only women, and she ought to have no fear of that physical revenge which Julia had spoken of, but she reflected that Miss Jeffcourt's unmistakable beauty, and what was believed to be a "truly Southern spirit," had gained her many admirers who might easily take her wrongs upon their shoulders. If her father had only given her that letter before, she might have stopped Corbin's coming at all; she might even have met him in time to hurry him and her cousin's provocative remains out of the country. In the midst of these reflections she had to pass the little hillside cemetery. It was a spot of great natural beauty, cypress-shadowed and luxuriant. It was justly celebrated in Pineville, and, but for its pretentious tombstones, might have been peaceful and suggestive. Here she recognized a figure just turning from its gate. It was Julia Jeffcourt.

Her first instinct — that she was too late and that her cousin had come to the cemetery to make some arrangements for the impending burial — was, however, quickly dissipated by the young girl's manner.

"Well, Sally Dows, *you* here! who'd have thought of seeing you to-day? Why, Chet Brooks allowed that you danced every set last night and did n't get home till daylight. And you — you that are going to show up at another party to-night too! Well, I reckon I have n't got that much ambition these times. And out with your new bonnet too."

There was a slight curl of her handsome lip as she looked at her cousin. She was certainly a more beautiful girl than Miss Sally; very tall, dark and luminous of eye, with a brunette pallor of complexion, suggesting, it was said, that remote mixture of blood which was one of the unproven counts of Miss Miranda's indictment against her family. Miss Sally smiled sweetly behind her big bow. "If you reckon to tie to everything that Chet Brooks says, you'll want lots of string, and you won't be safe then. You ought to have heard him run on about this one, and that one, and that other one, not an hour ago in our parlor. I had to pack him off, saying he was even making Judy's niggers tired." She stopped and added with polite languor, "I suppose there's no news up at yo' house either? Everything's going on as usual — and — you get yo' California draft regularly?"

A good deal of the white of Julia's beautiful eyes showed as she turned indignantly on the speaker. "I wish, cousin Sally, you'd just let up talking to me about that money. You know as well as I do that I allowed to maw I wouldn't take a cent of it from the first! I might have had all the gowns and bonnets " — with a look at Miss Sally's bows — " I wanted from her ; she even offered to take me to St. Louis for a rig-out — if I 'd been willing to take blood money. But I 'd rather stick to this old sleazy mou'nin' for Tom " — she gave a dramatic pluck at her faded black skirt — " than flaunt round in white muslins and China silks at ten dollars a yard, paid for by his murderer."

"You know black 's yo' color always, — taking in your height and complexion, Jule," said Miss Sally demurely, yet not without a feminine consciousness that it really did set off her cousin's graceful figure to perfection. " But you can't keep up this gait always. You know some day you might come upon this Mr. Corbin."

" He 'd better not cross my path," she said passionately.

" I 've heard girls talk like that about a man and then get just green and yellow after him," said Miss Sally critically. " But goodness me! speaking of meeting people reminds me I clean forgot to stop at the stage office and see about bringing over the new overseer. Lucky I met you, Jule! Good-by, dear. Come in to-night, and we 'll all go to the party together." And with a little nod she ran off before her indignant cousin could frame a suitably crushing reply to her Parthian insinuation.

But at the stage office Miss Sally only wrote a few lines on a card, put it in an envelope, which she addressed to Mr. Joseph Corbin, and then seating herself with easy carelessness on a long packing-box, languidly summoned the proprietor.

"You're always on hand yourself at Kirby station when the kyars come in to bring passengers to Pineville, Mr. Sledge?"

"Yes, Miss."

"Yo' haven't brought any strangers over lately?"

"Well, last week Squire Farnham of Green Ridge — if he kin be called a stranger — as used to live in the very house yo' father" —

"Yes, I know," said Miss Sally, impatiently, "but if an *entire* stranger comes to take a seat for Pineville, you ask him if that's his name," handing the letter, "and give it to him if it is. And — Mr. Sledge — it's nobody's business but — yours and mine."

"I understand, Miss Sally," with a slow, paternal, tolerating wink. "He'll get it, and nobody else, sure."

"Thank you; I hope Mrs. Sledge is getting round again."

"Pow'fully, Miss Sally."

Having thus, as she hoped, stopped the arrival of the unhappy Corbin, Miss Sally returned home to consider the best means of finally disposing of him. She had insisted upon his stopping at Kirby and holding no communication with the Jeffcourts until he heard from her, and had strongly pointed out the hopeless infelicity of his plan. She dare not tell her Aunt Miranda, knowing that she would be too happy to precipitate an interview that would terminate disastrously to both the Jeffcourts and Corbin. She might have to take her father into her confidence, — a dreadful contingency.

She was dressed for the evening party, which was provincially early; indeed, it was scarcely past nine o'clock when she had finished her toilet, when there came a rap at her door. It was one of Mammy Judy's children.

"Dey is a gemplum, Miss Sally."

"Yes, yes," said Miss Sally, impatiently, thinking only of her escort. "I'll be there in a minute. Run away. He can wait."

"And he said I was to guv yo' dis yer,"

continued the little negro with portentous gravity, presenting a card.

Miss Sally took it with a smile. It was a plain card on which was written with a pencil in a hand she hurriedly recognized, "Joseph Corbin."

Miss Sally's smile became hysterically rigid, and pushing the boy aside with a little cry, she darted along the veranda and entered the parlor from a side door and vestibule. To her momentary relief she saw that her friends had not yet arrived: a single figure — a stranger's — rose as she entered.

Even in her consternation she had time to feel the added shock of disappointment. She had always present in her mind an ideal picture of this man whom she had never seen or even heard described. Joseph Corbin had been tall, dark, with flowing hair and long mustache. He had flashing fiery eyes which were capable of being subdued by a single glance of gentleness — her own. He was tempestuous, quick, and passionate, but in quarrel would be led by a smile. He was a combination of an Italian brigand and a poker player whom she had once met on a Mississippi steamboat. He would wear a broad-brimmed soft hat, a red shirt, showing his massive throat and neck — and high boots! Alas! the man before her was of medium height, with light close-cut hair, hollow cheeks that seemed to have been lately scraped with a razor, and light gray troubled eyes. A suit of cheap black, ill fitting, hastily acquired, and provincial even for Pineville, painfully set off these imperfections, to which a white cravat in a hopelessly tied bow was superadded. A terrible idea that this combination of a country undertaker and an ill-paid circuit preacher on probation was his best holiday tribute to her, and not a funeral offering to Mr. Jeffcourt, took possession of her. And when, with feminine quickness, she saw his eyes wander over her own fine clothes and festal figure, and sink again upon the floor in a kind of hopeless disappointment equal to her own, she felt ready to cry. But the more terrible sound of laughter approaching the house from the garden recalled her. Her friends were coming.

"For Heaven's sake," she broke out desperately, "did n't you get my note at the station telling you not to come?"

His face grew darker, and then took up

its look of hopeless resignation, as if this last misfortune was only an accepted part of his greater trouble, as he sat down again, and to Miss Sally's horror, listlessly swung his hat to and fro under his chair.

"No," he said, gloomily, "I did n't go to no station. I walked here all the way from Shelbyville. I thought it might seem more like the square thing to her for me to do. I sent *him* by express ahead in the box. It 's been at the stage office all day."

With a sickening conviction that she had been sitting on her cousin's body while she wrote that ill-fated card, the young girl managed to gasp out impatiently: "But you must go — yes — go now, at once! Don't talk now, but go."

"I did n't come here," he said, rising with a kind of slow dignity, "to interfere with things I did n't kalkilate to see," glancing again at her dress, as the voices came nearer, "and that I ain't in touch with, — but to know if you think I 'd better bring him — or" —

He did not finish the sentence, for the door had opened suddenly, and a half-dozen laughing girls and their escorts burst into the room. But among them, a little haughty and still irritated from her last interview, was her cousin Julia Jeffcourt, erect and beautiful in a sombre silk.

"Go," repeated Miss Sally, in an agonized whisper. "You must not be known here."

But the attention of Julia had been arrested by her cousin's agitation, and her eye fell on Corbin, where it was fixed with some fatal fascination that seemed in turn to enthrall and possess him also. To Miss Sally's infinite dismay the others fell back and allowed these two black figures to stand out, then to move towards each other with the same terrible magnetism. They were so near she could not repeat her warning to him without the others hearing it. And all hope died when Corbin, turning deliberately towards her with a grave gesture in the direction of Julia, said quietly : —

"Interduce me."

Miss Sally hesitated, and then gasped hastily, "Miss Jeffcourt."

"Yer don't say *my* name. Tell her I'm Joseph Corbin of 'Frisco, California, who killed her brother." He stopped and turned towards her. "I came here to try and fix things again and I've brought *him*."

In the wondering silence that ensued the others smiled vacantly, breathlessly, and expectantly, until Corbin advanced and held out his hand, when Julia Jeffcourt, drawing hers back to her bosom with the palms outward, uttered an inarticulate cry and — and spat in his face!

With that act she found tongue — reviling him, the house that harbored him, the insolence that presented him, the insult that had been put upon her! "Are you men!" she added passionately, "who stand here with the man before you that killed my brother, and see him offer me his filthy villainous hand — and dare not strike him down!"

And they dared not. Violently, blindly, stupidly moved through all their instincts, though they gathered hysterically around him, there was something in his dull self-containment that was unassailable and awful. For he wiped his face and breast with his handkerchief without a tremor, and turned to them with even a suggestion of relief.

"She's right, gentlemen," he said gravely. "She's right. It might have been otherwise. I might have allowed that it might be otherwise, — but she's right. I'm a Soth'n man

COLONEL STARBOTTLE'S CLIENT. 55

myself, gentlemen, and I reckon to understand what she has done. I killed the only man that had a right to stand up for her, and she has now to stand up for herself. But if she wants — and you see she allows she wants — to pass that on to some of you, or all of you, I'm willing. As many as you like, and in what way you like — I waive any chyce of weapon — I'm ready, gentlemen. I came here — with *him* — for that purpose."

Perhaps it may have been his fateful resignation; perhaps it may have been his exceeding readiness, — but there was no response. He sat down again, and again swung his hat slowly and gloomily to and fro under his chair.

"I've got him in a box at the stage office," he went on, apparently to the carpet, "I had him dug up that I might bring him here, and mebbe bury some of the trouble and difference along with his friends. It might be," he added, with a slightly glowering upward glance, as to an overruling, but occasionally misdirecting Providence, — "it might be from the way things are piling up on me that some one might have rung in another corpse instead o' *him*, but so far as

I can judge, allowin' for the space of time and nat'ral wear and tear — it's *him!*"

He rose slowly and moved towards the door in a silence that was as much the result of some conviction that any violent demonstration against him would be as grotesque and monstrous as the situation, as of anything he had said. Even the flashing indignation of Julia Jeffcourt seemed to become suddenly as unnatural and incongruous as her brother's chief mourner himself, and although she shrank from his passing figure she uttered no word. Chester Brooks's youthful emotions, following the expression of Miss Sally's face, lost themselves in a vague hysteric smile, and the other gentlemen looked sheepish. Joseph Corbin halted at the door.

"Whatever," he said, turning to the company, " ye make up your mind to do about me, I reckon ye'd better do it *after* the funeral. *I'm* always ready. But *he*, what with being in a box and changing climate, had better go *first*." He paused, and with a suggestion of delicacy in the momentary dropping of his eyelids, added, — " for *reasons*."

He passed out through the door, on to

the portico and thence into the garden. It was noticed at the time that the half-dozen hounds lingering there rushed after him with their usual noisy demonstrations, but that they as suddenly stopped, retreated violently to the security of the basement, and there gave relief to their feelings in a succession of prolonged howls.

CHAPTER IV.

It must not be supposed that Miss Sally did not feel some contrition over the ineffective part she had played in this last episode. But Joseph Corbin had committed the unpardonable sin to a woman of destroying her own illogical ideas of him, which was worse than if he had affronted the preconceived ideas of others, in which case she might still defend him. Then, too, she was no longer religious, and had no " call " to act as peacemaker. Nevertheless she resented Julia Jeffcourt's insinuations bitterly, and the cousins quarreled — not the first time in their intercourse — and it was reserved for the latter to break the news of Corbin's arrival with the body to Mrs. Jeffcourt.

How this was done and what occurred at that interview has not been recorded. But it was known the next day that, while Mrs. Jeffcourt accepted the body at Corbin's hands, — and it is presumed the funeral expenses also, — he was positively forbidden to appear either at the services at the house or at the church. There had been some wild talk among the younger and many of the lower members of the community, notably the "poor" non-slave-holding whites, of tarring and feathering Joseph Corbin, and riding him on a rail out of the town on the day of the funeral, as a propitiatory sacrifice to the manes of Thomas Jeffcourt; but it being pointed out by the undertaker that it might involve some uncertainty in the settlement of his bill, together with some reasonable doubt of the thorough resignation of Corbin, whose previous momentary aberration in that respect they were celebrating, the project was postponed until *after the funeral*. And here an unlooked-for incident occurred.

There was to be a political meeting at Kirby on that day, when certain distinguished Southern leaders had gathered from the remoter Southern States. At the instigation of Captain Dows it was adjourned at the hour of the funeral to enable members to attend, and it was even rumored, to the great delight of Pineville, that a distinguished speaker or two might come over to "improve the occasion" with some slight allusion to the engrossing topic of "Southern Rights." This combined appeal to the domestic and political emotions of Pineville was irresistible. The Second Baptist Church was crowded. After the religious service there was a pause, and Judge Reed, stepping forward amid a breathless silence, said that they were peculiarly honored by the unexpected presence in their midst "of that famous son of the South, Colonel Starbottle," who had lately returned to his native soil from his adopted home in California. Every eye was fixed on the distinguished stranger as he rose.

Jaunty and gallant as ever, femininely smooth-faced, yet polished and high colored as a youthful mask; pectorally expansive, and unfolding the white petals of his waistcoat through the swollen lapels of his coat, like a bursting magnolia bud, Colonel Starbottle began. The present associations were, he might say, singularly hallowed to him; not only was Pineville — a Southern centre — the recognized nursery of Southern chivalry, Southern beauty (a stately inclination to the pew in which Miss Sally and Julia Jeffcourt sat), Southern intelligence, and Southern independence, but it was the home

of the lamented dead who had been, like
himself and another he should refer to later,
an adopted citizen of the Golden State, a
seeker of the Golden Fleece, a companion of
Jason. It was the home, fellow-citizens and
friends, of the sorrowing sister of the deceased, a young lady whom he, the speaker,
had as yet known only through the chivalrous blazon of her virtues and graces by her
attendant knights (a courteous wave towards the gallery where Joyce Masterton,
Chester Brooks, Calhoun Bungstarter, and
the embattled youth generally of Pineville
became empurpled and idiotic); it was the
home of the afflicted widowed mother, also
personally unknown to him, but with whom
he might say he had had — er — er — professional correspondence. But it was not
this alone that hallowed the occasion, it was
a sentiment that should speak in trumpet-
like tones throughout the South in this
uprising of an united section. It was the
forgetfulness of petty strife, of family feud,
of personal wrongs in the claims of party!
It might not be known that he, the speaker,
was professionally cognizant of one of these
regrettable — should he say accidents? —
arising from the chivalrous challenge and

equally chivalrous response of two fiery Southern spirits, to which they primarily owe their coming here that day. And he should take it as his duty, his solemn duty, in that sacred edifice to proclaim to the world that in his knowledge as a professional man — as a man of honor, as a Southerner, as a gentleman, that the — er — circumstances which three years ago led to the early demise of our lamented friend and brother, reflected only the highest credit equally on both of the parties. He said this on his own responsibility — in or out of this sacred edifice — and in or out of that sacred edifice he was personally responsible, and prepared to give the fullest satisfaction for it. He was also aware that it might not be known — or understood — that since that boyish episode the survivor had taken the place of the departed in the bereaved family and ministered to their needs with counsel and — er — er — pecuniary aid, and had followed the body afoot across the continent that it might rest with its kindred dust. He was aware that an unchristian — he would say but for that sacred edifice — a *dastardly* attempt had been made to impugn the survivor's motives — to suggest an unseemly discord between him and the family, but he, the speaker, would never forget the letter breathing with Christian forgiveness and replete with angelic simplicity sent by a member of that family to his client, which came under his professional eye (here the professional eye for a moment lingered on the hysteric face of Miss Sally); he did not envy the head or heart of a man who could peruse these lines — of which the mere recollection — er — er — choked the utterance of even a professional man like — er — himself — without emotion. "And what, my friends and fellow-citizens," suddenly continued the Colonel, replacing his white handkerchief in his coat-tail, "was the reason why *my* client, Mr. Joseph Corbin — whose delicacy keeps him from appearing among these mourners — comes here to bury all differences, all animosities, all petty passions? Because he is a son of the South; because as a son of the South, as the representative, and a distant connection, I believe, of my old political friend, Major Corbin, of Nashville, he wishes here and everywhere, at this momentous crisis, to sink everything in the one all-pervading, all-absorbing, one and indivisible *unity* of the South in its resistance to the Northern Usurper! That, my friends, is the great, the solemn, the Christian lesson of this most remarkable occasion in my professional, political, and social experience."

Whatever might have been the calmer opinion, there was no doubt that the gallant Colonel had changed the prevailing illogical emotion of Pineville by the substitution of another equally illogical, and Miss Sally was not surprised when her father, touched by the Colonel's allusion to his daughter's epistolary powers, insisted upon bringing Joseph Corbin home with him, and offering him the hospitality of the Dows mansion. Although the stranger seemed to yield rather from the fact that the Dows were relations of the Jeffcourts than from any personal preference, when he was fairly installed in one of the appropriately gloomy guest chambers, Miss Sally set about the delayed work of reconciliation — theoretically accepted by her father, and cynically tolerated by her Aunt Miranda. But here a difficulty arose which she had not foreseen. Although Corbin had evidently forgiven her defection on that memorable evening, he had not apparently got over the revelation of her giddy worldliness, and was resignedly apathetic and distrustful of her endeavors. She was at first amused, and then angry. And her patience was exhausted when she discovered that he actually seemed more anxious to conciliate Julia Jeffcourt than her mother.

"But she spat in your face," she said, indignantly.

"That's so," he replied, gloomily; "but I reckoned you said something in one of your letters about turning the other cheek when you were smitten. Of course, as you don't believe it now," he added with his upward glance, "I suppose *that*'s been played on me, too."

But here Miss Sally's spirit lazily rebelled.

"Look here, Mr. Joseph *Jeremiah* Corbin," she returned with languid impertinence, "if instead of cavortin' round on yo' knees trying to conciliate an old woman who never had a stroke of luck till you killed her son, and a young girl who won't be above letting on afore you think it that your conciliatin' her means *sparkin'* her; if instead of that foolishness you'd turn your hand to trying to conciliate the folks here and keep 'em from going into that fool's act of breaking up these United States; if instead of digging up second-hand corpses that's already been put out of sight once you'd set to work to try and prevent the folks about here from digging up their old cranks and their old whims, and their old women fancies, you'd be doing something like a Christian and a man! What's yo' blood-guiltiness — I'd like to know — alongside of the blood-guiltiness of those fools who are just wild to rush into it, led by such turkey-cocks as yo' friend Colonel Starbottle? And you've been five years in California — a free State — and that's all yo' 've toted out of it — a dead body! There now, don't sit there and swing yo' hat under that chyar, but rouse out and come along with me to the pawty if you can shake a foot, and show Miss Pinkney and the gyrls yo' fit for something mo' than to skirmish round as a black japanned spittoon for Julia Jeffcourt!" It is not recorded that Corbin accepted this cheerful invitation, but for a few days afterwards he was more darkly observant of, and respectful to, Miss Sally. Strange indeed if he had not noticed — although always in his resigned fashion — the dull green stagnation of the life around him, or when not accepting it as part of his trouble he had not chafed at the arrested youth and senile childishness of the people. Stranger still if he had not at times been startled to hear the outgrown superstitions and follies of his youth voiced again by grown-up men, and perhaps strangest of all if he had not vaguely accepted it all as the hereditary curse of that barbarism under which he himself had survived and suffered.

The reconciliation between himself and Mrs. Jeffcourt was superficially effected, so far as a daily visit by him to the house indicated it to the community, but it was also known that Julia was invariably absent on these occasions. What happened at those interviews did not transpire, but it may be surmised that Mrs. Jeffcourt, perhaps recognizing the fact that Corbin was really giving her all that he had to give, or possibly having some lurking fear of Colonel Starbottle, was so far placated as to exhibit only the average ingratitude of her species towards a regular benefactor. She consented to the erection of a small obelisk over her son's grave, and permitted Corbin to plant a few flowering shrubs, which he daily visited and took care of. It is said that on one of these pilgrimages he encountered Miss Julia, apparently on the same errand, who haughtily retired. It was further alleged, on the authority of one of Mammy Judy's little niggers, that those two black mourning figures had been seen at nightfall sitting opposite to each other at the head and foot of the grave, and "glowerin'" at one another "like two hants." But when it was asserted on the same authority that their voices had been later overheard uplifted in some vehement discussion over the grave of the impassive dead, great curiosity was aroused. Being pressed by the eager Miss Sally to repeat some words or any words he had heard them say, the little witness glibly replied, "Marse Linkum" (Lincoln), and "The Souf," and so, for the time, shipwrecked his testimony. But it was recalled six months afterwards. It was then that a pleasant spring day brought madness and enthusiasm to a majority of Pineville, and bated breath and awe to a few, and it was known with the tidings that the South had appealed to arms, that among those who had first responded to the call was Joseph Corbin, an alleged "Union man," who had, however, volunteered to take that place in her ranks which might *have been filled by the man he had killed.* And then people forgot all about him.

. . . .

A year passed. It was the same place; the old familiar outlines of home and garden and landscape. But seen now, in the choking breathlessness of haste, in the fitful changing flashes of life and motion around it, in intervals of sharp suspense or dazed bewilderment, it seemed to be recognized no longer. Men who had known it all their lives, hurrying to the front in compact masses, scurrying to the rear in straggling line, or opening their ranks to let artillery gallop by, stared at it vaguely, and clattered or scrambled on again. The smoke of a masked battery in the woods struggled and writhed to free itself from the clinging tree-tops behind it, and sank back into a gray encompassing cloud. The dust thrown up by a column of passing horse poured over the wall in one long wave, and whitened the garden with its ashes. Throughout the dim empty house one no longer heard the sound of cannon, only a dull intermittent concussion was felt, silently bringing flakes of plaster from the walls, or sliding fragments of glass from the shattered windows. A shell, lifted from the ominous distance, hung uncertain in the air and then descended swiftly through the roof; the whole house dilated with flame for an instant, smoke rolled slowly from the windows, and even the desolate chimneys started into a hideous mockery of life, and then all was still again. At such awful intervals the sun shone out brightly, touched the green of the still sleeping woods and the red and white of a flower in the garden, and something in a gray uniform writhed out of the dust of the road, staggered to the wall, and died.

A mile down this road, growing more and more obscure with those rising and falling apparitions or the shapeless and rugged heaps terrible in their helpless inertia by hedge and fence, arose the cemetery hill. Taken and retaken thrice that afternoon, the dead above it far outnumbered the dead below; and when at last the tide of battle swept around its base into the dull, reverberating woods, and it emerged from the smoke, silenced and abandoned, only a few stragglers remained. One of them, leaning on his musket, was still gloomily facing the woods.

"Joseph Corbin," said a low, hurried voice.

He started and glanced quickly at the tombs around him. Perhaps it was because he had been thinking of the dead, — but the voice sounded like *his*. Yet it was only the *sister*, who had glided, pale and haggard, from the thicket.

"They are coming through the woods," she said quickly. "Run, or you'll be taken. Why do you linger?"

"You know why," he said gloomily.

"Yes, but you have done yo' duty. You have done his work. The task is finished now, and yo' free."

He did not reply, but remained gazing at the woods.

"Joseph," she said more gently, laying her trembling hand on his arm, "Joseph, fly — and — take me with you. For I was wrong, and I want you to forgive me. I knew your heart was not in this, and I ought not to have asked you. Joseph — listen! I never wanted to avenge myself nor *him* when I spat on your face. I wanted to avenge myself on *her*. I hated her, because I thought she wanted to work upon you and use you for herself."

"Your mother," he said, looking at her.

"No," she said, with widely opened eyes; "you know who I mean — Miss Sally."

He looked at her wonderingly for a moment, but quickly bent his head again in the direction of the road. "They are coming," he said, starting. "*You* must go. This is no place for you. Stop! it's too late; you cannot go now until they have passed. Come here — crouch down here — over this grave — so."

He almost forced her — kneeling down — upon the mound below the level of the shrubs, and then ran quickly himself a few paces lower down the hill to a more exposed position. She understood it. He wished to attract attention to himself. He was successful — a few hurried shots followed from the road, but struck above him.

He clambered back quickly to where she was still crouching.

"They were the vedettes," he said, "but they have fallen back on the main skirmish line and will be here in force in a moment. Go — while you can." She had not moved. He tried to raise her — her hat fell off — he saw blood oozing from where the vedette's bullet that had missed him had pierced her brain.

And yet he saw in that pale dead face only the other face which he remembered now had been turned like this towards his own. It was very strange. And this was the end, and this was his expiation! He raised his own face humbly, blindly, despairingly to the inscrutable sky; it looked back upon him from above as coldly as the dead face had from below.

Yet out of this he struck a faint idea that he voiced aloud in nearly the same words which he had used to Colonel Starbottle only three years ago. "It was with his own pistol too," he said, and took up his musket.

He walked deliberately down the hill, occasionally trying the stock of his musket in the loose earth, and at last suddenly remained motionless, in the attitude of leaning over it. At the same moment there was a distant shout; two thin parallel streams of blue and steel came issuing through the woods like a river, appeared to join tumultuously in the open before the hill, and out of the tumult a mounted officer called upon him to surrender.

He did not reply.

"Come down from there, Johnny Reb, I want to speak to you," called a young corporal.

He did not move.

"It's time to go home, Johnny."

No response.

The officer, who had been holding down his men with an unsworded but masterful hand, raised it suddenly. A dozen shots followed. The men leaped forward, and dashing Corbin contemptuously aside streamed up the hill past him.

But he had neither heard nor cared. For they found he had already deliberately transfixed himself through the heart on his own bayonet.

THE
POSTMISTRESS OF LAUREL RUN.

CHAPTER I.

THE mail stage had just passed Laurel Run,—so rapidly that the whirling cloud of dust dragged with it down the steep grade from the summit hung over the level long after the stage had vanished, and then, drifting away, slowly sifted a red precipitate over the hot platform of the Laurel Run post-office.

Out of this cloud presently emerged the neat figure of the postmistress with the mail-bag which had been dexterously flung at her feet from the top of the passing vehicle. A dozen loungers eagerly stretched out their hands to assist her, but the warning: "It's agin the rules, boys, for any but her to touch it," from a bystander, and a coquettish shake of the head from the postmistress herself — much more effective than any official interdict — withheld them. The bag was not heavy, — Laurel Run was too recent a settlement to have attracted much correspondence, — and the young woman, having pounced upon her prey with a certain feline instinct, dragged it, not without difficulty, behind the partitioned inclosure in the office, and locked the door. Her pretty face, momentarily visible through the window, was slightly flushed with the exertion, and the loose ends of her fair hair, wet with perspiration, curled themselves over her forehead into tantalizing little rings. But the window shutter was quickly closed, and this momentary but charming vision withdrawn from the waiting public.

"Guv'ment oughter have more sense than to make a woman pick mail-bags outer the road," said Jo Simmons sympathetically. "'T ain't in her day's work anyhow; Guv'ment oughter hand 'em over to her like a lady; it's rich enough and ugly enough."

"'T ain't Guv'ment; it's that stage company's airs and graces," interrupted a newcomer. "They think it mighty fine to go beltin' by, makin' everybody take their dust, just because *stoppin'* ain't in their contract.

Why, if that expressman who chucked down
the bag had any feelin's for a lady " — but
he stopped here at the amused faces of his
auditors.

"Guess you don't know much o' that expressman's feelin's, stranger," said Simmons
grimly. "Why, you oughter see him just
nussin' that bag like a baby as he comes
tearin' down the grade, and then rise up and
sorter heave it to Mrs. Baker ez if it was
a five-dollar bokay! His feelin's for her!
Why, he's give himself so dead away to her
that we're looking for him to forget what
he's doin' next, and just come sailin' down
hisself at her feet."

Meanwhile, on the other side of the partition, Mrs. Baker had brushed the red dust
from the padlocked bag, and removed what
seemed to be a supplementary package attached to it by a wire. Opening it she
found a handsome scent-bottle, evidently a
superadded gift from the devoted expressman. This she put aside with a slight smile
and the murmured word, "Foolishness."
But when she had unlocked the bag, even
its sacred interior was also profaned by a
covert parcel from the adjacent postmaster
at Burnt Ridge, containing a gold "speci-

men" brooch and some circus tickets. It was laid aside with the other. This also was vanity and — presumably — vexation of spirit.

There were seventeen letters in all, of which five were for herself — and yet the proportion was small that morning. Two of them were marked "Official Business," and were promptly put by with feminine discernment; but in another compartment than that holding the presents. Then the shutter was opened, and the task of delivery commenced.

It was accompanied with a social peculiarity that had in time become a habit of Laurel Run. As the young woman delivered the letters, in turn, to the men who were patiently drawn up in Indian file, she made that simple act a medium of privileged but limited conversation on special or general topics,— gay or serious as the case might be, or the temperament of the man suggested. That it was almost always of a complimentary character on their part may be readily imagined; but it was invariably characterized by an element of refined restraint, and, whether from some implied understanding or individual sense of honour, it never passed the bounds of conventionality or a certain delicacy of respect. The delivery was consequently more or less protracted, but when each man had exchanged his three or four minutes' conversation with the fair postmistress, — a conversation at times impeded by bashfulness or timidity, on his part solely, or restricted often to vague smiling, — he resignedly made way for the next. It was a formal levee, mitigated by the informality of rustic tact, great good-humor, and infinite patience, and would have been amusing had it not always been terribly in earnest and at times touching. For it was peculiar to the place and the epoch, and indeed implied the whole history of Mrs. Baker.

She was the wife of John Baker, foreman of "The Last Chance," now for a year lying dead under half a mile of crushed and beaten-in tunnel at Burnt Ridge. There had been a sudden outcry from the depths at high hot noontide one day, and John had rushed from his cabin — his young, foolish, flirting wife clinging to him — to answer that despairing cry of his imprisoned men. There was one exit that he alone knew which might be yet held open, among falling walls and tottering timbers, long enough to set them free. For one moment only the strong man hesitated between her entreating arms and his brothers' despairing cry. But she rose suddenly with a pale face, and said, " Go, John ; I will wait for you here." He went, the men were freed — but she had waited for him ever since !

Yet in the shock of the calamity and in the after struggles of that poverty which had come to the ruined camp, she had scarcely changed. But the men had. Although she was to all appearances the same giddy, pretty Betsy Baker, who had been so disturbing to the younger members, they seemed to be no longer disturbed by her. A certain subdued awe and respect, as if the martyred spirit of John Baker still held his arm around her, appeared to have come upon them all. They held their breath as this pretty woman, whose brief mourning had not seemed to affect her cheerfulness or even playfulness of spirit, passed before them. But she stood by her cabin and the camp — the only woman in a settlement of forty men — during the darkest hours of their fortune. Helping them to wash and cook, and ministering to their domestic needs, the sanctity of her cabin was, however, always kept as inviolable as if it had been *his* tomb. No one exactly knew why, for it was only a tacit instinct; but even one or two who had not scrupled to pay court to Betsy Baker during John Baker's life, shrank from even a suggestion of familiarity towards the woman who had said that she would "wait for him there."

When brighter days came and the settlement had increased by one or two families, and laggard capital had been hurried up to relieve the still beleaguered and locked-up wealth of Burnt Ridge, the needs of the community and the claims of the widow of John Baker were so well told in political quarters that the post-office of Laurel Run was created expressly for her. Every man participated in the building of the pretty yet substantial edifice — the only public building of Laurel Run — that stood in the dust of the great highway, half a mile from the settlement. There she was installed for certain hours of the day, for she could not be prevailed upon to abandon John's cabin, and here, with all the added respect due to a public functionary, she was secure in her privacy.

But the blind devotion of Laurel Run to

John Baker's relict did not stop here. In its zeal to assure the Government authorities of the necessity for a post-office, and to secure a permanent competency to the postmistress, there was much embarrassing extravagance. During the first week the sale of stamps at Laurel Run post-office was unprecedented in the annals of the Department. Fancy prices were given for the first issue; then they were bought wildly, recklessly, unprofitably, and on all occasions. Complimentary congratulation at the little window invariably ended with "and a dollar's worth of stamps, Mrs. Baker." It was felt to be supremely delicate to buy only the highest priced stamps, without reference to their adequacy; then mere *quantity* was sought; then outgoing letters were all over-paid and stamped in outrageous proportion to their weight and even size. The imbecility of this, and its probable effect on the reputation of Laurel Run at the General Post-office, being pointed out by Mrs. Baker, stamps were adopted as local currency, and even for decorative purposes on mirrors and the walls of cabins. Everybody wrote letters, with the result, however, that those *sent* were ludicrously and suspiciously in excess of those received. To obviate this, select parties made forced journeys to Hickory Hill, the next post-office, with letters and circulars addressed to themselves at Laurel Run. How long the extravagance would have continued is not known, but it was not until it was rumored that, in consequence of this excessive flow of business, the Department had concluded that a post*master* would be better fitted for the place that it abated, and a compromise was effected with the General Office by a permanent salary to the postmistress.

Such was the history of Mrs. Baker, who had just finished her afternoon levee, nodded a smiling "good-by" to her last customer, and closed her shutter again. Then she took up her own letters, but, before reading them, glanced, with a pretty impatience, at the two official envelopes addressed to herself, which she had shelved. They were generally a "lot of new rules," or notifications, or "absurd" questions which had nothing to do with Laurel Run and only bothered her and "made her head ache," and she had usually referred them to her admiring neighbor at Hickory Hill for explanation, who had generally returned them to her with the brief indorsement, "Purp stuff, don't bother," or, "Hog wash, let it slide." She remembered now that he had not returned the last two. With knitted brows and a slight pout she put aside her private correspondence and tore open the first one. It referred with official curtness to an unanswered communication of the previous week, and was "compelled to remind her of rule 47." Again those horrid rules! She opened the other; the frown deepened on her brow, and became fixed.

It was a summary of certain valuable money letters that had miscarried on the route, and of which they had given her previous information. For a moment her cheeks blazed. How dare they; what did they mean! Her waybills and register were always right; she knew the names of every man, woman, and child in her district; no such names as those borne by the missing letters had ever existed at Laurel Run; no such addresses had ever been sent from Laurel Run post-office. It was a mean insinuation! She would send in her resignation at once! She would get "the boys" to write an insulting letter to Senator Slocumb, — Mrs. Baker had the feminine idea of Government as a purely personal institution, — and she would find out who it was that had put them up to this prying, crawling impudence! It was probably that wall-eyed old wife of the postmaster at Heavy Tree Crossing, who was jealous of her. "Remind her of their previous unanswered communication," indeed! Where was that communication, anyway? She remembered she had sent it to her admirer at Hickory Hill. Odd that he had n't answered it. Of course, he knew about this meanness — could he, too, have dared to suspect her! The thought turned her crimson again. He, Stanton Green, was an old "Laurel Runner," a friend of John's, a little "triflin'" and "presoomin'," but still an old loyal pioneer of the camp! "Why had n't he spoke up?"

There was the soft, muffled fall of a horse's hoof in the thick dust of the highway, the jingle of dismounting spurs, and a firm tread on the platform. No doubt one of the boys returning for a few supplemental remarks under the feeble pretense of forgotten stamps. It had been done before, and she had resented it as "cayotin' round;" but now she was eager to pour out her wrongs to the first comer. She had her hand impulsively on the door of the partition, when she stopped with a new sense of her impaired dignity. Could she confess this to her worshipers? But here the door opened in her very face, and a stranger entered.

He was a man of fifty, compactly and strongly built. A squarely-cut goatee, slightly streaked with gray, fell straight from his thin-lipped but handsome mouth; his eyes were dark, humorous, yet searching. But the distinctive quality that struck Mrs Baker was the blending of urban ease with frontier frankness. He was evidently a man who had seen cities and knew countries as well. And while he was dressed with the comfortable simplicity of a Californian mounted traveler, her inexperienced but feminine eye detected the keynote of his respectability in the carefully-tied bow of his cravat. The Sierrean throat was apt to be open, free, and unfettered.

"Good-morning, Mrs. Baker," he said, pleasantly, with his hat already in his hand. "I'm Harry Home, of San Francisco." As he spoke his eye swept approvingly over the neat inclosure, the primly-tied papers, and well-kept pigeon-holes; the pot of flowers on her desk; her china-silk mantle, and killing little chip hat and ribbons hanging against the wall; thence to her own pink, flushed face, bright blue eyes, tendriled clinging hair, and then — fell upon the leathern mailbag still lying across the table. Here it became fixed on the unfortunate wire of the amorous expressman that yet remained hanging from the brass wards of the lock, and he reached his hand toward it.

But little Mrs. Baker was before him, and had seized it in her arms. She had been too preoccupied and bewildered to resent his first intrusion behind the partition, but this last familiarity with her sacred official property — albeit empty — capped the climax of her wrongs.

"How dare you touch it!" she said indignantly. "How dare you come in here! Who are you, anyway? Go outside, at once!"

The stranger fell back with an amused, deprecatory gesture, and a long silent laugh. "I'm afraid you don't know me, after all!" he said pleasantly. "I'm Harry Home, the Department Agent from the San Francisco office. My note of advice, No. 201, with my name on the envelope, seems to have miscarried too."

Even in her fright and astonishment it flashed upon Mrs. Baker that she had sent that notice, too, to Hickory Hill. But with it all the feminine secretive instinct within her was now thoroughly aroused, and she kept silent.

"I ought to have explained," he went on smilingly; "but you are quite right, Mrs. Baker," he added, nodding towards the bag. "As far as you knew, I had no business to go near it. Glad to see you know how to defend Uncle Sam's property so well. I was only a bit puzzled to know" (pointing to the wire) "if that thing was on the bag when it was delivered to you?"

Mrs. Baker saw no reason to conceal the truth. After all, this official was a man like the others, and it was just as well that he should understand her power. "It's only the expressman's foolishness," she said, with a slightly coquettish toss of her head. "He thinks it smart to tie some nonsense on that bag with the wire when he flings it down."

Mr. Home, with his eyes on her pretty face, seemed to think it a not inhuman or unpardonable folly. "As long as he does n't meddle with the inside of the bag, I suppose you must put up with it," he said laughingly. A dreadful recollection, that the Hickory Hill postmaster had used the inside of the bag to convey *his* foolishness, came across her. It would never do to confess it now. Her face must have shown some agitation, for the official resumed with a half-paternal, half-reassuring air: "But enough of this. Now, Mrs. Baker, to come to my business here. Briefly, then, it does n't concern you in the least, except so far as it may relieve you and some others, whom the Department knows equally well, from a certain responsibility, and, perhaps, anxiety. We are pretty well posted down there in all that concerns Laurel Run, and I think" (with a slight bow) "we 've known all about you and John Baker. My only business here is to take your place to-night in receiving the "Omnibus Way Bag," that you know arrives here at 9.30, does n't it?"

"Yes, sir," said Mrs. Baker hurriedly; "but it never has anything for us, except" — (she caught herself up quickly, with a stammer, as she remembered the sighing Green's occasional offerings) "except a notification from Hickory Hill post-office. It leaves there," she went on with an affectation of precision, "at half past eight exactly, and it 's about an hour's run — seven miles by road."

"Exactly," said Mr. Home. "Well, *I*

will receive the bag, open it, and dispatch it again. You can, if you choose, take a holiday."

"But," said Mrs. Baker, as she remembered that Laurel Run always made a point of attending her evening levee on account of the superior leisure it offered, "there are the people who come for letters, you know."

"I thought you said there were no letters at that time," said Mr. Home quickly.

"No — but — but" — (with a slight hysterical stammer) "the boys come all the same."

"Oh!" said Mr. Home dryly.

"And — O Lord!" — But here the spectacle of the possible discomfiture of Laurel Run at meeting the bearded face of Mr. Home, instead of her own smooth cheeks, at the window, combined with her nervous excitement, overcame her so that, throwing her little frilled apron over her head, she gave way to a paroxym of hysterical laughter. Mr. Home waited with amused toleration for it to stop, and, when she had recovered, resumed. "Now, I should like to refer an instant to my first communication to you. Have you got it handy?"

Mrs. Baker's face fell. "No; I sent it over to Mr. Green, of Hickory Hill, for information."

"What!"

Terrified at the sudden seriousness of the man's voice, she managed to gasp out, however, that, after her usual habit, she had not opened the official letters, but had sent them to her more experienced colleague for advice and information; that she never could understand them herself, — they made her head ache, and interfered with her other duties, — but *he* understood them, and sent her word what to do. Remembering also his usual style of indorsement, she grew red again.

"And what did he say?"

"Nothing; he didn't return them."

"Naturally," said Mr. Home, with a peculiar expression. After a few moments' silent stroking of his beard, he suddenly faced the frightened woman.

"You oblige me, Mrs. Baker, to speak more frankly to you than I had intended. You have — unwittingly, I believe — given information to a man whom the Government suspects of peculation. You have, without knowing it, warned the postmaster at Hickory Hill that he is suspected; and, as you might have frustrated our plans for tracing a series of embezzlements to their proper source, you will see that you might have also done great wrong to yourself as his only neighbor and the next responsible person. In plain words, we have traced the disappearance of money letters to a point when it lies between these two offices. Now, I have not the least hesitation in telling you that we do not suspect Laurel Run, and never have suspected it. Even the result of your thoughtless act, although it warned him, confirms our suspicion of his guilt. As to the warning, it has failed, or he has grown reckless, for another letter has been missed since. To-night, however, will settle all doubt in the matter. When I open that bag in this office to-night, and do not find a certain decoy letter in it, which was last checked at Heavy Tree Crossing, I shall know that it remains in Green's possession at Hickory Hill."

She was sitting back in her chair, white and breathless. He glanced at her kindly, and then took up his hat. "Come, Mrs. Baker, don't let this worry you. As I told you at first, *you* have nothing to fear. Even your thoughtlessness and ignorance of rules

have contributed to show your own innocence.
Nobody will ever be the wiser for this; we
do not advertise our affairs in the Department.
Not a soul but yourself knows the
real cause of my visit here. I will leave you
here alone for a while, so as to divert any
suspicion. You will come, as usual, this
evening, and be seen by your friends; I will
only be here when the bag arrives, to open
it. Good-by, Mrs. Baker; it's a nasty bit
of business, but it's all in the day's work.
I've seen worse, and, thank God, you're out
of it."

She heard his footsteps retreat into the
outer office and die out of the platform; the
jingle of his spurs, and the hollow beat of his
horse's hoofs that seemed to find a dull echo
in her own heart, and she was alone.

The room was very hot and very quiet;
she could hear the warping and creaking of
the shingles under the relaxing of the nearly
level sunbeams. The office clock struck
seven. In the breathless silence that followed,
a woodpecker took up his interrupted
work on the roof, and seemed to beat out
monotonously on her ear the last words of the
stranger: Stanton Green — a thief! Stanton
Green, one of the "boys" John had

helped out of the falling tunnel! Stanton Green, whose old mother in the States still wrote letters to him at Laurel Run, in a few hours to be a disgraced and ruined man forever! She remembered now, as a thoughtless woman remembers, tales of his extravagance and fast living, of which she had taken no heed, and, with a sense of shame, of presents sent her, that she now clearly saw must have been far beyond his means. What would the boys say? What would John have said? Ah! what would John have *done!*

She started suddenly to her feet, white and cold as on that day that she had parted from John Baker before the tunnel. She put on her hat and mantle, and going to that little iron safe that stood in the corner, unlocked it and took out its entire contents of gold and silver. She had reached the door when another idea seized her, and opening her desk she collected her stamps to the last sheet, and hurriedly rolled them up under her cape. Then with a glance at the clock, and a rapid survey of the road from the platform, she slipped from it, and seemed to be swallowed up in the waiting woods beyond.

CHAPTER II.

ONCE within the friendly shadows of the long belt of pines, Mrs. Baker kept them until she had left the limited settlement of Laurel Run far to the right, and came upon an open slope of Burnt Ridge, where she knew Jo Simmons' mustang, Blue Lightning, would be quietly feeding. She had often ridden him before, and when she had detached the fifty-foot reata from his head-stall, he permitted her the further recognized familiarity of twining her fingers in his bluish mane and climbing on his back. The tool-shed of Burnt Ridge Tunnel, where Jo's saddle and bridle always hung, was but a canter farther on. She reached it unperceived, and — another trick of the old days — quickly extemporized a side-saddle from Simmons' Mexican tree, with its high cantle and horn bow, and the aid of a blanket. Then leaping to her seat, she rapidly threw off her mantle, tied it by its sleeves around her waist, tucked it under one knee, and let it fall over her horse's flanks. By this time Blue Lightning was also struck with a flash of equine recollection and pricked up his ears. Mrs. Baker uttered a little chirping cry which he remembered, and the next moment they were both careering over the Ridge.

The trail that she had taken, though precipitate, difficult, and dangerous in places, was a clear gain of two miles on the stage road. There was less chance of her being followed or meeting any one. The greater cañons were already in shadow; the pines on the farther ridges were separating their masses, and showing individual silhouettes against the sky, but the air was still warm, and the cool breath of night, as she well knew it, had not yet begun to flow down the mountain. The lower range of Burnt Ridge was still uneclipsed by the creeping shadow of the mountain ahead of her. Without a watch, but with this familiar and slowly changing dial spread out before her, she knew the time to a minute. Heavy Tree Hill, a lesser height in the distance, was already wiped out by that shadowy index finger — half past seven! The stage would be at Hickory Hill just before half past eight; she ought to anticipate it, if possible, — it would stay ten minutes to change horses, — she *must* arrive before it left!

There was a good two-mile level before the rise of the next range. Now, Blue Lightning! all you know! And that was much, — for with the little chip hat and fluttering ribbons well bent down over the bluish mane, and the streaming gauze of her mantle almost level with the horse's back, she swept down across the long tableland like a skimming blue-jay. A few more bird-like dips up and down the undulations, and then came the long, cruel ascent of the Divide.

Acrid with perspiration, caking with dust, slithering in the slippery, impalpable powder of the road, groggily staggering in a red dusty dream, coughing, snorting, head-tossing; becoming suddenly dejected, with slouching haunch and limp legs on easy slopes, or wildly spasmodic and agile on sharp acclivities, Blue Lightning began to have ideas and recollections! Ah! she was a devil for a lark — this lightly-clinging, caressing, blarneying, cooing creature — up there! He remembered her now. Ha! very well then. Hoop-la! And suddenly leaping out like a rabbit, bucking, trotting hard, ambling lightly, "loping" on three legs and recreating himself, — as only a California mustang could, — the invincible Blue Lightning at last stood triumphantly upon the summit. The evening star had just pricked itself through the golden mist of the horizon line, — eight o'clock! She could do it now! But here, suddenly, her first hesitation seized her. She knew her horse, she knew the trail, she knew herself, — but did she know *the man* to whom she was riding? A cold chill crept over her, and then she shivered in a sudden blast; it was Night at last swooping down from the now invisible Sierras, and possessing all it touched. But it was only one long descent to Hickory Hill now, and she swept down securely on its wings. Half-past eight! The lights of the settlement were just ahead of her — but so, too, were the two lamps of the waiting stage before the post-office and hotel.

Happily the lounging crowd were gathered around the hotel, and she slipped into the post-office from the rear, unperceived. As she stepped behind the partition, its only occupant — a good-looking young fellow with a reddish mustache — turned towards her

with a flush of delighted surprise. But it
changed at the sight of the white, determined
face and the brilliant eyes that had never
looked once towards him, but were fixed
upon a large bag, whose yawning mouth was
still open and propped up beside his desk.

"Where is the through money letter that
came in that bag?" she said quickly.

"What — do — you — mean?" he stammered, with a face that had suddenly grown
whiter than her own.

"I mean that it's a *decoy*, checked at
Heavy Tree Crossing, and that Mr. Home, of
San Francisco, is now waiting at my office
to know if you have taken it!"

The laugh and lie that he had at first
tried to summon to mouth and lips never
reached them. For, under the spell of her
rigid, truthful face, he turned almost mechanically to his desk, and took out a package.

"Good God! you've opened it already!"
she cried, pointing to the broken seal.

The expression on her face, more than
anything she had said, convinced him that
she knew all. He stammered under the new
alarm that her despairing tone suggested.
"Yes! — I was owing some bills — the collector was waiting here for the money, and

I took something from the packet. But I was going to make it up by next mail — I swear it."

"How much have you taken?"

"Only a trifle. I" —

"How much?"

"A hundred dollars!"

She dragged the money she had brought from Laurel Run from her pocket, and counting out the sum, replaced it in the open package. He ran quickly to get the sealing-wax, but she motioned him away as she dropped the package back into the mail-bag. "No; as long as the money is found in the bag the package may have been broken *accidentally*. Now burst open one or two of those other packages a little — so;" she took out a packet of letters and bruised their official wrappings under her little foot until the tape fastening was loosened. "Now give me something heavy." She caught up a brass two-pound weight, and in the same feverish but collected haste wrapped it in paper, sealed it, stamped it, and, addressing it in a large printed hand to herself at Laurel Hill, dropped it in the bag. Then she closed it and locked it; he would have assisted her, but she again waved him away. "Send for the expressman, and keep yourself out of the way for a moment," she said curtly.

An attitude of weak admiration and foolish passion had taken the place of his former tremulous fear. He obeyed excitedly, but without a word. Mrs. Baker wiped her moist forehead and parched lips, and shook out her skirt. Well might the young expressman start at the unexpected revelation of those sparkling eyes and that demurely smiling mouth at the little window.

"Mrs. Baker!"

She put her finger quickly to her lips, and threw a world of unutterable and enigmatical meaning into her mischievous face.

"There's a big San Francisco swell takin' my place at Laurel to-night, Charley."

"Yes, ma'am."

"And it's a pity that the Omnibus Way Bag happened to get such a shaking up and banging round already, coming here."

"Eh?"

"I say," continued Mrs. Baker, with great gravity and dancing eyes, "that it would be just *awful* if that keerful city clerk found things kinder mixed up inside when he comes to open it. I wouldn't give him trouble for the world, Charley."

"No, ma'am, it ain't like you."

"So you'll be particularly careful on *my* account."

"Mrs. Baker," said Charley, with infinite gravity, "if that bag *should tumble off a dozen times* between this and Laurel Hill, I'll hop down and pick it up myself."

"Thank you! shake!"

They shook hands gravely across the window-ledge.

"And you ain't going down with us, Mrs. Baker?"

"Of course not; it wouldn't do, — for *I ain't here*, — don't you see?"

"Of course!"

She handed him the bag through the door. He took it carefully, but in spite of his great precaution fell over it twice on his way to the road, where from certain exclamations and shouts it seemed that a like miserable mischance attended its elevation to the boot. Then Mrs. Baker came back into the office, and, as the wheels rolled away, threw herself into a chair, and inconsistently gave way for the first time to an outburst of tears. Then her hand was grasped suddenly and she found Green on his knees before her. She started to her feet.

"Don't move," he said, with weak hysteric passion, "but listen to me, for God's sake! I am ruined, I know, even though you have just saved me from detection and disgrace. I have been mad! — a fool, to do what I have done, I know, but you do not know all — you do not know why I did it — you cannot think of the temptation that has driven me to it. Listen, Mrs. Baker. I have been striving to get money, honestly, dishonestly — any way, to look well in *your* eyes — to make myself worthy of you — to make myself rich, and to be able to offer you a home and take you away from Laurel Run. It was all for *you*, it was all for love of *you*, Betsy, my darling. Listen to me!"

In the fury, outraged sensibility, indignation, and infinite disgust that filled her little body at that moment, she should have been large, imperious, goddess-like, and commanding. But God is at times ironical with suffering womanhood. She could only writhe her hand from his grasp with childish contortions; she could only glare at him with eyes that were prettily and piquantly brilliant; she could only slap at his detaining hand with a plump and velvety palm, and when she found her voice it was high falsetto. And all she could say was, "Leave me be, looney, or I'll scream!"

He rose, with a weak, confused laugh, half of miserable affectation and half of real anger and shame.

"What did you come riding over here for, then? What did you take all this risk for? Why did you rush over here to share my disgrace — for *you* are as much mixed up with this now as *I* am — if you didn't calculate to share *everything else* with me? What did you come here for, then, if not for *me?*"

"What did *I* come here for?" said Mrs. Baker, with every drop of red blood gone from her cheek and trembling lip. "What — did — I — come here for? Well! — I came here for *John Baker's* sake! John Baker, who stood between you and death at Burnt Ridge, as I stand between you and damnation at Laurel Run, Mr. Green! Yes, John Baker, lying under half of Burnt Ridge, but more to me this day than any living man crawling over it — in — in" — oh, fatal climax! — "in a month o' Sundays! What did I come here for? I came here as John Baker's livin' wife to carry on dead John Baker's work. Yes, dirty work this time, may be, Mr. Green! but his work and for *him* only — precious! That's what I came here for; that's what I *live* for; that's what I'm waiting for — to be up to *him* and his work always! That's me — Betsy Baker!"

She walked up and down rapidly, tying her chip hat under her chin again. Then she stopped, and taking her chamois purse from her pocket, laid it sharply on the desk.

"Stanton Green, don't be a fool! Rise up out of this, and be a man again. Take enough out o' that bag to pay what you owe Gov'ment, send in your resignation, and keep the rest to start you in an honest life elsewhere. But light out o' Hickory Hill afore this time to-morrow."

She pulled her mantle from the wall and opened the door.

"You are going?" he said bitterly.

"Yes." Either she could not hold seriousness long in her capricious little fancy, or, with feminine tact, she sought to make the parting less difficult for him, for she broke into a dazzling smile. "Yes, I'm goin' to run Blue Lightning agin Charley and that way bag back to Laurel Run, and break the record."

. . . .

It is said that she did! Perhaps owing to the fact that the grade of the return journey to Laurel Run was in her favor, and that she could avoid the long, circuitous ascent to the summit taken by the stage, or that, owing to the extraordinary difficulties in the carriage of the way bag, — which had to be twice rescued from under the wheels of the stage, — she entered the Laurel Run post-office as the coach leaders came trotting up the hill. Mr. Home was already on the platform.

"You'll have to ballast your next way bag, boss," said Charley, gravely, as it escaped his clutches once more in the dust of the road, "or you'll have to make a new contract with the company. We've lost ten minutes in five miles over that bucking thing."

Home did not reply, but quickly dragged his prize into the office, scarcely noticing Mrs. Baker, who stood beside him pale and breathless. As the bolt of the bag was drawn, revealing its chaotic interior, Mrs. Baker gave a little sigh. Home glanced quickly at her, emptied the bag upon the floor, and picked up the broken and half-filled money parcel. Then he collected the scattered coins and counted them. "It's all right, Mrs. Baker," he said gravely. "*He*'s safe this time."

"I'm so glad!" said little Mrs. Baker, with a hypocritical gasp.

"So am I," returned Home, with increasing gravity, as he took the coin, "for, from all I have gathered this afternoon, it seems he was an old pioneer of Laurel Run, a friend of your husband's, and, I think, more fool than knave!" He was silent for a moment, clicking the coins against each other; then he said carelessly: "Did he get quite away, Mrs. Baker?"

"I'm sure I don't know what you're talking about," said Mrs. Baker, with a lofty air of dignity, but a somewhat debasing color. "I don't see why *I* should know anything about it, or why he should go away at all."

"Well," said Mr. Home, laying his hand gently on the widow's shoulder, "well, you see, it might have occurred to his friends that the *coins were marked!* That is, no doubt, the reason why he would take their good advice and go. But, as I said before, Mrs. Baker, *you*'re all right, whatever happens,—the Government stands by *you!*"

A NIGHT AT "HAYS."

CHAPTER I.

It was difficult to say if Hays' farmhouse, or "Hays," as it was familiarly called, looked any more bleak and cheerless that winter afternoon than it usually did in the strong summer sunshine. Painted a cold merciless white, with scant projections for shadows, a roof of white-pine shingles, bleached lighter through sun and wind, and covered with low, white-capped chimneys, it looked even more stark and chilly than the drifts which had climbed its low roadside fence, and yet seemed hopeless of gaining a foothold on the glancing walls, or slippery, wind-swept roof. The storm, which had already heaped the hollows of the road with snow, hurled its finely-granulated flakes against the building, but they were whirled along the gutters and ridges, and disappeared in smokelike puffs across the icy roof. The granite outcrop in the hilly field beyond had long ago whitened and vanished; the dwarf firs and larches which had at first taken uncouth shapes in the drift blended vaguely together, and then merged into an unbroken formless wave. But the gaunt angles and rigid outlines of the building remained sharp and unchanged. It would seem as if the rigors of winter had only accented their hardness, as the fierceness of summer had previously made them intolerable.

It was believed that some of this unyielding grimness attached to Hays himself. Certain it is that neither hardship nor prosperity had touched his character. Years ago his emigrant team had broken down in this wild but wooded defile of the Sierras, and he had been forced to a winter encampment, with only a rude log-cabin for shelter, on the very verge of the promised land. Unable to enter it himself, he was nevertheless able to assist the better-equipped teams that followed him with wood and water and a coarse forage gathered from a sheltered slope of wild oats. This was the beginning of a rude " supply station " which afterwards became so profitable that when spring came and Hays' team were sufficiently recruited to follow the flood of immigrating gold-seekers to the placers and valleys, there seemed no occasion for it. His fortune had been already found in the belt of arable slope behind the wooded defile, and in the miraculously located coign of vantage on what was now the great highway of travel and the only oasis and first relief of the weary journey; the breaking down of his own team at that spot had not only been the salvation of those who found at "Hays" the means of prosecuting the last part of their pilgrimage, but later provided the equipment of returning teams.

The first two years of this experience had not been without hardship and danger. He had been raided by Indians and besieged for three days in his stockaded cabin; he had been invested by wintry drifts of twenty feet of snow, cut off equally from incoming teams from the pass and the valley below. During the second year his wife had joined him with four children, but whether the enforced separation had dulled her conjugal affection, or whether she was tempted by a natural feminine longing for the land of promise beyond, she sought it one morning with a fascinating teamster, leaving her two sons and two daughters behind her; two years later the elder of the daughters followed the mother's example, with such maidenly discretion, however, as to forbear compromising herself by any previous matrimonial formality whatever. From that day Hays had no further personal intercourse with the valley below. He put up a hotel a mile away from the farmhouse that he might not have to dispense hospitality to his customers, nor accept their near companionship. Always a severe Presbyterian, and an uncompromising deacon of a far-scattered and scanty community who occasionally held their service in one of his barns, he grew more rigid, sectarian, and narrow day by day. He was feared, and although neither respected nor loved, his domination and endurance were accepted. A grim landlord, hard creditor, close-fisted patron, and a smileless neighbor who neither gambled nor drank, "Old Hays," as he was called, while yet scarce fifty, had few acquaintances and fewer friends. There were those who believed that his domestic infelicities were the result of his unsympathetic nature; it never occurred to any one (but himself probably) that they might have been the cause. In those Sierran altitudes, as elsewhere, the belief in original sin — popularly known as " pure cussedness"

— dominated and overbore any consideration of passive, impelling circumstances or temptation, unless they had been actively demonstrated with a revolver. The passive expression of harshness, suspicion, distrust, and moroseness was looked upon as inherent wickedness.

The storm raged violently as Hays emerged from the last of a long range of outbuildings and sheds, and crossed the open space between him and the farmhouse. Before he had reached the porch, with its scant shelter, he had floundered through a snowdrift, and faced the full fury of the storm. But the snow seemed to have glanced from his hard angular figure as it had from his roof-ridge, for when he entered the narrow hall-way his pilot jacket was unmarked, except where a narrow line of powdered flakes outlined the seams as if worn. To the right was an apartment, half office, half sitting-room, furnished with a dark and chilly iron safe, a sofa and chairs covered with black and coldly shining horsehair. Here Hays not only removed his upper coat but his under one also, and drawing a chair before the fire sat down in his shirt-sleeves. It was his usual rustic pioneer habit, and might have been some lingering reminiscence of certain remote ancestors to whom clothes were an impediment. He was warming his hands and placidly ignoring his gaunt arms in their thinly-clad "hickory" sleeves, when a young girl of eighteen sauntered, half perfunctorily, half inquisitively into the room. It was his only remaining daughter. Already elected by circumstances to a dry household virginity, her somewhat large features, sallow complexion, and tasteless, unattractive dress, did not obviously suggest a sacrifice. Since her sister's departure she had taken sole charge of her father's domestic affairs and the few rude servants he employed, with a certain inherited following of his own moods and methods. To the neighbors she was known as " Miss Hays," — a dubious respect that, in a community of familiar " Sallies," "Mamies," " Pussies," was grimly prophetic. Yet she rejoiced in the Oriental appellation of "Zuleika." To this it is needless to add that it was impossible to conceive any one who looked more decidedly Western.

" Ye kin put some things in my carpet bag agin the time the sled comes round," said her father meditatively, without looking up.

"Then you're not coming back to-night?" asked the girl curiously. "What's goin' on at the summit, father?"

"*I* am," he said grimly. "You don't reckon I kalkilate to stop thar! I'm going on as far as Horseley's to close up that contract afore the weather changes."

"I kinder allowed it was funny you'd go to the hotel to-night. There's a dance there; those two Wetherbee girls and Mamie Harris passed up the road an hour ago on a wood-sled, nigh blown to pieces and sittin' up in the snow like skeert white rabbits."

Hays' brow darkened heavily.

"Let 'em go," he said, in a hard voice that the fire did not seem to have softened. "Let 'em go for all the good their fool-parents will ever get outer them, or the herd of wayside cattle they've let them loose among."

"I reckon they haven't much to do at home, or are hard put for company, to travel six miles in the snow to show off their prinkin' to a lot of idle louts shiny with bear's grease and scented up with doctor's stuff," added the girl, shrugging her shoulders, with a touch of her father's mood and manner.

Perhaps it struck Hays at that moment that her attitude was somewhat monstrous and unnatural for one still young and presumably like other girls, for, after glancing at her under his heavy brows, he said, in a gentler tone: —

"Never *you* mind, Zuly. When your brother Jack comes home he'll know what's what, and have all the proper New York ways and style. It's nigh on three years now that he's had the best training Dr. Dawson's Academy could give, — sayin' nothing of the pow'ful Christian example of one of the best preachers in the States. They may n't have worldly, ungodly fandangoes where he is, and riotous livin', and scarlet abominations, but I've been told that they've 'tea circles,' and 'assemblies,' and 'harmony concerts' of young folks — and dancin' — yes, fine square dancin' under control. No, I ain't stinted him in anythin'. You kin remember that, Zuleika, when you hear any more gossip and backbitin' about your father's meanness. I ain't spared no money for him."

"I reckon not," said the girl, a little sharply. "Why, there's that draft fur two hundred and fifty dollars that kem only last week from the Doctor's fur extras."

"Yes," replied Hays, with a slight knitting of the brows, "the Doctor mout hev writ more particklers, but parsons ain't allus business men. I reckon these here extrys were to push Jack along in the term, as the Doctor knew I wanted him back here in the spring, now that his brother has got to be too stiff-necked and self-opinionated to do his father's work." It seemed from this that there had been a quarrel between Hays and his eldest son, who conducted his branch business at Sacramento, and who had in a passion threatened to set up a rival establishment to his father's. And it was also evident from the manner of the girl that she was by no means a strong partisan of her father in the quarrel.

"You'd better find out first how all the schoolin' and trainin' of Jack's is goin' to jibe with the Ranch, and if he ain't been eddicated out of all knowledge of station business or keer for it. New York ain't Hays' Ranch, and these yer 'assemblies' and 'harmony' doin's and their airs and graces may put him out of conceit with our plain ways. I reckon ye did n't take that to mind when you've been hustlin' round payin' two hundred and fifty dollar drafts for Jack and quo'llin' with Bijah! I ain't sayin' nothin', father, only mebbe if Bijah had had drafts and extrys flourished around him a little more, mebbe he'd have been more polite and not so rough spoken. Mebbe," she continued with a little laugh, " even *I*'d be a little more in the style to suit Master Jack when he comes ef I had three hundred dollars' worth of convent schoolin' like Mamie Harris."

"Yes, and you'd have only made yourself fair game for ev'ry schemin', lazy sport or counter-jumper along the road from this to Sacramento!" responded Hays savagely.

Zuleika laughed again constrainedly, but in a way that might have suggested that this dreadful contingency was still one that it was possible to contemplate without entire consternation. As she moved slowly towards the door she stopped, with her hand on the lock, and said tentatively: "I reckon you won't be wantin' any supper before you go? You're almost sure to be offered suthin' up at Horseley's, while if I have to cook you up suthin' now and still have the men's regular supper to get at seven, it makes all the expense of an extra meal."

Hays hesitated. He would have preferred

his supper now, and had his daughter pressed him would have accepted it. But economy, which was one of Zuleika's inherited instincts, vaguely appearing to him to be a virtue, interchangeable with chastity and abstemiousness, was certainly to be encouraged in a young girl. It hardly seems possible that with an eye single to the integrity of the larder she could ever look kindly on the blandishments of his sex, or, indeed, be exposed to them. He said simply: "Don't cook for me," and resumed his attitude before the fire as the girl left the room.

As he sat there, grim and immovable as one of the battered fire-dogs before him, the wind in the chimney seemed to carry on a deep-throated, dejected, and confidential conversation with him, but really had very little to reveal. There were no haunting reminiscences of his married life in this room, which he had always occupied in preference to the company or sitting-room beyond. There were no familiar shadows of the past lurking in its corners to pervade his reverie. When he did reflect, which was seldom, there was always in his mind a vague idea of a central injustice to which he had been subjected, that was to be avoided by circuitous movement, to be hidden by work, but never to be surmounted. And to-night he was going out in the storm, which he could understand and fight, as he had often done before, and he was going to drive a bargain with a man like himself and get the better of him if he could, as he had done before, and another day would be gone, and that central injustice which he could not understand would be circumvented, and he would still be holding his own in the world. And the God of Israel whom he believed in, and who was a hard but conscientious Providence, something like himself, would assist him perhaps some day to the understanding of this same vague injustice which He was, for some strange reason, permitting. But never more unrelenting and unsparing of others than when under conviction of Sin himself, and never more harsh and unforgiving than when fresh from the contemplation of the Divine Mercy, he still sat there grimly holding his hand to a warmth that never seemed to get nearer his heart than that, when his daughter reëntered the room with his carpet-bag.

To rise, put on his coat and overcoat, secure a fur cap on his head by a woolen comforter, covering his ears and twined round his throat, and to rigidly offer a square and weather-beaten cheek to his daughter's dusty kiss, did not, apparently, suggest any lingering or hesitation. The sled was at the door, which, for a tumultuous moment, opened on the storm and the white vision of a horse knee-deep in a drift, and then closed behind him. Zuleika shot the bolt, brushed some flakes of the invading snow from the mat, and, after frugally raking down the fire on the hearth her father had just quitted, retired through the long passage to the kitchen and her domestic supervision.

It was a few hours later, supper had long past; the "hands" had one by one returned to their quarters under the roof or in the adjacent lofts, and Zuleika and the two maids had at last abandoned the kitchen for their bedrooms beyond. Zuleika herself, by the light of a solitary candle, had entered the office and had dropped meditatively into a chair, as she slowly raked the warm ashes over the still smouldering fire. The barking of dogs had momentarily attracted her attention, but it had suddenly ceased. It was followed, however, by a more startling incident, — a slight movement outside, and an attempt to raise the window!

She was not frightened; perhaps there was little for her to fear; it was known that Hays kept no money in the house, the safe was only used for securities and contracts, and there were half a dozen men within call. It was, therefore, only her usual active, burning curiosity for novel incident that made her run to the window and peer out; but it was with a spontaneous cry of astonishment she turned and darted to the front door, and opened it to the muffled figure of a young man.

"Jack! Saints alive! Why, of all things!" she gasped, incoherently.

He stopped her with an impatient gesture and a hand that prevented her from closing the door again.

"Dad ain't here?" he asked quickly.

"No."

"When 'll he be back?"

"Not to-night."

"Good," he said, turning to the door again. She could see a motionless horse and sleigh in the road, with a woman holding the reins.

He beckoned to the woman, who drove to the door and jumped out. Tall, handsome, and audacious, she looked at Zuleika with a quick laugh of confidence, as at some recognized absurdity.

"Go in there," said the young man, opening the door of the office; "I'll come back in a minute."

As she entered, still smiling, as if taking part in some humorous but risky situation, he turned quickly to Zuleika and said in a low voice: "Where can we talk?"

The girl held out her hand and glided hurriedly through the passage until she reached a door, which she opened. By the light of a dying fire he could see it was her bedroom. Lighting a candle on the mantel, she looked eagerly in his face as he threw aside his muffler and opened his coat. It disclosed a spare, youthful figure, and a thin, weak face that a budding mustache only seemed to make still more immature. For an instant brother and sister gazed at each other. Astonishment on her part, nervous impatience on his, apparently repressed any demonstration of family affection. Yet when she was about to speak he stopped her roughly.

"There now; don't talk. I know what you're goin' to say — could say it myself if I wanted to — and it's no use. Well then, here I am. You saw *her*. Well, she's *my wife* — we've been married three months. Yes, my *wife;* married three months ago. I'm here because I ran away from school — that is, I *have n't been there* for the last three months. I came out with her last steamer; we went up to the Summit Hotel last night — where they did n't know me — until we could see how the land lay, before popping down on dad. I happened to learn that he was out to-night, and I brought her down here to have a talk. We can go back again before he comes, you know, unless" —

"But," interrupted the girl, with sudden practicality, "you say you ain't been at Doctor Dawson's for three months! Why, only last week he drew on dad for two hundred and fifty dollars for your extras!"

He glanced around him and then arranged his necktie in the glass above the mantel with a nervous laugh.

"*Oh, that!* I fixed that up, and got the money for it in New York to pay our passage with. It's all right, you know."

CHAPTER II.

THE girl stood looking at the ingenious forger with an odd, breathless smile. It was difficult to determine, however, if gratified curiosity were not its most dominant expression.

"And you've got a wife — and *that*'s her?" she resumed.

"Yes."

"Where did you first meet her? Who is she?"

"She's an actress — mighty popular in 'Frisco — I mean New York. Lot o' chaps tried to get her — I cut 'em out. For all dad's trying to keep me at Dawson's — I ain't such a fool, eh?"

Nevertheless, as he stood there stroking his fair mustache, his astuteness did not seem to impress his sister to enthusiastic assent. Yet she did not relax her breathless, inquisitive smile as she went on: —

"And what are you going to do about dad?"

He turned upon her querulously.

"Well, that's what I want to talk about."

"You'll catch it!" she said impressively.

But here her brother's nervousness broke out into a weak, impotent fury. It was evident, too, that in spite of its apparent spontaneous irritation its intent was studied. Catch it! Would he? Oh, yes! Well, she'd see *who* 'd catch it! Not him. No, he'd had enough of this meanness, and wanted it ended! He was n't a woman to be treated like his sister, — like their mother — like their brother, if it came to that, for he knew how he was to be brought back to take Bijah's place in the spring; he'd heard the whole story. No, he was going to stand up for his rights, — he was going to be treated as the son of a man who was worth half a million ought to be treated! He was n't going to be skimped, while his father was wallowing in money that he did n't know what to do with, — money that by rights ought to have been given to their mother and their sister. Why, even the law would n't permit such meanness — if he was dead. No, he'd come back with Lottie, his wife, to show his father that there was one of the family that could n't be fooled and bullied, and would n't put up with it any longer. There was going to be a fair division of the property, and his sister Annie's property, and hers — Zuleika's — too, if she 'd have the pluck to speak up for herself. All this and much more he said. Yet even while his small fury was genuine and characteristic, there was such an evident incongruity between himself and his speech that it seemed to fit him loosely, and in a measure flapped in his gestures like another's garment. Zuleika, who had exhibited neither disgust nor sympathy with his rebellion, but had rather appeared to enjoy it as a novel domestic performance, the morality of which devolved solely upon the performer, retained her curious smile. And then a knock at the door startled them.

It was the stranger, — slightly apologetic and still humorous, but firm and self-confident withal. She was sorry to interrupt their family council, but the fire was going out where she sat, and she would like a cup of tea or some refreshment. She did not look at Jack, but, completely ignoring him, addressed herself to Zuleika with what seemed to be a direct challenge; in that feminine eye-grapple there was a quick, instinctive, and final struggle between the two women. The stranger triumphed. Zuleika's vacant smile changed to one of submission, and then, equally ignoring her brother in this double defeat, she hastened to the kitchen to do the visitor's bidding. The woman closed the door behind her, and took Zuleika's place before the fire.

"Well?" she said, in a half-contemptuous toleration.

"Well?" said Jack, in an equally ill-disguised discontent, but an evident desire to placate the woman before him. "It's all right, you know. I've had my say. It'll come right, Lottie, you'll see."

The woman smiled again, and glanced around the bare walls of the room.

"And I suppose," she said, drily, "when it comes right I'm to take the place of your sister in the charge of this workhouse and succeed to the keys of that safe in the other room?"

"It'll come all right, I tell you; you can fix things up here any way you'll like when we get the old man straight," said Jack, with the iteration of feebleness. "And as to that safe, I've seen it chock full of securities."

"It'll hold one less to-night," she said, looking at the fire.

"What are you talking about?" he asked, in querulous suspicion.

She drew a paper from her pocket.

"It's that draft of yours that you were crazy enough to sign Dawson's name to. It was lying out there on the desk. I reckon it is n't a thing you care to have kept as evidence, even by your father."

She held it in the flames until it was consumed.

"By Jove, your head is level, Lottie!" he said, with an admiration that was not, however, without a weak reserve of suspicion.

"No, it is n't, or I would n't be here," she said, curtly. Then she added, as if dismissing the subject, "Well, what did you tell her?"

"Oh, I said I met you in New York. You see I thought she might think it queer if she knew I only met you in San Francisco three weeks ago. Of course I said we were married."

She looked at him with weary astonishment.

"And of course, whether things go right or not, she'll find out that I've got a husband living, that I never met you in New

York, but on the steamer, and that you've lied. I don't see the *use* of it. You said you were going to tell the whole thing squarely and say the truth, and that's why I came to help you."

"Yes; but don't you see, hang it all!" he stammered, in the irritation of weak confusion, "I had to tell her *something*. Father won't dare to tell her the truth, no more than he will the neighbors. He'll hush it up, you bet; and when we get this thing fixed you'll go and get your divorce, you know, and we'll be married privately on the square."

He looked so vague, so immature, yet so fatuously self-confident, that the woman extended her hand with a laugh and tapped him on the back as she might have patted a dog. Then she disappeared to follow Zuleika in the kitchen.

When the two women returned together they were evidently on the best of terms. So much so that the man, with the easy reaction of a shallow nature, became sanguine and exalted, even to an ostentatious exhibition of those New York graces on which the paternal Hays had set such store. He complacently explained the methods by which he had deceived Dr. Dawson; how he had himself written a letter from his father commanding him to return to take his brother's place, and how he had shown it to the Doctor and been three months in San Francisco looking for work and assisting Lottie at the theatre, until a conviction of the righteousness of his cause, perhaps combined with the fact that they were also short of money and she had no engagement, impelled him to his present heroic step. All of which Zuleika listened to with childish interest, but superior appreciation of his companion. The fact that this woman was an actress, an abomination vaguely alluded to by her father as being even more mysteriously wicked than her sister and mother, and correspondingly exciting, as offering a possible permanent relief to the monotony of her home life, seemed to excuse her brother's weakness. She was almost ready to become his partisan — *after* she had seen her father.

They had talked largely of their plans; they had settled small details of the future and the arrangement of the property; they had agreed that Zuleika should be relieved of her household drudgery, and sent to a fashionable school in San Francisco with a music teacher and a dressmaker. They had discussed everything but the precise manner in which the revelation should be conveyed to Hays. There was still plenty of time for that, for he would not return until to-morrow at noon, and it was already tacitly understood that the vehicle of transmission should be a letter from the Summit Hotel. The possible contingency of a sudden outburst of human passion not entirely controlled by religious feeling was to be guarded against.

They were sitting comfortably before the replenished fire; the wind was still moaning in the chimney, when, suddenly, in a lull of the storm the sound of sleigh-bells seemed to fill the room. It was followed by a voice from without, and, with a hysterical cry, Zuleika started to her feet. The same breathless smile with which she had greeted her brother an hour ago was upon her lips as she gasped: —

"Lord, save us! — but it's dad come back!"

I grieve to say that here the doughty redresser of domestic wrongs and retriever of the family honor lapsed white-faced in his chair idealess and tremulous. It was his frailer companion who rose to the occasion

and even partly dragged him with her.
"Go back to the hotel," she said quickly,
"and take the sled with you, — you are not
fit to face him now! But he does not know
me, and I will stay!" To the staring Zuleika: "I am a stranger stopped by a broken sleigh on my way to the hotel. Leave
the rest to me. Now clear out, both of you.
I'll let him in."

She looked so confident, self-contained,
and superior, that the thought of opposition
never entered their minds, and as an impatient rapping rose from the door they let
her, with a half-impatient, half-laughing gesture, drive them before her from the room.
When they had disappeared in the distance,
she turned to the front door, unbolted and
opened it. Hays blundered in out of the
snow with a muttered exclamation, and then,
as the light from the open office door revealed a stranger, started and fell back.

"Miss Hays is busy," said the woman
quietly, "I am afraid, on my account. But
my sleigh broke down on the way to the
hotel and I was forced to get out here. I
suppose this is Mr. Hays?"

A strange woman — by her dress and appearance a very worldling — and even braver in looks and apparel than many he had seen in the cities — seemed, in spite of all his precautions, to have fallen short of the hotel and been precipitated upon him! Yet under the influence of some odd abstraction he was affected by it less than he could have believed. He even achieved a rude bow as he bolted the door and ushered her into the office. More than that, he found himself explaining to the fair trespasser the reasons of his return to his own home. For, like a direct man, he had a consciousness of some inconsistency in his return — or in the circumstances that induced a change- of plans which might conscientiously require an explanation.

"You see, ma'am, a rather singular thing happened to me after I passed the summit. Three times I lost the track, got off it somehow, and found myself traveling in a circle. The third time, when I struck my own tracks again, I concluded I 'd just follow them back here. I suppose I might have got the road again by tryin' and fightin' the snow — but ther's some things not worth the fightin'. This was a matter of business, and, after all, ma'am, business ain't everythin', is it?"

He was evidently in some unusual mood,

the mood that with certain reticent natures often compels them to make their brief confidences to utter strangers rather than impart them to those intimate friends who might remind them of their weakness. She agreed with him pleasantly, but not so obviously as to excite suspicion. "And you preferred to let your business go, and come back to the comfort of your own home and family."

"The comfort of my home and family?" he repeated in a dry, deliberate voice. "Well, I reckon I ain't been tempted much by *that*. That isn't what I meant." But he went back to the phrase, repeating it grimly, as if it were some mandatory text. "The comfort of my *own home and family!* Well, Satan hasn't set *that* trap for my feet yet, ma'am. No; ye saw my daughter? well, that's all my family; ye see this room? that's all my home. My wife ran away from me; my daughter cleared out too, my eldest son as was with me here has quo'lled with me and reckons to set up a rival business agin me. No," he said, still more meditatively and deliberately; "it wasn't to come back to the comforts of my own home and family that I faced round on Heavy Tree Hill, I reckon."

As the woman, for certain reasons, had no desire to check this auspicious and unlooked for confidence, she waited patiently. Hays remained silent for an instant, warming his hands before the fire, and then looked up interrogatively.

"A professor of religion, ma'am, or under conviction?"

"Not exactly," said the lady smiling.

"Excuse me, but in spite of your fine clothes I reckoned you had a serious look just now. A reader of Scripture, may be?"

"I know the Bible."

"You remember when the angel with the flamin' sword appeared unto Saul on the road to Damascus?"

"Yes."

"It mout hev been suthin' in that style that stopped me," he said slowly and tentatively. "Though nat'rally *I* did n't *see* anything, and only had the queer feelin'. It might hev been *that* shied my mare off the track."

"But Saul was up to some wickedness, was n't he?" said the lady smilingly, "while *you* were simply going somewhere on business?"

"Yes," said Hays thoughtfully, "but my

business might hev seemed like persecution.
I don't mind tellin' you what it was if you'd
care to listen. But mebbe you're tired.
Mebbe you want to retire. You know,"
he went on with a sudden hospitable outburst, " you need n't be in any hurry to go;
we kin take care of you here to-night, and
it 'll cost you nothin'. And I 'll send you
on with my sleigh in the mornin'. Per'aps
you 'd like suthin' to eat — a cup of tea —
or — I 'll call Zuleika; " and he rose with an
expression of awkward courtesy.

But the lady, albeit with a self-satisfied
sparkle in her dark eyes, here carelessly assured him that Zuleika had already given
her refreshment, and, indeed, was at that
moment preparing her own room for her.
She begged he would not interrupt his interesting story.

Hays looked relieved.

" Well, I reckon I won't call her, for what
I was goin' to say ain't exackly the sort o'
thin' for an innocent, simple sort o' thing
like her to hear — I mean," he interrupted
himself hastily — " that folks of more experience of the world like you and me don't
mind speakin' of — I 'm sorter takin' it for
granted that you 're a married woman,
ma'am."

The lady, who had regarded him with a sudden rigidity, here relaxed her expression and nodded.

"Well," continued Hays, resuming his place by the fire, "you see this yer man I was goin' to see lives about four miles beyond the summit on a ranch that furnishes most of the hay for the stock that side of the Divide. He 's bin holdin' off his next year's contracts with me, hopin' to make better terms from the prospects of a late spring and higher prices. He held his head mighty high and talked big of waitin' his own time. I happened to know he could n't do it."

He put his hands on his knees and stared at the fire, and then went on: —

"Ye see this man had had crosses and family trials. He had a wife that left him to jine a lot of bally dancers and painted women in the 'Frisco playhouses when he was livin' in the southern country. You 'll say that was like *my* own case, — and mebbe that was why it came to him to tell me about it, — but the difference betwixt *him* and *me* was that instead of restin' unto the Lord and findin' Him, and pluckin' out the eye that offended him 'cordin' to Scripter, as I did, *he* followed after *her* tryin' to get her back, until, findin' that was n't no use, he took a big disgust and came up here to hide hisself, where there was n't no playhouse nor playactors, and no wimmen but Injin squaws. He preëmpted the land, and nat'rally, there bein' no one ez cared to live there but himself, he had it all his own way, made it pay, and, as I was sayin' before, held his head high for prices. Well — you ain't gettin' tired, ma'am?"

"No," said the lady, resting her cheek on her hand and gazing on the fire, "it's all very interesting; and so odd that you two men, with nearly the same experiences, should be neighbors."

"Say buyer and seller, ma'am, not neighbors — at least Scriptoorily — nor friends. Well, — now this is where the Speshal Providence comes in, — only this afternoon Jim Briggs, hearin' me speak of Horseley's offishness" —

"*Whose* offishness?" asked the lady.

"Horseley's offishness, — Horseley's the name of the man I'm talkin' about. Well, hearin' that, he says: "You hold on, Hays, and he'll climb down. That wife of his has left the stage — got sick of it — and is driftin' round in 'Frisco with some fellow.

When Horseley gets to hear that, you can't keep him here, — he'll settle up, sell out, and realize on everything he's got to go after her agin, — you bet. That's what Briggs said. Well, that's what sent me up to Horseley's to-night — to get there, drop the news, and then pin him down to that contract."

"It looked like a good stroke of business and a fair one," said the lady in an odd voice. It was so odd that Hays looked up. But she had somewhat altered her position, and was gazing at the ceiling, and with her hand to her face seemed to have just recovered from a slight yawn, at which he hesitated with a new and timid sense of politeness.

"You're gettin' tired, ma'am?"

"Oh dear, no!" she said in the same voice, but clearing her throat with a little cough. "And why did n't you see this Mr. Horseley after all? Oh, I forgot! — you said you changed your mind from something you'd heard."

He had turned his eyes to the fire again, but without noticing as he did so that she slowly moved her face, still half hidden by her hand, towards him and was watching him intently.

"No," he said, slowly, "nothin' I heard,

somethin' I felt. It mout hev been that that set me off the track. It kem to me all of a sudden that he might be sittin' thar calm and peaceful like ez I might be here, hevin' forgot all about her and his trouble, and here was me goin' to drop down upon him and start it all fresh agin. It looked a little like persecution — yes, like persecution. I got rid of it, sayin' to myself it was business. But I'd got off the road meantime, and had to find it again, and whenever I got back to the track and was pointed for his house, it all seemed to come back on me and set me off agin. When that had happened three times, I turned round and started for home."

"And do you mean to say," said the lady, with a discordant laugh, "that you believe, because *you* did n't go there and break the news, that nobody else will? That he won't hear of it from the first man he meets?"

"He don't meet any one up where he lives, and only Briggs and myself know it, and I'll see that Briggs don't tell. But it was mighty queer this whole thing comin' upon me suddenly, — was n't it?"

"Very queer," replied the lady; "for" — with the same metallic laugh — "you don't seem to be given to this kind of weakness with your own family."

If there was any doubt as to the sarcastic suggestion of her voice, there certainly could be none in the wicked glitter of her eyes fixed upon his face under her shading hand. But haply he seemed unconscious of both, and even accepted her statement without an ulterior significance.

"Yes," he said, communingly, to the glaring embers of the hearth, " it must have been a special revelation."

There was something so fatuous and one-idea'd in his attitude and expression, so monstrously inconsistent and inadequate to what was going on around him, and so hopelessly stupid — if a mere simulation — that the angry suspicion that he was acting a part slowly faded from her eyes, and a hysterical smile began to twitch her set lips. She still gazed at him. The wind howled drearily in the chimney; all that was economic, grim, and cheerless in the room seemed to gather as flitting shadows around that central figure. Suddenly she arose with such a quick rustling of her skirts that he lifted his eyes with a start; for she was standing immediately before him, her hands behind her, her handsome, audacious face bent smilingly forward, and her bold, brilliant eyes within a foot of his own.

"Now, Mr. Hays, do you want to know what this warning or special revelation of yours *really* meant? Well, it had nothing whatever to do with that man on the summit. No. The whole interest, gist, and meaning of it was simply this, that you should turn round and come straight back here and " — she drew back and made him an exaggerated theatrical curtsey — " have the supreme pleasure of making *my* acquaintance! That was all. And now, as you 've *had it*, in five minutes I must be off. You 've offered me already your horse and sleigh to go to the summit. I accept it and go! Good-by!"

He knew nothing of a woman's coquettish humor; he knew still less of that mimic stage from which her present voice, gesture, and expression were borrowed; he had no knowledge of the burlesque emotions which that voice, gesture, and expression were supposed to portray, and finally and fatally he was unable to detect the feminine hysteric jar and discord that underlay it all. He thought it was strong, characteristic, and real, and accepted it literally. He rose.

"Ef you allow you can't stay, why I'll go and get the horse. I reckon he ain't bin put up yet."

"Do, please."

He grimly resumed his coat and hat and disappeared through the passage into the kitchen, whence, a moment later, Zuleika came flying.

"Well, what has happened?" she said eagerly.

"It's all right," said the woman quickly, "though he knows nothing yet. But I've got things fixed generally, so that he'll be quite ready to have it broken to him by this time to-morrow. But don't you say anything till I've seen Jack and you hear from *him*. Remember."

She spoke rapidly; her cheeks were quite glowing from some sudden energy; so were Zuleika's with the excitement of curiosity. Presently the sound of sleigh-bells again filled the room. It was Hays leading the horse and sleigh to the door, beneath a sky now starlit and crisp under a northeast wind. The fair stranger cast a significant glance at Zuleika, and whispered hurriedly, "You know he must not come with me. You must keep him here."

She ran to the door muffled and hooded, leaped into the sleigh, and gathered up the reins.

"But you cannot go alone," said Hays, with awkward courtesy. "I was kalkilatin'" —

"You're too tired to go out again, dad," broke in Zuleika's voice quickly. "You ain't fit; you're all gray and krinkly now, like as when you had one of your last spells. She'll send the sleigh back to-morrow."

"I can find my way," said the lady briskly; "there's only one turn off, I believe, and that " —

"Leads to the stage station three miles west. You need n't be afraid of gettin' off on that, for you'll likely see the down stage crossin' your road ez soon ez you get clear of the ranch."

"Good-night," said the lady. An arc of white spray sprang before the forward runner, and the sleigh vanished in the road.

Father and daughter returned to the office.

"You did n't get to know her, dad, did ye?" queried Zuleika.

"No," responded Hays gravely, "except to see she was n't no backwoods or mountaineering sort. Now, there's the kind of woman, Zuly, as knows her own mind and yours too; that a man like your brother Jack oughter pick out when he marries."

Zuleika's face beamed behind her father. "You ain't goin' to sit up any longer, dad?" she said, as she noticed him resume his seat by the fire. "It's gettin' late, and you look mighty tuckered out with your night's work."

"Do you know what she said, Zuly?" returned her father, after a pause, which turned out to have been a long, silent laugh.

"No."

"She said," he repeated slowly, "that she reckoned I came back here to-night to have the pleasure of her acquaintance!" He brought his two hands heavily down upon his knees, rubbing them down deliberately towards his ankles, and leaning forward with his face to the fire and a long-sustained smile of complete though tardy appreciation.

He was still in this attitude when Zuleika left him. The wind crooned over him confidentially, but he still sat there, given up apparently to some posthumous enjoyment of his visitor's departing witticism.

It was scarcely daylight when Zuleika, while dressing, heard a quick tapping upon her shutter. She opened it to the scared and bewildered face of her brother.

"What happened with her and father last night?" he said hoarsely.

"Nothing — why?"

"Read that. It was brought to me half an hour ago by a man in dad's sleigh, from the stage station."

He handed her a crumpled note with trembling fingers. She took it and read: —

"The game's up and I'm out of it! Take my advice and clear out of it too, until you can come back in better shape. Don't be such a fool as to try and follow me. Your father isn't one, and that's where you've slipped up."

"He shall pay for it, whatever he's done," said her brother with an access of wild passion. "Where is he?"

"Why, Jack, you wouldn't dare to see him now?"

"Wouldn't I?" He turned and ran, convulsed with passion, before the windows towards the front of the house. Zuleika slipped out of her bedroom and ran to her father's room. He was not there. Already

A NIGHT AT "HAYS."

she could hear her brother hammering frantically against the locked front door.

The door of the office was partly open. Her father was still there. Asleep? Yes, for he had apparently sunk forward before the cold hearth. But the hands that he had always been trying to warm were colder than the hearth or ashes, and he himself never again spoke nor stirred.

. . . .

It was deemed providential by the neighbors that his youngest and favorite son, alarmed by news of his father's failing health, had arrived from the Atlantic States just at the last moment. But it was thought singular that after the division of the property he entirely abandoned the Ranch, and that even pending the division his beautiful but fastidious Eastern bride declined to visit it with her husband.

JOHNSON'S "OLD WOMAN."

It was growing dark, and the Sonora trail was becoming more indistinct before me at every step. The difficulty had increased over the grassy slope, where the overflow from some smaller watercourse above had worn a number of diverging gullies so like the trail as to be undistinguishable from it. Unable to determine which was the right one, I threw the reins over the mule's neck and resolved to trust to that superior animal's sagacity, of which I had heard so much. But I had not taken into account the equally well-known weaknesses of sex and species, and Chu Chu had already shown uncontrollable signs of wanting her own way. Without a moment's hesitation, feeling the relaxed bridle, she lay down and rolled over.

In this perplexity the sound of horse's hoofs ringing out of the rocky cañon beyond was a relief, even if momentarily embarrassing. An instant afterwards a horse and rider appeared cantering round the hill on what was evidently the lost trail, and pulled up as I succeeded in forcing Chu Chu to her legs again.

"Is that the trail from Sonora?" I asked.

"Yes;" but with a critical glance at the mule, "I reckon you ain't going thar to-night."

"Why not?"

"It's a matter of eighteen miles, and most of it a blind trail through the woods after you take the valley."

"Is it worse than this?"

"What's the matter with this trail? Ye ain't expecting a racecourse or a shell road over the foothills — are ye?"

"No. Is there any hotel where I can stop?"

"Nary."

"Nor any house?"

"No."

"Thank you. Good-night."

He had already passed on, when he halted again and turned in his saddle. "Look yer. Just a spell over yon cañon ye'll find a patch o' buckeyes; turn to the right and ye'll see a trail. That'll take ye to a shanty. You ask if it's Johnson's."

"Who's Johnson?"

"I am. You ain't lookin' for Vanderbilt or God Almighty up here, are you? Well, then, you hark to me, will you? You say to my old woman to give you supper and a shakedown somewhar to-night. Say *I* sent you. So long."

He was gone before I could accept or decline. An extraordinary noise proceeded from Chu Chu, not unlike a suppressed chuckle. I looked sharply at her; she coughed affectedly, and, with her head and neck stretched to their greatest length, appeared to contemplate her neat little off fore shoe with admiring abstraction. But as soon as I had mounted she set off abruptly, crossed the rocky cañon, apparently sighted the patch of buckeyes of her own volition, and without the slightest hesitation found the trail to the right, and in half an hour stood before the shanty.

It was a log cabin with an additional "lean-to" of the same material, roofed with bark, and on the other side a larger and more ambitious "extension" built of rough, unplaned, and unpainted redwood boards, lightly shingled. The "lean-to" was evidently used as a kitchen, and the central cabin as a living-room. The barking of a dog as I approached called four children of different sizes to the open door, where already an enterprising baby was feebly essaying to crawl over a bar of wood laid across the threshold to restrain it.

"Is this Johnson's house?"

My remark was really addressed to the eldest, a boy of apparently nine or ten, but I felt that my attention was unduly fascinated by the baby, who at that moment had toppled over the bar, and was calmly eyeing me upside down, while silently and heroically suffocating in its petticoats. The boy disappeared without replying, but presently returned with a taller girl of fourteen or fifteen. I was struck with the way that, as she reached the door, she passed her hands rapidly over the heads of the others as if counting them, picked up the baby, reversed it, shook out its clothes, and returned it to the inside, without even looking at it. The act was evidently automatic and habitual.

I repeated my question timidly.

Yes, it *was* Johnson's, but he had just gone to King's Mills. I replied, hurriedly, that I knew it, — that I had met him beyond the cañon. As I had lost my way and

could n't get to Sonora to-night, he had been
good enough to say that I might stay there
until morning. My voice was slightly raised
for the benefit of Mr. Johnson's "old woman," who, I had no doubt, was inspecting
me furtively from some corner.

The girl drew the children away, except
the boy. To him she said simply, "Show
the stranger whar to stake out his mule,
'Dolphus," and disappeared in the "extension" without another word. I followed my
little guide, who was perhaps more actively
curious, but equally unresponsive. To my
various questions he simply returned a smile
of exasperating vacuity. But he never took
his eager eyes from me, and I was satisfied
that not a detail of my appearance escaped
him. Leading the way behind the house to
a little wood, whose only "clearing" had
been effected by decay or storm, he stood
silently apart while I picketed Chu Chu,
neither offering to assist me nor opposing
any interruption to my survey of the locality. There was no trace of human cultiva-
tion in the surroundings of the cabin; the
wilderness still trod sharply on the heels
of the pioneer's fresh footprints, and even
seemed to obliterate them. For a few yards

around the actual dwelling there was an unsavory fringe of civilization in the shape of cast-off clothes, empty bottles, and tin cans, and the adjacent thorn and elder bushes blossomed unwholesomely with bits of torn white paper and bleaching dish-cloths. This hideous circle never widened; Nature always appeared to roll back the intruding débris; no bird nor beast carried it away; no animal ever forced the uncleanly barrier; civilization remained grimly trenched in its own exuvia. The old terrifying girdle of fire around the hunter's camp was not more deterring to curious night prowlers than this coarse and accidental outwork.

When I regained the cabin I found it empty, the doors of the lean-to and extension closed, but there was a stool set before a rude table, upon which smoked a tin cup of coffee, a tin dish of hot saleratus biscuit, and a plate of fried beef. There was something odd and depressing in this silent exclusion of my presence. Had Johnson's "old woman" from some dark post of observation taken a dislike to my appearance, or was this churlish withdrawal a peculiarity of Sierran hospitality? Or was Mrs. Johnson young and pretty, and hidden under the restricting ban of Johnson's jealousy, or was she a deformed cripple, or even a bedridden crone? From the extension at times came a murmur of voices, but never the accents of adult womanhood. The gathering darkness, relieved only by a dull glow from the smouldering logs in the adobe chimney, added to my loneliness. In the circumstances I knew I ought to have put aside the repast and given myself up to gloomy and pessimistic reflection; but Nature is often inconsistent, and in that keen mountain air, I grieve to say, my physical and moral condition was not in that perfect accord always indicated by romancers. I had an appetite and I gratified it; dyspepsia and ethical reflections might come later. I ate the saleratus biscuit cheerfully, and was meditatively finishing my coffee when a gurgling sound from the rafters above attracted my attention. I looked up; under the overhang of the bark roof three pairs of round eyes were fixed upon me. They belonged to the children I had previously seen, who, in the attitude of Raphael's cherubs, had evidently been deeply interested spectators of my repast. As our eyes met an inarticulate giggle escaped the lips of the youngest.

I never could understand why the shy amusement of children over their elders is not accepted as philosophically by its object as when it proceeds from an equal. We fondly believe that when Jones or Brown laughs at us it is from malice, ignorance, or a desire to show his superiority, but there is always a haunting suspicion in our minds that these little critics *really* see something in us to laugh at. I, however, smiled affably in return, ignoring any possible grotesqueness in my manner of eating in private.

"Come here, Johnny," I said blandly.

The two elder ones, a girl and a boy, disappeared instantly, as if the crowning joke of this remark was too much for them. From a scraping and kicking against the log wall I judged that they had quickly dropped to the ground outside. The younger one, the giggler, remained fascinated, but ready to fly at a moment's warning.

"Come here, Johnny, boy," I repeated gently. "I want you to go to your mother, please, and tell her" —

But here the child, who had been working its face convulsively, suddenly uttered a lugubrious howl and disappeared also. I ran to the front door and looked out in time to see the tallest girl, who had received me, walking away with it under her arm, pushing the boy ahead of her and looking back over her shoulder, not unlike a youthful she-bear conducting her cubs from danger. She disappeared at the end of the extension, where there was evidently another door.

It was very extraordinary. It was not strange that I turned back to the cabin with a chagrin and mortification which for a moment made me entertain the wild idea of saddling Chu Chu, and shaking the dust of that taciturn house from my feet. But the ridiculousness of such an act, to say nothing of its ingratitude, as quickly presented itself to me. Johnson had offered me only food and shelter; I could have claimed no more from the inn I had asked him to direct me to. I did not reënter the house, but, lighting my last cigar, began to walk gloomily up and down the trail. With the outcoming of the stars it had grown lighter; through a wind opening in the trees I could see the heavy bulk of the opposite mountain, and beyond it a superior crest defined by a red line of forest fire, which, however, cast no reflection on the surrounding earth or sky. Faint woodland currents of air, still warm from the afternoon sun, stirred the leaves around me with long-drawn aromatic breaths. But these in time gave way to the steady Sierran night wind sweeping down from the higher summits, and rocking the tops of the tallest pines, yet leaving the tranquillity of the dark lower aisles unshaken. It was very quiet; there was no cry nor call of beast or bird in the darkness; the long rustle of the tree-tops sounded as faint as the far-off wash of distant seas. Nor did the resemblance cease there; the close-set files of the pines and cedars, stretching in illimitable ranks to the horizon, were filled with the immeasurable loneliness of an ocean shore. In this vast silence I began to think I understood the taciturnity of the dwellers in the solitary cabin.

When I returned, however, I was surprised to find the tallest girl standing by the door. As I approached she retreated before me, and pointing to the corner where a common cot bed had been evidently just put up, said, "Ye can turn in thar, only ye'll have to rouse out early when 'Dolphus does the chores," and was turning towards the extension again, when I stopped her almost appealingly.

"One moment, please. Can I see your mother?"

She stopped and looked at me with a singular expression. Then she said sharply: —

"You know, fust rate, she's dead."

She was turning away again, but I think she must have seen my concern in my face, for she hesitated. "But," I said quickly, "I certainly understood your father, that is, Mr. Johnson," I added, interrogatively, "to say that — that I was to speak to" — I didn't like to repeat the exact phrase — "his *wife*."

"I don't know what he was playin' ye for," she said shortly. "Mar has been dead mor 'n a year."

"But," I persisted, "is there no grown-up woman here?"

"No."

"Then who takes care of you and the children?"

"I do."

"Yourself and your father — eh?"

"Dad ain't here two days running, and then on'y to sleep."

"And you take the entire charge of the house?"

"Yes, and the log tallies."

"The log tallies?"

"Yes; keep count and measure the logs that go by the slide."

It flashed upon me that I had passed the slide or declivity on the hillside, where logs were slipped down into the valley, and I inferred that Johnson's business was cutting timber for the mill.

"But you're rather young for all this work," I suggested.

"I'm goin' on sixteen," she said gravely.

Indeed, for the matter of that, she might have been any age. Her face, on which sunburn took the place of complexion, was already hard and set. But on a nearer view I was struck with the fact that her eyes, which were not large, were almost indistinguishable from the presence of the most singular eyelashes I had ever seen. Intensely black, intensely thick, and even tangled in their profusion, they bristled rather than fringed her eyelids, obliterating everything but the shining black pupils beneath, which were like certain lustrous hairy mountain berries. It was this woodland suggestion that seemed to uncannily connect her with the locality. I went on playfully: —

"That's not *very* old — but tell me —

does your father, or *did* your father, ever speak of you as his 'old woman?'"

She nodded. "Then you thought I was mar?" she said, smiling.

It was such a relief to see her worn face relax its expression of pathetic gravity — although this operation quite buried her eyes in their black thickest hedge again — that I continued cheerfully: "It wasn't much of a mistake, considering all you do for the house and family."

"Then you didn't tell Billy 'to go and be dead in the ground with mar,' as he 'lows you did?" she said half suspiciously, yet trembling on the edge of a smile.

No, I had not, but I admitted that my asking him to go to his mother might have been open to this dismal construction by a sensitive infant mind. She seemed mollified, and again turned to go.

"Good-night, Miss — you know your father didn't tell me your real name," I said.

"Karline!"

"Good-night, Miss Karline."

I held out my hand.

She looked at it and then at me through her intricate eyelashes. Then she struck it **aside briskly,** but not unkindly, said "Quit foolin', now," as she might have said to one of the children, and disappeared through the inner door. Not knowing whether to be amused or indignant, I remained silent a moment. Then I took a turn outside in the increasing darkness, listened to the now hurrying wind over the tree-tops, reëntered the cabin, closed the door, and went to bed.

But not to sleep. Perhaps the responsibility towards these solitary children, which Johnson had so lightly shaken off, devolved upon me as I lay there, for I found myself imagining a dozen emergencies of their unprotected state, with which the elder girl could scarcely grapple. There was little to fear from depredatory man or beast — desperadoes of the mountain trail never stooped to ignoble burglary, bear or panther seldom approached a cabin — but there was the chance of sudden illness, fire, the accidents that beset childhood, to say nothing of the narrowing moral and mental effect of their isolation at that tender age. It was scandalous in Johnson to leave them alone.

In the silence I found I could hear quite distinctly the sound of their voices in the extension, and it was evident that Caroline was putting them to bed. Suddenly a voice was uplifted — her own! She began to sing and the others to join her. It was the repetition of a single verse of a well-known lugubrious negro melody. "All the world am sad and dreary," wailed Caroline, in a high head-note, "everywhere I roam." "Oh, darkieth," lisped the younger girl in response, "how my heart growth weary, far from the old folkth at h-o-o-me." This was repeated two or three times before the others seemed to get the full swing of it, and then the lines rose and fell sadly and monotonously in the darkness. I don't know why, but I at once got the impression that those motherless little creatures were under a vague belief that their performance was devotional, and was really filling the place of an evening hymn. A brief and indistinct kind of recitation, followed by a dead silence, broken only by the slow creaking of new timber, as if the house were stretching itself to sleep too, confirmed my impression. Then all became quiet again.

But I was more wide awake than before. Finally I rose, dressed myself, and dragging my stool to the fire, took a book from my knapsack, and by the light of a guttering candle, which I discovered in a bottle in the corner of the hearth, began to read. Presently I fell into a doze. How long I slept I could not tell, for it seemed to me that a dreamy consciousness of a dog barking at last forced itself upon me so strongly that I awoke. The barking appeared to come from behind the cabin in the direction of the clearing where I had tethered Chu Chu. I opened the door hurriedly, ran round the cabin towards the hollow, and was almost at once met by the bulk of the frightened Chu Chu, plunging out of the darkness towards me, kept only in check by her reata in the hand of a blanketed shape slowly advancing with a gun over its shoulder out of the hollow. Before I had time to recover from my astonishment I was thrown into greater confusion by recognizing the shape as none other than Caroline!

Without the least embarrassment or even self-consciousness of her appearance, she tossed the end of the reata to me with the curtest explanation as she passed by. Some prowling bear or catamount had frightened the mule. I had better tether it before the cabin away from the wind.

"But I thought wild beasts never came so near," I said quickly.

"Mule meat's mighty temptin'," said the girl sententiously and passed on. I wanted to thank her; I wanted to say how sorry I was that she had been disturbed; I wanted to compliment her on her quiet midnight courage, and yet warn her against recklessness; I wanted to know whether she had been accustomed to such alarms; and if the gun she carried was really a necessity. But I could only respect her reticence, and I was turning away when I was struck by a more inexplicable spectacle. As she neared the end of the extension I distinctly saw the tall figure of a man, moving with a certain diffidence and hesitation that did not, however, suggest any intention of concealment, among the trees; the girl apparently saw him at the same moment and slightly slackened her pace. Not more than a dozen feet separated them. He said something that was inaudible to my ears, — but whether from his hesitation or the distance I could not determine. There was no such uncertainty in her reply, however, which was given in her usual curt fashion: "All right. You can trapse along home now and turn in."

She turned the corner of the extension and disappeared. The tall figure of the man wavered hesitatingly for a moment, and then vanished also. But I was too much excited by curiosity to accept this unsatisfactory conclusion, and, hastily picketing Chu Chu a few rods from the front door, I ran after him, with an instinctive feeling that he had not gone far. I was right. A few paces distant he had halted in the same dubious, lingering way. "Hallo!" I said.

He turned towards me in the like awkward fashion, but with neither astonishment nor concern.

"Come up and take a drink with me before you go," I said, "if you're not in a hurry. I'm alone here, and since I *have* turned out I don't see why we might n't have a smoke and a talk together."

"I durs n't."

I looked up at the six feet of strength before me and repeated wonderingly, "Dare not?"

"*She* would n't like it." He made a movement with his right shoulder towards the extension.

"Who?"

"Miss Karline."

"Nonsense!" I said. "She is n't in the cabin, — you won't see *her*. Come along."

He hesitated, although from what I could discern of his bearded face it was weakly smiling.

"Come."

He obeyed, following me not unlike Chu Chu, I fancied, with the same sense of superior size and strength and a slight whitening of the eye, as if ready to shy at any moment. At the door he "backed." Then he entered sideways. I noticed that he cleared the doorway at the top and the sides only by a hair's breadth.

By the light of the fire I could see that, in spite of his full first growth of beard, he was young, — even younger than myself, — and that he was by no means bad-looking. As he still showed signs of retreating at any moment, I took my flask and tobacco from my saddle-bags, handed them to him, pointed to the stool, and sat down myself upon the bed.

"You live near here?"

"Yes," he said a little abstractedly, as if listening for some interruption, "at Ten Mile Crossing."

"Why, that's two miles away."

"I reckon."

"Then you don't live here — on the clearing?"

"No. I b'long to the mill at ' T'en Mile.' "

"You were on your way home?"

"No," he hesitated, looking at his pipe; "I kinder meander round here at this time, when Johnson's away, to see if everything's goin' straight."

"I see — you're a friend of the family."

"'Deed no!" He stopped, laughed, looked confused, and added, apparently to his pipe, "That is, a sorter friend. Not much. *She*" — he lowered his voice as if that potential personality filled the whole cabin — "would n't like it."

"Then at night, when Johnson's away, you do sentry duty round the house?"

"Yes, 'sentry dooty,' that's it," — he seemed impressed with the suggestion — "that's it! Sentry dooty. You've struck it, pardner."

"And how often is Johnson away?"

"'Bout two or three times a week on an average."

"But Miss Caroline appears to be able to take care of herself. She has no fear."

"Fear! Fear was n't hangin' round when *she* was born!" He paused. "No, sir. Did ye ever look into them eyes?"

I had n't, on account of the lashes. But I did n't care to say this, and only nodded.

"There ain't the created thing livin' or dead, that she can't stand straight up to and look at."

I wondered if he had fancied she experienced any difficulty in standing up before that innocently good-humored face, but I could not resist saying: —

"Then I don't see the use of your walking four miles to look after her."

I was sorry for it the next minute, for he seemed to have awkwardly broken his pipe, and had to bend down for a long time afterwards to laboriously pick up the smallest fragments of it. At last he said, cautiously:

"Ye noticed them bits o' flannin' round the chillern's throats?"

I remembered that I had, but was uncertain whether it was intended as a preventive of cold or a child's idea of decoration. I nodded.

"That's their trouble. One night, when old Johnson had been off for three days to Coulterville, I was prowling round here and I did n't git to see no one, though there was a light burnin' in the shanty all night. The next night I was here again, — the same light twinklin', but no one about. I reckoned that was mighty queer, and I jess crep' up to the house an' listened. I heard suthin' like a little cough oncet in a while, and at times suthin' like a little moan. I did n't durst to sing out for I knew *she* would n't like it, but whistled keerless like, to let the chillern know I was there. But it didn't seem to take. I was jess goin' off, when — darn my skin! — if I did n't come across the bucket of water I 'd fetched up from the spring *that mornin'*, standin' there full, and *never taken in!* When I saw that I reckoned I 'd jess wade in, anyhow, and I knocked. Pooty soon the door was half opened, and I saw her eyes blazin' at me like them coals. Then *she* 'lowed I 'd better 'git up and git,' and shet the door to! Then I 'lowed she might tell me what was up — through the door. Then she said, through the door, as how the chillern lay all sick with that hoss-distemper, diphthery. Then she 'lowed she 'd use a doctor ef I 'd fetch him. Then she 'lowed again I 'd better take the baby that had n't ketched it yet along with me, and leave it where it was safe. Then she passed out the baby through the door all wrapped up in a blankit like a papoose, and you bet I made tracks with it. I knowed thar was n't no good going to the mill, so I let out for White's, four miles beyond, whar there was White's old mother. I told her how things were pointin', and she lent me a hoss, and I jess rounded on Doctor Green at Mountain Jim's, and had him back here afore sun-up! And then I heard she wilted, — regularly played out, you see, — for she had it all along wuss than the lot, and never let on or whimpered!"

"It was well you persisted in seeing her that night," I said, watching the rapt expression of his face. He looked up quickly, became conscious of my scrutiny, and dropped his eyes again, smiled feebly, and drawing a circle in the ashes with the broken pipe-stem, said:—

"But *she* did n't like it, though."

I suggested, a little warmly, that if she allowed her father to leave her alone at night with delicate children, she had no right to choose *who* should assist her in an emergency. It struck me afterwards that this was not very complimentary to him, and I added hastily that I wondered if she expected some young lady to be passing along the trail at midnight! But this reminded me of Johnson's style of argument, and I stopped.

"Yes," he said meekly, "and ef she did n't keer enough for herself and her brothers and sisters, she orter remember them Beazeley chillern."

"Beazeley children?" I repeated wonderingly.

"Yes; them two little ones, the size of Mirandy; they're Beazeley's."

"Who is Beazeley, and what are his children doing here?"

"Beazeley up and died at the mill, and she bedevilled her father to let her take his two young 'uns here."

"You don't mean to say that with her other work she's taking care of other people's children too?"

"Yes, and eddicatin' them."

"Educating them?"

"Yes; teachin' them to read and write and do sums. One of our loggers ketched her at it when she was keepin' tally."

We were both silent for some moments.

"I suppose you know Johnson?" I said finally.

"Not much."

"But you call here at other times than when you're helping her?"

"Never been in the house before."

He looked slowly around him as he spoke, raising his eyes to the bare rafters above, and drawing a few long breaths, as if he were inhaling the aura of some unseen presence. He appeared so perfectly gratified and contented, and I was so impressed with this humble and silent absorption of the sacred interior, that I felt vaguely conscious that any interruption of it was a profanation, and I sat still, gazing at the dying fire. Presently he arose, stretched out his hand, shook mine warmly, said, "I reckon I'll meander along," took another long breath, this time secretly, as if conscious of my eyes, and then slouched sideways out of the house into the darkness again, where he seemed suddenly to attain his full height, and so looming, disappeared. I shut the door, went to bed, and slept soundly.

So soundly that when I awoke the sun was streaming on my bed from the open door. On the table before me my breakfast was already laid. When I had dressed and eaten it, struck by the silence, I went to the door and looked out. 'Dolphus was holding Chu Chu by the reata a few paces from the cabin.

"Where's Caroline?" I asked.

He pointed to the woods and said: "Over yon: keeping tally."

"Did she leave any message?"

"Said I was to git your mule for you."

"Anything else?"

"Yes; said you was to go."

I went, but not until I had scrawled a few words of thanks on a leaf of my note-book, which I wrapped about my last Spanish dollar, addressed it to "Miss Johnson," and laid it upon the table.

. . . .

It was more than a year later that in the bar-room of the Mariposa Hotel a hand was laid upon my sleeve. I looked up. It was Johnson.

He drew from his pocket a Spanish dollar. "I reckoned," he said, cheerfully, "I'd run again ye somewhar some time. My old woman told me to give ye that when I did, and say that she 'didn't keep no hotel.' But she allowed she'd keep the letter, and has spelled it out to the chillern."

Here was the opportunity I had longed for to touch Johnson's pride and affection in the brave but unprotected girl. "I want to talk to you about Miss Johnson," I said, eagerly.

"I reckon so," he said, with an exasperating smile. "Most fellers do. But she ain't *Miss* Johnson no more. She's married."

"Not to that big chap over from Ten Mile Mills?" I said breathlessly.

"What's the matter with *him*," said Johnson. "Ye didn't expect her to marry a nobleman, did ye?"

I said I didn't see why she shouldn't — and believed that she *had*.

THE NEW ASSISTANT AT PINE CLEARING SCHOOL.

CHAPTER I.

THE schoolmistress of Pine Clearing was taking a last look around her schoolroom before leaving it for the day. She might have done so with pride, for the schoolroom was considered a marvel of architectural elegance by the citizens, and even to the ordinary observer was a pretty, villa-like structure, with an open cupola and overhanging roof of diamond-shaped shingles and a deep Elizabethan porch. But it was the monument of a fierce struggle between a newer civilization and a barbarism of the old days, which had resulted in the clearing away of the pines — and a few other things as incongruous to the new life and far less innocent, though no less sincere. It had cost the community fifteen thousand dollars, and the lives of two of its citizens.

Happily there was no stain of this on the clean white walls, the beautifully-written gilt texts, or the shining blackboard that had offered no record which could not be daily wiped away. And, certainly, the last person in the world to suggest any reminiscences of its belligerent foundation was the person of the schoolmistress. Mature, thin, precise, — not pretty enough to have excited Homeric feuds, nor yet so plain as to preclude certain soothing graces, — she was the widow of a poor Congregational minister, and had been expressly imported from San Francisco to squarely mark the issue between the regenerate and unregenerate life. Low-voiced, gentlewomanly, with the pallor of ill-health perhaps unduly accented by her mourning, which was still cut modishly enough to show off her spare but good figure, she was supposed to represent the model of pious, scholastic refinement. The Opposition — sullen in ditches and at the doors of saloons, or in the fields truculent as their own cattle — nevertheless had lowered their crests and buttoned their coats over their revolutionary red shirts when *she* went by.

As she was stepping from the threshold, she was suddenly confronted by a brisk business-looking man, who was about to enter. "Just in time to catch you, Mrs. Martin," he said hurriedly; then, quickly correcting his manifest familiarity, he added: "I mean, I took the liberty of running in here on my way to the stage office. That matter you spoke of is all arranged. I talked it over with the other trustees, wrote to Sam Barstow, and he's agreeable, and has sent somebody up, and," he rapidly consulted his watch, "he ought to be here now; and I'm on my way to meet him with the other trustees."

Mrs. Martin, who at once recognized her visitor as the Chairman of the School Board, received the abrupt information with the slight tremulousness, faint increase of color, and hurried breathing of a nervous woman.

"But," she said, "it was only a *suggestion* of mine, Mr. Sperry; I really have no right to ask — I had no idea" —

"It's all right, ma'am, — never you mind. We put the case square to Barstow. We allowed that the school was getting too large for you to tackle, — I mean, you know, to superintend single-handed; and that these Pike County boys they're running in on us are a little too big and sassy for a lady like you to lasso and throw down — I mean, to sorter control — don't you see? But, bless you, Sam Barstow saw it all in a minit! He just jumped at it. I've got his letter here — hold on"— he hastily produced a letter from his pocket, glanced over it, suddenly closed it again with embarrassed quickness, yet not so quickly but that the woman's quicker eyes were caught, and nervously fascinated by the expression "I'm d—d" in a large business hand — and said in awkward haste, "No matter about reading it now — keep you too long — but he's agreed all right, you know. Must go now — they'll be waiting. Only I thought I'd drop in a-passin', to keep you posted;" and, taking off his hat, he began to back from the porch.

"Is — is — this gentleman who is to assist me — a — a mature professional man — or a — graduate?" hesitated Mrs. Martin, with a faint smile.

"Don't really know — I reckon Sam — Mr. Barstow — fixed that all right. Must really go now;" and, still holding his hat in his hand as a polite compromise for his undignified haste, he fairly ran off.

Arrived at the stage office, he found the **two** other trustees awaiting him, and the still more tardy stage-coach. One, a large, smooth-faced, portly man, was the Presbyterian minister; the other, of thinner and more serious aspect, was a large mill-owner.

"I presume," said the Rev. Mr. Peaseley, slowly, "that as our good brother Barstow, in the urgency of the occasion, has, to some extent, anticipated *our* functions in engaging this assistant, he is — a — a — satisfied with his capacity?"

"Sam knows what he's about," said the mill-owner cheerfully, "and as he's regularly buckled down to the work here, and will go his bottom dollar on it, you can safely leave things to him."

"He certainly has exhibited great zeal," said the reverend gentleman patronizingly.

"Zeal," echoed Sperry enthusiastically, "zeal? Why, he runs Pine Clearing as he runs his bank and his express company in Sacramento, and he's as well posted as if he were here all the time. Why, look here;" he nudged the mill-owner secretly, and, as the minister's back was momentarily turned, pulled out the letter he had avoided reading to Mrs. Martin, and pointed to a paragraph. "I'll be d—d," said the writer, "but I'll have peace and quietness at Pine Clearing, if

I have to wipe out or make over the whole Pike County gang. Draw on me for a piano if you think Mrs. Martin can work it. But don't say anything to Peaseley first, or he'll want it changed for a harmonium, and that lets us in for psalm-singing till you can't rest. Mind! I don't object to Church influence — it's a good hold! — but you must run *it* with other things equal, and not let it run *you*. I've got the schoolhouse insured for thirty thousand dollars — special rates too."

The mill-owner smiled. "Sam's head is level! But," he added, "he don't say much about the new assistant he's sending."

"Only here," he says, "I reckon the man I send will do all round; for Pike County has its claims as well as Boston."

"What does that mean?" asked the mill-owner.

"I reckon he means he don't want Pine Clearing to get too high-toned any more than he wants it too low down. He's mighty square in his averages — is Sam."

Here speculation was stopped by the rapid oncoming of the stage-coach in all the impotent fury of a belated arrival. "Had to go round by Montezuma to let off Jack Hill," curtly explained the driver, as he swung himself from the box, and entered the hotel bar-room in company with the new expressman, who had evidently taken Hill's place on the box-seat. Autocratically indifferent to further inquiry, he called out cheerfully: "Come along, boys, and hear this yer last new yarn about Sam Barstow, — it's the biggest thing out." And in another moment the waiting crowd, with glasses in their hands, were eagerly listening to the repetition of the "yarn" from the new expressman, to the apparent exclusion of other matters, mundane and practical.

Thus debarred from information, the three trustees could only watch the passengers as they descended, and try to identify their expected stranger. But in vain: the bulk of the passengers they already knew, the others were ordinary miners and laborers; there was no indication of the new assistant among them. Pending further inquiry they were obliged to wait the conclusion of the expressman's humorous recital. This was evidently a performance of some artistic merit, depending upon a capital imitation of an Irishman, a German Jew, and another voice, which was universally recognized and applauded as being "Sam's style all over!" But for the presence of the minister, Sperry and the mill-owner would have joined the enthusiastic auditors, and inwardly regretted the respectable obligations of their official position.

When the story-teller had concluded amidst a general call for more drinks, Sperry approached the driver. The latter recognizing him, turned to his companion carelessly, said, "Here's one of 'em," and was going away when Sperry stopped him.

"We were expecting a young man."

"Yes," said the driver, impatiently, "and there he is, I reckon."

"We don't mean the new expressman," said the minister, smiling blandly, "but a young man who" —

"*That* ain't no new expressman," returned the driver in scornful deprecation of his interlocutor's ignorance. "He only took Hill's place from Montezuma. He's the new kid reviver and polisher for that University you're runnin' here. I say — you fellers oughter get him to tell you that story of Sam Barstow and the Chinaman. It'd limber you fellers up to hear it."

"I fear there's some extraordinary mis-

AT PINE CLEARING SCHOOL. 183

take here," said Mr. Peaseley, with a chilling Christian smile.

"Not a bit of it. He's got a letter from Sam for one of ye. Yere, Charley — what's your name! Com yere. Yere's all yer three bosses waiting for ye."

And the supposed expressman and late narrator of amusing stories came forward and presented his credentials as the assistant teacher of Pine Clearing.

CHAPTER II.

EVEN the practical Mr. Sperry was taken aback. The young man before him was squarely built, with broad shoulders, and a certain air of muscular activity. But his face, although good-humored, was remarkable for offering not the slightest indication of studious preoccupation or mental training. A large mouth, light blue eyes, a square jaw, the other features being indistinctive — were immobile as a mask — except that, unlike a mask, they seemed to actually reflect the vacuity of the mood within, instead of concealing it. But as he saluted the trustees they each had the same feeling that even this expression was imported and not instinctive. His face was clean-shaven, and his hair cut so short as to suggest that a wig of some kind was necessary to give it characteristic or even ordinary human semblance. His manner, self-assured yet lacking reality, and his dress of respectable cut and material, yet worn as if it did not belong to him, completed a picture as unlike a student or schoolmaster as could be possibly conceived.

Yet there was the letter in Mr. Peaseley's hands from Barstow, introducing Mr. Charles Twing as the first assistant teacher in the Pine Clearing Free Academy!

The three men looked hopelessly at each other. An air of fatigued righteousness and a desire to be spiritually at rest from other trials pervaded Mr. Peaseley. Whether or not the young man felt the evident objection he had raised, he assumed a careless position, with his back and elbows against the bar; but even the attitude was clearly not his own.

"Are you personally known to Mr. Barstow?" asked Sperry, with a slight business asperity.

"Yes."

"That is — you are quite well acquainted with him?"

"If you'd heard me gag his style a minute ago, so that everybody here knew who it was, you'd say so."

Mr. Peaseley's eyes sought the ceiling, and rested on the hanging lamp, as if nothing short of direct providential interference could meet the occasion. Yet, as the eyes of his brother trustees were bent on him expectantly, he nerved himself to say something.

"I suppose, Mr. — Mr. Twing, you have properly understood the great — I may say, very grave, intellectual, and moral responsibilities of the work you seek to undertake — and the necessity of supporting it by *example*, by practice, by personal influence both in the school and *out of it*. Sir, I presume, sir, you feel that you are fully competent to undertake this?"

"I reckon *he* does!"

"*Who* does?"

"Sam Barstow, or he wouldn't have selected me. I presume" (with the slightest possible and almost instinctive imitation of the reverend gentleman's manner) "his head is considered level."

Mr. Peaseley withdrew his eyes from the ceiling. "I have," he said to his companions, with a pained smile, "an important choir meeting to attend this afternoon. I fear I must be excused." As he moved towards the door, the others formally following him, until out of the stranger's hearing, he added: "I wash my hands of this. After so wanton and unseemly an exhibition of utter incompetency, and even of understanding of the trust imposed upon him — upon *us* — *my* conscience forbids me to interfere further. But the real arbiter in this matter will be — thank Heaven! — the mistress herself. You have only to confront her at once with this man. *Her* decision will be speedy and final. For even Mr. Barstow will not dare to force so outrageous a character upon a delicate, refined woman, in a familiar and confidential capacity."

"That's so," said Sperry eagerly; "she'll settle it. And, of course," added the millowner, "that will leave *us* out of any difficulty with Sam."

The two men returned to the hapless stranger, relieved, yet constrained by the sacrifice to which they felt they were leading him. It would be necessary, they said, to introduce him to his principal, Mrs. Martin, at once. They might still find her at the schoolhouse, distant but a few steps. They said little else, the stranger keeping up an ostentatious whistling, and becoming more and more incongruous, they thought, as they neared the pretty schoolhouse. Here they *did* find Mrs. Martin, who had, naturally, lingered after the interview with Sperry.

She came forward to meet them, with the nervous shyness and slightly fastidious hesitation that was her nature. They saw, or fancied they saw, the same surprise and disappointment they had themselves experienced pass over her sensitive face, as she looked at him; they felt that their vulgar charge appeared still more outrageous by contrast with this delicate woman and her pretty, refined surroundings; but they saw that *he* enjoyed it, and was even — if such a word could be applied to so self-conscious a man — more at ease in her presence!

"I reckon you and me will pull together very well, ma'am," he said confidently.

They looked to see her turn her back upon him; faint, or burst out crying; but she did neither, and only gazed at him quietly.

"It's a mighty pretty place you've got here — and I like it, and if *we* can't run it, I don't know who can. Only just let me know *what* you want, ma'am, and you can count on me every time."

To their profound consternation Mrs. Martin smiled faintly.

"It rests with *you* only, Mrs. Martin," said Sperry quickly and significantly. "It's *your* say, you know; you're the only one to be considered or consulted here."

"Only just say what you want me to do," continued Twing, apparently ignoring the trustees; "pick out the style of job; give me a hint or two how to work it, or what you'd think would be the proper gag to fetch 'em, and I'm there, ma'am. It may be new at first, but I'll get at the business of it quick enough."

Mrs. Martin smiled — this time quite perceptibly — with the least little color in her cheeks and eyes. "Then you've had no experience in teaching?" she said.

"Well — no."

"You are not a graduate of any college?"

"Not much."

The two trustees looked at each other. Even Mr. Peaseley had not conceived such a damning revelation.

"Well," said Mrs. Martin slowly, "perhaps Mr. Twing had better *come early tomorrow morning and begin.*"

"Begin?" gasped Mr. Sperry in breathless astonishment.

"Certainly," said Mrs. Martin in timid explanation. "If he is new to the work the sooner the better."

Mr. Sperry could only gaze blankly at his brother official. Had they heard aright? Was this the recklessness of nervous excitement in a woman of delicate health, or had the impostor cast some glamour upon her? Or was she frightened of Sam Barstow and afraid to reject his candidate? The last thought was an inspiration. He drew her quickly aside. "One moment, Mrs. Martin! You said to me an hour ago that you did n't intend to have asked Mr. Barstow to send you an assistant. I hope that, merely because he *has* done so, you don't feel obliged to accept this man against your better judgment?"

"Oh no," said Mrs. Martin quietly.

The case seemed hopeless. And Sperry had the miserable conviction that by having insisted upon Mrs. Martin's judgment being final they had estopped their own right to object. But how could they have foreseen her extraordinary taste? He, however, roused himself for a last appeal.

"Mrs. Martin," he said in a lower voice, "I ought to tell you that the Reverend Mr. Peaseley strongly doubts the competency of that young man."

"Did n't Mr. Barstow make a selection at

your request?" asked Mrs. Martin, with a faint little nervous cough.

"Yes — but" —

"Then his competency only concerns *me* — and I don't see what Mr. Peaseley has to say about it."

Could he believe his senses? There was a decided flush in the woman's pale face, and the first note of independence and asperity in her voice.

That night, in the privacy of his conjugal chamber, Mr. Sperry relieved his mind to another of the enigmatical sex, — the stout Southwestern partner of his joys and troubles. But the result was equally unsatisfactory. "Well, Abner," said the lady, " I never could see, for all your men's praises of Mrs. Martin, what that feller can see in *her* to like!"

CHAPTER III.

MRS. MARTIN was early at the schoolhouse the next morning, yet not so early but that she discovered that the new assistant had been there before her. This was shown in some rearrangement of the school seats and benches. They were placed so as to form a horseshoe before her desk, and at the further extremity of this semicircle was a chair evidently for himself. She was a little nettled at his premature action, although admitting the utility of the change, but she was still more annoyed at his absence at such a moment. It was nearly the school hour when he appeared, to her surprise, marshaling a file of some of the smaller children whom he had evidently picked up *en route*, and who were, to her greater surprise, apparently on the best of terms with him. "Thought I'd better rake 'em in, introduce myself to 'em, and get 'em to know me before school begins. Excuse me," he went on hastily, "but I've a lot more coming up, and I'd better make myself square with them *outside*." But Mrs. Martin had apparently developed a certain degree of stiffness since their evening's interview.

"It seems to me quite as important, Mr. Twing," she said drily, "that you should first learn some of your own duties, which I came here early to teach you."

"Not at all," he said cheerfully. "To-day I take my seat, as I've arranged it, you see, over there with them, and watch 'em go through the motions. One rehearsal's enough for *me*. At the same time, I can chip in if necessary." And before she could reply he was out of the schoolhouse again, hailing the new-comers. This was done with apparently such delight to the children and with some evidently imported expression into his smooth mask-like face, that Mrs. Martin had to content herself with watching him with equal curiosity. She was turning away with a sudden sense of forgotten dignity, when a shout of joyous, childish laughter attracted her attention to the window. The new assistant, with half a dozen small children on his square shoulders, walking with bent back and every simulation of advanced senility, was evidently personating, with the assistance of astonishingly distorted features, the ogre of a Christmas pantomime. As his eye caught hers the expression vanished, the mask-like face returned; he set the children down, and moved away. And when school began, although he marshaled them triumphantly to the very door, — with what contortion of face or simulation of character she was unable to guess, — after he had entered the schoolroom and taken his seat every vestige of his previous facial aberration was gone, and only his usual stolidity remained. In vain, as Mrs. Martin expected, the hundred delighted little eyes before her dwelt at first eagerly and hopefully upon his face, but, as she *had not* expected, recognizing from the blankness of his demeanor that the previous performance was intended for them exclusively, the same eager eyes were presently dropped again upon their books in simple imitation, as if he were one of themselves. Mrs. Martin breathed freely, and lessons began.

Yet she was nervously conscious, meanwhile, of a more ill-omened occurrence. This was the non-arrival of several of her oldest pupils, notably, the refractory and incorrigible Pike County contingent to whom Sperry had alluded. For the past few days they had hovered on the verge of active insubordination, and had indulged in vague mutterings which she had resolutely determined not to hear. It was, therefore, with some inward trepidations, not entirely relieved by Twing's presence, that she saw the three Mackinnons and the two Hardees slouch into the school a full hour after the lessons had begun. They did not even excuse themselves, but were proceeding with a surly and ostentatious defiance to their seats, when Mrs. Martin was obliged to look up, and — as the eldest Hardee filed before her — to demand an explanation. The culprit addressed — a dull, heavy-looking youth of nineteen — hesitated with an air of mingled doggedness and sheepishness, and then, without replying, nudged his companion. It was evidently a preconcerted signal of rebellion, for the boy nudged stopped, and, turning a more intelligent, but equally dissatisfied, face upon the schoolmistress, began determinedly: —

"Wot's our excuse for coming an hour late? Well, we ain't got none. *We* don't call it an hour late — *we* don't. We call it

the right time. We call it the right time for
our lessons, for we don't allow to come here
to sing hymns with babbies. We don't want
to know 'where, oh where, are the Hebrew
children?' They ain't nothin' to us Ameri-
cans. And we don't want any more Daniels
in the Lions' Den played off on us. We have
enough of 'em in Sunday-school. We ain't
hankerin' much for grammar and dictionary
hogwash, and we don't want no Boston parts
o' speech rung in on us the first thing in the
mo'nin'. We ain't Boston — we're Pike
County — *we* are. We reckon to do our
sums, and our figgerin', and our sale and
barter, and our interest tables and weights
and measures when the time comes, and our
geograffy when it's on, and our readin' and
writin' and the American Constitution in
reg'lar hours, and then we calkilate to git
up and git afore the po'try and the Boston
airs and graces come round. That's our
rights and what our fathers pay school taxes
for, and we want 'em."

He stopped, looking less towards the
schoolmistress than to his companions, for
whom perhaps, after the schoolboy fashion,
this attitude was taken. Mrs. Martin sat,
quite white and self-contained, with her eyes

fixed on the frayed rim of the rebel's straw hat which he still kept on his head. Then she said quietly : —

"Take off your hat, sir."

The boy did not move.

"He can't," said a voice cheerfully.

It was the new assistant. The whole school faced rapidly towards him. The rebel leader and his followers, who had not noticed him before, stared at the interrupter, who did not, however, seem to exhibit any of the authority of office, but rather the comment and criticism of one of themselves. "Wot you mean?" asked the boy indignantly.

"I mean you can't take off your hat because you've got some things stowed away in it you don't want seen," said Twing, with an immovable face.

"Wot things?" exclaimed the boy angrily. Then suddenly recollecting himself, he added, "Go along! You can't fool me! Think you'll make me take off my hat — don't you?"

"Well," said Twing, advancing to the side of the rebel, "look here then!" With a dexterous movement and a slight struggle from the boy, he lifted the hat. A half-dozen apples, a bird's nest, two birds' eggs, and a fluttering half-fledged bird fell from it. A wave of delight and astonishment ran along the benches, a blank look of hopeless bewilderment settled upon the boy's face, and the gravity of the situation disappeared forever in the irrepressible burst of laughter, in which even his brother rebels joined. The smallest child who had been half-frightened, half-fascinated by the bold, bad, heroic attitude of the mutineer, was quick to see the ridiculousness of that figure crowned with cheap schoolboy plunder. The eloquent protest of his wrongs was lost in the ludicrous appearance of the protester. Even Mrs. Martin felt that nothing she could say at that moment could lift the rebellion into seriousness again. But Twing was evidently not satisfied.

"Beg Mrs. Martin's pardon, and say you were foolin' with the boys," he said in a low voice.

The discomfited rebel hesitated.

"Say it, or I'll *show what you've got in your pockets!*" said Twing in a terribly significant aside.

The boy mumbled an apology to Mrs. Martin, scrambled in a blank, hopeless way to his seat, and the brief rebellion ignominiously ended. But two things struck Mrs. Martin as peculiar. She overheard the culprit say, with bated breath and evident sincerity, to his comrades: "Had n't nothing in my hat, anyway!" and one of the infant class was heard to complain, in a deeply-injured way, that the bird's nest was *his*, and had been "stoled" from his desk. And there still remained the fact for which Twing's undoubted fascination over the children had somewhat prepared her — that at recess the malcontents — one and all — seemed to have forgiven the man who had overcome them, and gathered round him with unmistakable interest. All this, however, did not blind her to the serious intent of the rebellion, or of Twing's unaccountable assumption of her prerogative. While he was still romping with the children she called him in.

"I must remind you," she said, with a slight nervous asperity, "that this outrageous conduct of Tom Hardee was evidently deliberated and prepared by the others, and cannot end in this way."

He looked at her with a face so exasperatingly expressionless that she could have slapped it as if it had belonged to one of the older scholars, and said, — "But it *has* ended. It 's a dead frost."

"I don't know what you mean; and I must remind you also that in this school we neither teach nor learn slang."

His immobile face changed for an instant to a look of such decided admiration that she felt her color rise; but he wiped his expression away with his hand as if it had been some artificial make-up, and said awkwardly, but earnestly: —

"Excuse me — won't you? But, look here, Mrs. Martin, I found out early this morning, when I was squaring myself with the other children, that there was this row hangin' on — in fact, that there was a sort of idea that Pike County wasn't having a fair show — excuse me — in the running of the school, and that Peaseley and Barstow were a little too much on in every scene. In fact, you see, it was just what Tom said."

"This is insufferable," said Mrs. Martin, her eyes growing darker as her cheeks grew red. "They shall go home to their parents, and tell them from me" —

"That they're all mistaken — excuse me — but that's just what *they're goin'* to do. I tell you, Mrs. Martin, their little game's busted — I beg pardon — but it's all over. You'll have no more trouble with them."

"And you think that just because you found Tom had something in his hat, and exposed him?" said Mrs. Martin scornfully.

"Tom *hadn't* anything in his hat," said Twing, wiping his mouth slowly.

"Nothing?" repeated Mrs. Martin.

"No."

"But I *saw* you take the things out."

"That was only a *trick!* He had nothing except what I had up my sleeve, and forced on him. He knew it, and that frightened him, and made him look like a fool, and so bursted up his conspiracy. There's nothin' boys are more afraid of than ridicule, or the man or boy that make 'em ridiculous."

"I won't ask you if you call this *fair* to the boy, Mr. Twing?" said Mrs. Martin hotly; "but is this your idea of discipline?"

"I call it fair, because Tom knew it was some kind of a trick, and wasn't deceived. I call it discipline if it made him do what was right afterwards, and makes him afraid or unwilling to do anything to offend me or you again. He likes me none the worse for giving him a chance of being laughed out of a thing instead of being *driven* out of it. And," he added, with awkward earnestness, "if you'll just leave all this to *me*, and only consider me here to take this sort of work — which ain't a lady's — off your hands, we'll just strike our own line between the Peaseleys and Pike County — and run this school in spite of both."

A little mollified, a good deal puzzled, and perhaps more influenced by the man's manner than she had imagined, Mrs. Martin said nothing, but let the day pass without dismissing the offenders. And on returning home that evening she was considerably surprised to receive her landlady's extravagant congratulations on the advent of her new assistant. "And they do say, Mrs. Martin," continued that lady enthusiastically, "that your just setting your foot down square on that Peaseley and that Barstow, *both of 'em* — and choosing your own assistant yourself — a plain young fellow with no frills and fancies, but one that you could set about making all the changes you like, was just the biggest thing you ever did for Pine Clearing."

"And — they — consider him quite — competent?" said Mrs. Martin, with timid color and hesitating audacity.

"Competent! You ask my Johnny."

Nevertheless, Mrs. Martin was somewhat formally early at the schoolhouse the next morning. "Perhaps," she said, with an odd mixture of dignity and timidity, "we'd better, before school commences, go over the lessons for the day."

"I *have*," he said quickly. "I told you *one* rehearsal was enough for me."

"You mean you have looked over them?"

"Got 'em by heart. Letter perfect. Want to hear me? Listen."

She did. He had actually committed to memory, and without a lapse, the entire text of rules, questions, answers, and examples of the lessons for the day.

CHAPTER IV.

BEFORE a month had passed, Mr. Twing's success was secure and established. So were a few of the changes he had quietly instituted. The devotional singing and Scripture reading which had excited the discontent of the Pike County children and their parents was not discontinued, but half an hour before recess was given up to some secular choruses, patriotic or topical, in which the little ones under Twing's really wonderful practical tuition exhibited such quick and pleasing proficiency, that a certain negro minstrel camp-meeting song attained sufficient popularity to be lifted by general accord to promotion to the devotional exercises, where it eventually ousted the objectionable " Hebrew children " on the question of melody alone. Grammar was still taught at Pine Clearing School in spite of the Hardees and Mackinnons, but Twing had managed to import into the cognate exercises of recitation a wonderful degree of enthusiasm and excellence. Dialectical Pike County, that had refused to recognize the governing powers of the nominative case, nevertheless came out strong in classical elocution, and Tom Hardee, who had delivered his ungrammatical protest on behalf of Pike County, was no less strong, if more elegant, in his impeachment of Warren Hastings as Edmund Burke, with the equal sanction of his parents. The trustees, Sperry and Jackson, had marveled, but were glad enough to accept the popular verdict — only Mr. Peaseley still retained an attitude of martyr-like forbearance and fatigued toleration towards the new assistant and his changes. As to Mrs. Martin, she seemed to accept the work of Mr. Twing after his own definition of it — as of a masculine quality ill-suited to a lady's tastes and inclinations; but it was noticeable that while she had at first repelled any criticism of him whatever, she had lately been given to explaining his position to her friends, and had spoken of him with somewhat labored and ostentatious patronage. Yet when they were alone together she frankly found him very amusing, and his presumption and vulgarity so clearly unintentional that it no longer offended her.

They were good friends without having any confidences beyond the duties of the school; she had asked no further explanation of the fact that he had been selected by Mr. Barstow without reference to any special antecedent training. What his actual antecedents were she had never cared to know, nor he apparently to reveal; that he had been engaged in some other occupations of superior or inferior quality would not have been remarkable in a community where the principal lawyer had been a soldier, and the miller a doctor. The fact that he admired her was plain enough to *her*; that it pleased her, but carried with it no ulterior thought or responsibility, might have been equally clear to others. Perhaps it was so to *him*.

Howbeit, this easy mutual intercourse was one day interrupted by what seemed a trifling incident. The piano, which Mr. Barstow had promised, duly made its appearance in the schoolhouse, to the delight of the scholars and the gentle satisfaction of Mrs. Martin, who, in addition to the rudimentary musical instruction of the younger girls, occasionally played upon it herself in a prim, refined, and conscientious fashion. To this, when she was alone after school hours, she sometimes added a faint, colorless voice of limited range and gentlewomanly expression. It was on one of these occasions that Twing, becoming an accidental auditor of this chaste, sad piping, was not only permitted to remain to hear the end of a love song of strictly guarded passion in the subjunctive mood, but at the close was invited to try his hand — a quick, if not a cultivated one — at the instrument. He did so. Like her, he added his voice. Like hers, it was a love song. But there the similitude ended. Negro in dialect, illiterate in construction, idiotic in passion, and presumably addressed to the "Rose of Alabama," in the very extravagance of its childish infatuation it might have been a mockery of the schoolmistress's song but for one tremendous fact! In unrestrained feeling, pathetic yearning, and exquisite tenderness of expression, it was unmistakably and appallingly personal and sincere. It was true the lips spoken of were "lubly," the eyes alluded to were like "lightenin' bugs," but from the voice and gestures of the singer Mrs. Martin confusedly felt that they were intended for *hers*, and even the refrain that "she dressed so neat and looked so sweet" was glaringly allusive to her own modish mourning. Alternately flushing and paling, with a hysteric smile hovering round her small reserved mouth, the unfortunate gentlewoman was fain to turn to the window to keep her countenance until it was concluded. She did not ask him to repeat it, nor did she again subject herself to this palpable serenade, but a few days afterwards, as she was idly striking the keys in the interval of a music lesson, one of her little pupils broke out, " Why, Mrs. Martin, if yo ain't a pickin' out that pow'ful pretty tune that Mr. Twing sings!"

Nevertheless, when Twing, a week or two later, suggested that he might sing the same song as a solo at a certain performance to be given by the school children in aid of a local charity, she drily intimated that it was hardly of a character to suit the entertainment. " But," she added, more gently, "you recite so well; why not give a recitation?"

He looked at her with questioning and troubled eyes, — the one expression he seemed to have lately acquired. " But that would be *in public!* There 'll be a lot of people there," he said doubtfully.

A little amused at this first apparent sign of a want of confidence in himself, she said, with a reassuring smile, "So much the better, — you do it really too well to have it thrown away entirely on children."

"Do *you* wish it?" he said suddenly.

Somewhat confused, but more irritated by his abruptness, she replied, "Why not?" But when the day came, and before a crowded audience, in which there was a fair sprinkling of strangers, she regretted her rash suggestion. For when the pupils had gone through certain calisthenic exercises — admirably taught and arranged by him — and "spoken their pieces," he arose, and, fixing his eyes on her, began Othello's defense before the Duke and Council. Here, as on the previous occasion, she felt herself personally alluded to in his account of his wooing. Desdemona, for some occult reason, vicariously appeared for her in the unwarrantable picture of his passion, and to this was added the absurd consciousness which she could not put aside that the audience, following with enthusiasm his really strong declamation, was also following his suggestion and adopting it. Yet she was also conscious, and, as she thought, as inconsistently, of being pleased and even proud of his success. At the conclusion the applause was general, and a voice added with husky admiration and familiarity: —

"Brayvo, Johnny Walker!"

Twing's face became suddenly white as a Pierrot mask. There was a dead silence, in which the voice continued, "Give us 'Sugar in the Gourd,' Johnny."

A few hisses, and cries of "Hush!" "Put him out!" followed. Mrs. Martin raised her eyes quickly to where her assistant had stood bowing his thanks a moment before. He was gone!

More concerned than she cared to confess, vaguely fearful that she was in some way connected with his abrupt withdrawal, and perhaps a little remorseful that she had allowed her personal feelings to interfere with her frank recognition of his triumph, she turned back to the schoolroom, after the little performers and their audience had departed, in the hope that he might return. It was getting late, the nearly level rays of the sun were lying on the empty benches at the lower end of the room, but the desk where she sat with its lid raised was in deep shadow. Suddenly she heard his voice in a rear hall, but it was accompanied by another's, — the same voice which had interrupted the applause. Before she could either withdraw, or make herself known, the two men had entered the room, and were passing slowly through it. She understood at once that Twing had slipped out into a janitor's room in the rear, where he had evidently forced an interview and explanation from his interrupter, and now had been waiting for the audience to disperse before emerging by the front door. They had evidently overlooked her in the shadow.

"But," said the stranger, as if following an aggrieved line of apology, "if Barstow knew who you were, and what you'd done, and still thought you good enough to rastle round here and square up them Pike County fellers and them kids — what in thunder do you care if the others *do* find you out, as long as Barstow sticks to you?"

"I've told you why, Dick," returned Twing gloomily.

"Oh, the schoolma'am!"

"Yes, she's a saint, an angel. More than that — she's a lady, Dick, to the tip of her fingers, who knows nothing of the world outside a parson's study. She took me on trust — without a word — when the trustees hung back and stared. She's never asked me about myself, and now when she knows who and what I have been — she'll loathe me!"

"But look here, Jim," said the stranger anxiously. "I'll say it's all a lie. I'll come here and apologize to you afore *her*, and say I took you for somebody else. I'll" —

"It's too late," said Twing moodily.

"And what'll you do?"

"Leave here."

They had reached the door together. To Mrs. Martin's terror, as the stranger passed out, Twing, instead of following him as she expected, said "Good-night," and gloomily reëntered the schoolroom. Here he paused a moment, and then throwing himself on one of the benches, dropped his head upon a desk with his face buried in his hands — like a very schoolboy.

What passed through Mrs. Martin's mind I know not. For a moment she sat erect and rigid at her desk. Then she slipped quietly down, and, softly as one of the last shadows cast by the dying sun, glided across the floor to where he sat.

"Mrs. Martin," he said, starting to his feet.

"I have heard all," she said faintly. "I could n't help it. I was here when you came in. But I want to tell you that I am content to know you only as you seem to be, — as I have always found you here, — strong and loyal to a duty laid upon you by those who had a full knowledge of all you had been."

"Did you? Do you know what I have been?"

Mrs. Martin looked frightened, trembled a moment, and, recovering herself with an effort, said gently, "I know nothing of your past."

"Nothing?" he repeated, with a mirthless attempt at laughter, and a quick breath. "Not that I've been a — a — mountebank, a variety actor — a clown, you know, for the amusement of the lowest, at twenty-five cents a ticket. That I'm 'Johnny Walker,' the song and dance man — the all-round man — selected by Mr. Barstow to teach these boors a lesson as to what they wanted!"

She looked at him a moment — timidly, yet thoughtfully. "Then you are an actor — a person who simulates what he does not feel?"

"Yes."

"And all the time you have been here you have been acting the schoolmaster — playing a part — for — for Mr. Barstow?"

"Yes."

"Always?"

"Yes."

The color came softly to her face again, and her voice was very low. "And when you sang to me that day, and when you looked at me — as you did — an hour or two ago — while you were entertaining — you were — only — acting?"

Mr. Twing's answer was not known, but it must have been a full and complete one, for it was quite dark when he left the schoolroom — *not* for the last time — with its mistress on his arm.

IN A PIONEER RESTAURANT.

CHAPTER I.

THERE was probably no earthly reason why the "Poco Más ó Menos" Club of San Francisco should have ever existed, or why its five harmless, indistinctive members should not have met and dined together as ordinary individuals. Still less was there any justification for the gratuitous opinion which obtained, that it was bold, bad, and brilliant. Looking back upon it over a quarter of a century and half a globe, I confess I cannot recall a single witticism, audacity, or humorous characteristic that belonged to it. Yet there was no doubt that we were thought to be extremely critical and satirical, and I am inclined to think we honestly believed it. To take our seats on Wednesdays and Saturdays at a specially reserved table at the restaurant we patronized, to be conscious of being observed by the other guests, and of our waiter confidentially imparting our fame to strangers behind the shaken-out folds of a napkin, and of knowing that the faintest indication of merriment from our table thrilled the other guests with anticipatory smiles, was, I am firmly convinced, all that we ever did to justify our reputations. Nor, strictly speaking, were we remarkable as individuals; an assistant editor, a lawyer, a young army quartermaster, a bank clerk and a mining secretary — we could not separately challenge any special social or literary distinction. Yet I am satisfied that the very name of our Club — a common Spanish colloquialism, literally meaning "a little more or less," and adopted in Californian slang to express an unknown quantity — was supposed to be replete with deep and convulsing humor.

My impression is that our extravagant reputation, and, indeed, our continued existence as a Club, was due solely to the proprietor of the restaurant and two of his waiters, and that we were actually "run" by them. When the suggestion of our meeting regularly there was first broached to the proprietor — a German of slow but deep emotions — he received it with a "So" of such impressive satisfaction that it might have

been the beginning of our vainglory. From
that moment he became at once our patron
and our devoted slave. To linger near our
table once or twice during dinner with an
air of respectful vacuity, — as of one who
knew himself too well to be guilty of the
presumption of attempting to understand
our brilliancy, — to wear a certain parental
pride and unconsciousness in our fame, and
yet to never go further in seeming to com-
prehend it than to obligingly translate the
name of the Club as "a leedle more and nod
quide so much" — was to him sufficient happiness. That he ever experienced any business profit from the custom of the Club, or
its advertisement, may be greatly doubted;
on the contrary, that a few plain customers,
nettled at our self-satisfaction, might have
resented his favoritism seemed more probable. Equally vague, disinterested, and
loyal was the attachment of the two waiters,
— one an Italian, faintly reminiscent of better days and possibly superior extraction;
the other a rough but kindly Western man,
who might have taken this menial position
from temporary stress of circumstances, yet
who continued in it from sheer dominance
of habit and some feebleness of will. They

both vied with each other to please us. It may have been they considered their attendance upon a reputed intellectual company less degrading than ministering to the purely animal and silent wants of the average customers. It may have been that they were attracted by our general youthfulness. Indeed, I am inclined to think that they themselves were much more distinctive and interesting than any members of the Club, and it is to introduce *them* that I venture to recall so much of its history.

A few months after our advent at the restaurant, one evening, Joe Tallant, the mining secretary, one of our liveliest members, was observed to be awkward and distrait during dinner, forgetting even to offer the usual gratuity to the Italian waiter who handed him his hat, although he stared at him with an imbecile smile. As we chanced to leave the restaurant together, I was rallying him upon his abstraction, when to my surprise he said gravely: "Look here, one of two things has got to happen: either we must change our restaurant or I'm going to resign."

"Why?"

"Well, to make matters clear, I'm obliged

to tell you something that in our business we usually keep a secret. About three weeks ago I had a notice to transfer twenty feet of Gold Hill to a fellow named 'Tournelli.' Well, Tournelli happened to call for it himself, and who the devil do you suppose Tournelli was? Why our Italian waiter. I was regularly startled, and so was he. But business is business; so I passed him over the stock and said nothing — nor did he — neither there nor here. Day before yesterday he had thirty feet more transferred to him, and sold out."

"Well?" I said impatiently.

"Well," repeated Tallant indignantly. "Gold Hill's worth six hundred dollars a foot. That's eighteen thousand dollars cash. And a man who's good enough for that much money is too good to wait upon me. Fancy a man who could pay my whole year's salary with five feet of stock slinging hash to *me*. Fancy *you* tipping him with a quarter!"

"But if *he* don't mind it — and prefers to continue a waiter — why should *you* care? And *we*'re not supposed to know."

"That's just it," groaned Tallant. "That's just where the sell comes in. Think how he must chuckle over us! No, sir!

There's nothing aristocratic about me; but, by thunder, if I can't eat my dinner, and feel I am as good as the man who waits on me, I'll resign from the Club."

After endeavoring to point out to him the folly of such a proceeding, I finally suggested that we should take the other members of our Club into our confidence, and abide by their decision; to which he agreed. But, to his chagrin, the others, far from participating in his delicacy, seemed to enjoy Tournelli's unexpected wealth with a vicarious satisfaction and increase of dignity as if we were personally responsible for it. Although it had been unanimously agreed that we should make no allusions, jocose or serious, to him, nor betray any knowledge of it before him, I am afraid our attitude at the next dinner was singularly artificial. A nervous expectancy when he approached us, and a certain restraint during his presence, a disposition to check any discussion of shares or "strikes" in mining lest he should think it personal, an avoidance of unnecessary or trifling "orders," and a singular patience in awaiting their execution when given; a vague hovering between sympathetic respect and the other extreme of indifferent bluntness in our requests, tended, I think, to make that meal far from exhilarating. Indeed, the unusual depression affected the unfortunate cause of it, who added to our confusion by increased solicitude of service and — as if fearful of some fault, or having incurred our disfavor — by a deprecatory and exaggerated humility that in our sensitive state seemed like the keenest irony. At last, evidently interpreting our constraint before him into a desire to be alone, he retired to the door of a distant pantry, whence he surveyed us with dark and sorrowful Southern eyes. Tallant, who in this general embarrassment had been imperfectly served, and had eaten nothing, here felt his grievance reach its climax, and in a sudden outbreak of recklessness he roared out, " Hi, waiter — you, Tournelli. He may," he added, turning darkly to us, " buy up enough stock to control the board and dismiss *me ;* but, by thunder, if it costs me my place, I 'm going to have some more chicken ! "

It was probably this sensitiveness that kept us from questioning him, even indirectly, and perhaps led us into the wildest surmises. He was acting secretly for a brotherhood or society of waiters; he was a silent partner of his German employer; he was a disguised Italian stockbroker, gaining "points" from the unguarded conversation of "operating" customers; he was a political refugee with capital; he was a fugitive Sicilian bandit, investing his ill-gotten gains in California; he was a dissipated young nobleman, following some amorous intrigue across the ocean, and acting as his own Figaro or Leporello. I think a majority of us favored the latter hypothesis, possibly because we were young, and his appearance gave it color. His thin black mustaches and dark eyes, we felt, were Tuscan and aristocratic; at least, they were like the baritone who played those parts, and *he* ought to know. Yet nothing could be more exemplary and fastidious than his conduct towards the few lady frequenters of the "Poodle Dog" restaurant, who, I regret to say, were not puritanically reserved or conventual in manner.

But an unexpected circumstance presently changed and divided our interest. It was alleged by Clay, the assistant editor, that entering the restaurant one evening he saw the back and tails of a coat that seemed familiar to him half-filling a doorway leading to the restaurant kitchen. It was unmistakably the figure of one of our Club members, — the young lawyer, — Jack Manners. But what was he doing there? While the Editor was still gazing after him, he suddenly disappeared, as if some one had warned him that he was observed. As he did not reappear, when Tournelli entered from the kitchen a few moments later, the Editor called him and asked for his fellow-member. To his surprise the Italian answered, with every appearance of truthfulness, that he had not seen Mr. Manners at all! The Editor was staggered; but as he chanced, some hours later, to meet Manners, he playfully rallied him on his mysterious conference with the Italian. Manners replied briefly that he had had no interview whatever with Tournelli, and changed the subject quickly. The mystery — as we persisted in believing it — was heightened when another member deposed that he had seen "Tom," the Western waiter, coming from Manners's office. As Manners had volunteered no information of this, we felt that we could not without indelicacy ask him if Tom was a client, or a messenger from Tournelli. The only result was that our Club dinner was even more constrained than before. Not only was "Tom" now invested with a dark importance, but it was evident that the harmony of the Club was destroyed by these singular secret relations of two of its members with their employés.

It chanced that one morning, arriving from a delayed journey, I dropped into the restaurant. It was that slack hour between the lingering breakfast and coming luncheon when the tables are partly stripped and unknown doors, opened for ventilation, reveal the distant kitchen, and a mingled flavor of cold coffee-grounds and lukewarm soups hangs heavy on the air. To this cheerlessness was added a gusty rain without, that filmed the panes of the windows and doors, and veiled from the passer-by the usual tempting display of snowy cloths and china.

As I seemed to be the only customer at that hour, I selected a table by the window for distraction. Tom had taken my order; the other waiters, including Tournelli, were absent, with the exception of a solitary German, who, in the interlude of perfunctory trifling with the casters, gazed at me with that abstracted irresponsibility which one waiter assumes towards another's customer. Even the proprietor had deserted his desk at the counter. It seemed to be a favorable opportunity to get some information from Tom.

But he anticipated me. When he had dealt a certain number of dishes around me, as if they were cards and he was telling my fortune, he leaned over the table and said, with interrogating confidence: —

"I reckon you call that Mr. Manners of yours a good lawyer?"

We were very loyal to each other in the Club, and I replied with youthful enthusiasm that he was considered one of the most promising at the bar. And, remembering Tournelli, I added confidently that whoever engaged him to look after their property interests had secured a treasure.

"But is he good in criminal cases — before a police court, for instance?" continued Tom.

I believed — I don't know on what grounds — that Manners was good in insurance and admiralty law, and that he looked upon criminal practice as low; but I answered briskly — though a trifle startled — that as a criminal lawyer he was perfect.

"He could advise a man, who had a row hanging on, how to steer clear of being up for murder — eh?"

I trusted, with a desperate attempt at jocosity, that neither he nor Tournelli had been doing anything to require Manners's services in that way.

"It would be too late, *then*," said Tom, coolly, "and *anybody* could tell a man what he ought to have done, or how to make the best of what he had done; but the smart thing in a lawyer would be to give a chap points *beforehand*, and sorter tell him how far he could go, and yet keep inside the law. How he might goad a fellow to draw on him, and then plug him — eh?"

I looked up quickly. There was nothing in his ordinary, good-humored, but not very strong face to suggest that he himself was the subject of this hypothetical case. If he were speaking for Tournelli, the Italian certainly was not to be congratulated on his ambassador's prudence; and, above all, Manners was to be warned of the interpretation which might be put upon his counsels, and disseminated thus publicly. As I was thinking what to say, he moved away, but suddenly returned again.

"What made you think Tournelli had been up to anything?" he asked sharply.

"Nothing," I answered; "I only thought you and he, being friends" —

"You mean we're both waiters in the same restaurant. Well, I don't know him any better than I know that chap over there," pointing to the other waiter. "He's a Greaser or an Italian, and, I reckon, goes with his kind."

Why had we not thought of this before? Nothing would be more natural than that the rich and imperious Tournelli should be exclusive, and have no confidences with his enforced associates. And it was evident that Tom had noticed it and was jealous.

"I suppose he's rather a swell, isn't he?" I suggested tentatively.

A faint smile passed over Tom's face. It was partly cynical and partly suggestive of that amused toleration of our youthful credulity which seemed to be a part of that discomposing patronage that everybody extended to the Club. As he said nothing, I continued encouragingly:—

"Because a man's a waiter, it doesn't follow that he's always been one, or always will be."

"No," said Tom, abstractedly; "but it's about as good as anything else to lie low and wait on." But here two customers entered, and he turned to them, leaving me in doubt whether to accept this as a verbal pleasantry or an admission. Only one thing seemed plain: I had certainly gained no information, and only added a darker mystery to his conference with Manners, which I determined I should ask Manners to explain.

I finished my meal in solitude. The rain was still beating drearily against the windows with an occasional accession of impulse that seemed like human impatience. Vague figures under dripping umbrellas, that hid their faces as if in premeditated disguise, hurried from the main thoroughfare. A woman in a hooded waterproof like a domino, a Mexican in a black *serape*, might have been stage conspirators hastening to a rendezvous. The cavernous chill and odor which I had before noted as coming from some sarcophagus of larder or oven, where "funeral baked meats" might have been kept in stock, began to oppress me. The hollow and fictitious domesticity of this common board had never before seemed so hopelessly displayed. And Tom, the waiter, his napkin twisted in his hand and his face turned with a sudden dark abstraction towards the window, appeared to be really "lying low," and waiting for something outside his avocation.

CHAPTER II.

THE fact that Tom did not happen to be on duty at the next Club dinner gave me an opportunity to repeat his mysterious remark to Manners, and to jokingly warn that rising young lawyer against the indiscretion of vague counsel. Manners, however, only shrugged his shoulders. "I don't know what he meant," he said carelessly; "but since *he* chooses to talk of his own affairs publicly, *I* don't mind saying that they are neither very weighty nor very dangerous. It's only the old story: the usual matrimonial infidelities that are mixed up with the Californian emigration. He leaves the regular wife behind, — fairly or unfairly, I can't say. She gets tired waiting, after the usual style, and elopes with somebody else. The Western Penelope is n't built for waiting. But she seems to have converted some of his property into cash when she skipped from St. Louis, and that's where his chief concern comes in. That's what he wanted to see me for; that's why he inveigled me into that infernal pantry of his one day to show me a plan of his property, as if that was any good."

He paused disgustedly. We all felt, I think, that Tom was some kind of an impostor, claiming the sympathies of the Club on false pretenses. Nevertheless, the Quartermaster said, "Then you did n't do anything for him — give him any advice, eh?"

"No; for the property's as much hers as his, and he has n't got a divorce; and, as it's doubtful whether he did n't desert her first, he can't get one. He was surprised," he added, with a grim smile, "when I told him that he was obliged to support her, and was even liable for her debts. But people who are always talking of invoking the law know nothing about it." We were surprised too, although Manners was always convincing us, in some cheerful but discomposing way, that we were all daily and hourly, in our simplest acts, making ourself responsible for all sorts of liabilities and actions, and even generally preparing ourselves for arrest and imprisonment. The Quartermaster continued lazily: —

"Then you did n't give him any points about shooting?"

"No; he does n't even know the man she went off with. It was eighteen months ago, and I don't believe he'd even know her again if he met her. But, if he is n't much of a client, we shall miss him to-night as a waiter, for the place is getting full, and there are not enough to serve."

The restaurant was, indeed, unusually crowded that evening; the more so that, the private rooms above being early occupied, some dinner parties and exclusive couples had been obliged to content themselves with the public dining saloon. A small table nearest us, usually left vacant to insure a certain seclusion to the Club, was arranged, with a deprecatory apology from the proprietor, for one of those couples, a man and woman. The man was a well-known speculator, — cool, yet reckless and pleasure-loving; the woman, good-looking, picturesquely attractive, self-conscious, and self-possessed. Our propinquity was evidently neither novel nor discomposing. As she settled her skirts in her place, her bright, dark eyes swept our table with a frank, almost childish, familiarity. The younger members of the Club quite unconsciously pulled up their collars and settled their neckties; the elders as unconsciously raised their voices slightly, and somewhat arranged their sentences. Alas! the simplicity and unaffectedness of the Club were again invaded.

Suddenly there was a crash, the breaking of glass, and an exclamation. Tournelli, no doubt disorganized by the unusual hurry, on his way to our table had dropped his tray, impartially distributed a plate of asparagus over an adjoining table, and, flushed and nervous, yet with an affectation of studied calmness, was pouring the sauce into the young Quartermaster's plate, in spite of his languid protests. At any other time we would have laughed, but there was something in the exaggerated agitation of the Italian that checked our mirth. Why should he be so upset by a trifling accident? He could afford to pay for the breakage; he would laugh at dismissal. Was it the sensitiveness of a refined nature, or — he was young and good-looking — was he disconcerted by the fact that our handsome neighbor had witnessed his awkwardness? But she was not laughing, and, as far as I could see, was intently regarding the bill of fare.

"Waiter!" called her companion, hailing Tournelli. "Here!" The Italian, with a face now distinctly white, leaned over the table, adjusting the glasses, but did not reply.

"Waiter!" repeated the stranger, sharply. Tournelli's face twitched, then became set as a mask; but he did not move. The stranger leaned forward and pulled his apron from behind. Tournelli started with flashing eyes, and turned swiftly round. But the Quartermaster's hand had closed on his wrist.

"That's my knife, Tournelli."

The knife dropped from the Italian's fingers.

"Better see *what* he wants. It may not be *that*," said the young officer, coolly but kindly.

Tournelli turned impatiently towards the stranger. We alone had witnessed this incident, and were watching him breathlessly. Yet what bade fair a moment ago to be a tragedy, seemed now to halt grotesquely. For Tournelli, throwing open his linen jacket with a melodramatic gesture, tapped his breast, and with flashing eyes and suppressed accents said, "Sare; you wantah me? Look — I am herre!"

The speculator leaned back in his chair in good-humored astonishment. The lady's black eyes, without looking at Tournelli, glanced backward round the room, and slipped along our table, with half-defiant unconcern; and then she uttered a short hysterical laugh.

"Ah! ze lady — madame — ze signora — eh — she wantah me?" continued Tournelli, leaning on the table with compressed fingers, and glaring at her. "Perhaps *she* wantah Tournelli — eh?"

"Well, you might bring some with the soup," blandly replied her escort, who seemed to enjoy the Italian's excitement as a national eccentricity; "but hurry up and set the table, will you?"

Then followed, on the authority of the Editor, who understood Italian, a singular scene. Secure, apparently, in his belief that his language was generally uncomprehended, Tournelli brought a decanter, and, setting it on the table, said, "Traitress!" in an intense whisper. This was followed by the cruets, which he put down with the exclamation, "Perjured fiend!" Two glasses, placed on either side of her, carried the word "Apostate!" to her ear; and three knives and forks, rattling more than was necessary, and laid crosswise before her plate, were accompanied with "Tremble, wanton!" Then, as he pulled the tablecloth straight, and ostentatiously concealed a wine-stain with a clean napkin, scarcely whiter than his lips, he articulated under his breath: "Let him beware! he goes not hence alive! I will slice his craven heart — thus — and thou shalt see it." He turned quickly to a side table and brought back a spoon. "And *this* is why I have not found you;" another spoon, "For *this* you have disappeared;" a purely perfunctory polishing of her fork, "For *him*, bah!" an equally unnecessary wiping of her glass, "Blood of God!" — more wiping — "It will end! Yes" — general wiping and a final flourish over the whole table with a napkin — "I go, but at the door I shall await you both."

She had not spoken yet, nor even lifted her eyes. When she did so, however, she raised them level with his, showed all her white teeth — they were small and cruel-looking — and said smilingly in his own dialect: —

"Thief!"

Tournelli halted, rigid.

"You're talking his lingo, eh?" said her escort good-humoredly.

"Yes."

"Well — tell him to bustle around and be a little livelier with the dinner, won't you? This is only skirmishing."

"You hear," she continued to Tournelli in a perfectly even voice; "or shall it be a policeman, and a charge of stealing?"

"Stealing!" gasped Tournelli. "*You* say stealing!"

"Yes — ten thousand dollars. You are well disguised here, my little fellow; it is a good business — yours. Keep it while you can."

I think he would have sprung upon her there and then, but that the Quartermaster, who was nearest him, and had been intently watching his face, made a scarcely perceptible movement as if ready to anticipate him. He caught the officer's eye; caught, I think, in ours the revelation that he had been understood, drew back with a sidelong, sinuous movement, and disappeared in the passage to the kitchen.

I believe we all breathed more freely, although the situation was still full enough of impending possibilities to prevent peaceful enjoyment of our dinner. As the Editor finished his hurried translation, it was suggested that we ought to warn the unsuspecting escort of Tournelli's threats. But it was pointed out that this would be betraying the woman, and that Jo Hays (her companion) was fully able to take care of himself. "Besides," said the Editor, aggrievedly, " you fellows only think of *yourselves*, and you don't understand the first principles of journalism. Do you suppose I'm going to do anything to spoil a half-column of leaded brevier copy — from an eye-witness, too? No; it's a square enough fight as it stands. We must look out for the woman, and not let Tournelli get an unfair drop on Hays. That is, if the whole thing isn't a bluff."

But the Italian did not return. Whether he had incontinently fled, or was nursing his wrath in the kitchen, or already fulfilling his threat of waiting on the pavement outside the restaurant, we could not guess. Another waiter appeared with the dinners they had ordered. A momentary thrill of excitement passed over us at the possibility that Tournelli had poisoned their soup; but it presently lapsed, as we saw the couple partaking of it comfortably, and chatting with apparent unconcern. Was the scene we had just witnessed only a piece of Southern exaggeration? Was the woman a creature devoid of nerves or feeling of any kind; or was she simply a consummate actress? Yet she was clearly not acting, for in the intervals of conversation, and even while talking, her dark eyes wandered carelessly around the room, with the easy self-confidence of a pretty woman. We were beginning to talk of something else, when the Editor said suddenly, in a suppressed voice: —

"Hullo! What's the matter now?"

The woman had risen, and was hurriedly throwing her cloak over her shoulders. But it was *her* face that was now ashen and agitated, and we could see that her hands were trembling. Her escort was assisting her, but was evidently as astonished as ourselves. "Perhaps," he suggested hopefully, "if you wait a minute it will pass off."

"No, no," she gasped, still hurriedly wrestling with her cloak. "Don't you see I'm suffocating here — I want air. You can follow!" She began to move off, her face turned fixedly in the direction of the door. We instinctively looked there — perhaps for Tournelli. There was no one. Nevertheless, the Editor and Quartermaster had half-risen from their seats.

"Helloo!" said Manners suddenly. "There's Tom just come in. Call him!"

Tom, evidently recalled from his brief furlough by the proprietor on account of the press of custom, had just made his appearance from the kitchen.

"Tom, where's Tournelli?" asked the Lawyer hurriedly, but following the retreating woman with his eyes.

"Skipped, they say. Somebody insulted him," said Tom curtly.

"You didn't see him hanging round outside, eh? Swearing vengeance?" asked the Editor.

"No," said Tom scornfully.

The woman had reached the door, and darted out of it as her escort paused a moment at the counter to throw down a coin. Yet in that moment she had hurried before him through the passage into the street. I turned breathlessly to the window. For an instant her face, white as a phantom's, appeared pressed rigidly against the heavy plate-glass, her eyes staring with a horrible fascination back into the room — I even imagined at us. Perhaps, as it was evident that Tournelli was not with her, she fancied he was still here; perhaps she had mistaken Tom for him! However, her escort quickly rejoined her; their shadows passed the window together — they were gone.

Then a pistol-shot broke the quiet of the street.

The Editor and Quartermaster rose and ran to the door. Manners rose also, but lingered long enough to whisper to me, "Don't lose sight of Tom," and followed them. But to my momentary surprise no one else moved. I had forgotten, in the previous excitement, that in those days a pistol-shot was not unusual enough to attract attention. A few raised their heads at the sound of running feet on the pavement, and the flitting of black shadows past the windows. Tom had not stirred, but, napkin in hand, and eyes fixed on vacancy, was standing, as I had seen him once before, in an attitude of listless expectation.

In a few minutes Manners returned. I thought he glanced oddly at Tom, who was still lingering in attendance, and I even fancied he talked to us ostentatiously for his benefit. "Yes, it was a row of Tournelli's. He was waiting at the corner; had rushed at Hays with a knife, but had been met with a derringer-shot through his hat. The lady, who, it seems, was only a chance steamer acquaintance of Hays', thought the attack must have been meant for *her*, as she had recognized in the Italian a man who had stolen from her divorced husband in the States, two years ago, and was a fugitive from justice. At least that was the explanation given by Hays, for the woman had fainted and been driven off to her hotel by the Quartermaster, and Tournelli had escaped. But the Editor was on his track. "You didn't notice that lady, Tom, did you?"

Tom came out of an abstracted study, and said: "No, she had her back to me all the time."

Manners regarded him steadily for a moment without speaking, but in a way that I could not help thinking was much more embarrassing to the bystanders than to him. When we rose to leave, as he placed his usual gratuity into Tom's hand, he said carelessly, "You might drop into my office to-morrow if you have anything to tell *me*."

"I haven't," said Tom quietly.

"Then I may have something to tell *you*."

Tom nodded, and turned away to his duties.

The Mining Secretary and myself could scarcely wait to reach the street before we turned eagerly on Manners.

"Well?"

"Well; the woman you saw was Tom's runaway wife, and Tournelli the man she ran away with."

"And Tom knew it?"

"Can't say."

"And you mean to say that all this while Tom never suspected *him*, and even did not recognize *her* just now?"

Manners lifted his hat and passed his fingers through his hair meditatively. "Ask me something easier, gentlemen."

A TREASURE OF THE GALLEON.

Her father's house was nearly a mile from the sea, but the breath of it was always strong at the windows and doors in the early morning, and when there were heavy "southwesters" blowing in the winter, the wind brought the sharp sting of sand to her cheek, and the rain an odd taste of salt to her lips. On this particular December afternoon, however, as she stood in the doorway, it seemed to be singularly calm; the southwest trades blew but faintly, and scarcely broke the crests of the long Pacific swell that lazily rose and fell on the beach, which only a slanting copse of scrub-oak and willow hid from the cottage. Nevertheless, she knew this league-long strip of shining sand much better, it is to be feared, than the scanty flower-garden, arid and stunted by its contiguity. It had been her playground when she first came there, a motherless girl of twelve, and she had helped her father gather its scattered driftwood — as the fortunes of the Millers were not above accepting these occasional offerings of their lordly neighbor.

"I would n't go far to-day, Jenny," said her father, as the girl stepped from the threshold. "I don't trust the weather at this season; and besides you had better be looking over your wardrobe for the Christmas Eve party at Sol. Catlin's."

"Why, father, you don't intend to go to that man's?" said the girl, looking up with a troubled face.

"Lawyer Miller," as he was called by his few neighbors, looked slightly embarrassed. "Why not?" he asked in a faintly irritated tone.

"Why not? Why, father, you know how vulgar and conceited he is, — how everybody here truckles to him!"

"Very likely; he 's a very superior man of his kind, — a kind they understand here, too, — a great trapper, hunter, and pioneer."

"But I don't believe in his trapping, hunting, and pioneering," said the girl, petulantly. "I believe it 's all as hollow and boisterous as himself. It 's no more real, or what one thinks it should be, than he is. And he dares to patronize you — you, father, an educated man and a gentleman!"

"Say rather an unsuccessful lawyer who was fool enough to believe that buying a ranch could make him a farmer," returned her father, but half jestingly. "I only wish I was as good at my trade as he is."

"But you never liked him, — you always used to ignore him; you've changed, father"— She stopped suddenly, for her recollection of her father's quiet superiority and easy independence when he first came there was in such marked contrast to his late careless and weak concession to the rude life around them, that she felt a pang of vague degradation, which she feared her voice might betray.

"Very well! Do as you like," he replied, with affected carelessness; "only I thought, as we cannot afford to go elsewhere this Christmas, it might be well for us to take what we could find here."

"Take what we could find here!" It was so unlike him — he who had always been so strong in preserving their little domestic refinements in their rude surroundings, that their poverty had never seemed mean, nor their seclusion ignoble. She turned away to conceal her indignant color. She could share the household work with a squaw and

Chinaman, she could fetch wood and water. Catlin had patronizingly seen her doing it, but to dance to his vulgar piping — never!

She was not long in reaching the sands that now lay before her, warm, sweet-scented from short beach grass, stretching to a dim rocky promontory, and absolutely untrod by any foot but her own. It was this virginity of seclusion that had been charming to her girlhood; fenced in between the impenetrable hedge of scrub-oaks on the one side, and the lifting green walls of breakers tipped with *chevaux de frise* of white foam on the other, she had known a perfect security for her sports and fancies that had captivated her town-bred instincts and native fastidiousness. A few white-winged sea-birds, as proud, reserved, and maidenlike as herself, had been her only companions. And it was now the custodian of her secret, — a secret as innocent and childlike as her previous youthful fancies, — but still a secret known only to herself.

One day she had come upon the rotting ribs of a wreck on the beach. Its distance from the tide line, its position, and its deep imbedding of sand, showed that it was of ancient origin. An omnivorous reader of all that pertained to the history of California, Jenny had in fancy often sailed the seas in one of those mysterious treasure-ships that had skirted the coast in bygone days, and she at once settled in her mind that her discovery was none other than a castaway Philippine galleon. Partly from her reserve, and partly from a suddenly conceived plan, she determined to keep its existence unknown to her father, as careful inquiry on her part had found it was equally unknown to the neighbors. For this shy, imaginative young girl of eighteen had convinced herself that it might still contain a part of its old treasure. She would dig for it herself, without telling anybody. If she failed, no one would know it; if she were successful, she would surprise her father and perhaps retrieve their fortune by less vulgar means than their present toil. Thanks to the secluded locality and the fact that she was known to spend her leisure moments in wandering there, she could work without suspicion. Secretly conveying a shovel and a few tools to the spot the next day, she set about her prodigious task. As the upper works were gone, and the galleon not large, in three weeks, working an hour or two each day, she had made a deep excavation in the stern. She had found many curious things, — the flotsam and jetsam of previous storms, — but as yet, it is perhaps needless to say, not the treasure.

To-day she was filled with the vague hope of making her discovery before Christmas Day. To have been able to take her father something on that day — if only a few old coins — the fruit of her own unsuspected labor and intuition — not the result of vulgar barter or menial wage — would have been complete happiness. It was perhaps a somewhat visionary expectation for an educated girl of eighteen, but I am writing of a young Californian girl, who had lived in the fierce glamour of treasure-hunting, and in whose sensitive individuality some of its subtle poison had been instilled. Howbeit, to-day she found nothing. She was sadly hiding her pick and shovel, as was her custom, when she discovered the fresh track of an alien foot in the sand. Robinson Crusoe was not more astounded at the savage footprint than Jenny Miller at this damning proof of the invasion of her sacred territory. The footprints came from and returned to the copse of shrubs. Some one might have seen her at work!

But a singular change in the weather, overlooked in her excitement, here forced itself upon her. A light film over sea and sky, lifted only by fitful gusts of wind, seemed to have suddenly thickened until it became an opaque vault, narrowing in circumference as the wind increased. The promontory behind her disappeared, as if swallowed up, the distance before her seemed to contract; the ocean at her side, the color of dull pewter, vanished in a sheet of slanting rain, and by the time she reached the house, half running, half carried along by the quartering force of the wind, a full gale was blowing.

It blew all the evening, reaching a climax and fury at past midnight that was remembered for many years along that coast. In the midst of it they heard the booming of cannon, and then the voices of neighbors in the road. "There was," said the voices, "a big steamer ashore just afore the house," They dressed quickly and ran out.

Hugging the edge of the copse to breathe and evade the fury of the wind, they struggled to the sands. At first, looking out to sea, the girl w n thing but foam. But, following the direction of a neighbor's arm, for in that wild tumult man alone seemed speechless, she saw directly before her, so close upon her that she could have thrown a pebble on board, the high bows of a ship. Indeed, its very nearness gave her the feeling that it was already saved, and its occasional heavy roll to leeward, drunken, helpless, ludicrous, but never awful, brought a hysteric laugh to her lips. But when a livid blue light, lit in the swinging top, showed a number of black objects clinging to bulwarks and rigging, and the sea, with languid, heavy cruelty, pushing rather than beating them away, one by one, she knew that Death was there.

The neighbors, her father with the others, had been running hopelessly to and fro, or cowering in groups against the copse, when suddenly they uttered a cry — their first — of joyful welcome. And with that shout, the man she most despised and hated, Sol. Catlin, mounted on a "calico" mustang, as outrageous and bizarre as himself, dashed among them.

In another moment, what had been fear, bewilderment, and hesitation was changed to courage, confidence, and action. The men pressed eagerly around him, and as eagerly dispersed under his quick command. Galloping at his heels was a team with the whale-boat, brought from the river, miles away. He was here, there, and everywhere; catching the line thrown by the rocket from the ship, marshaling the men to haul it in, answering the hail from those on board above the tempest, pervading everything and everybody with the fury of the storm; loud, imperious, domineering, self-asserting, all-sufficient, and successful! And when the boat was launched, the last mighty impulse came from his shoulder. He rode at the helm into the first hanging wall of foam, erect and triumphant! Dazzled, bewildered, crying and laughing, she hated him more than ever.

The boat made three trips, bringing off, with the aid of the hawser, all but the sailors she had seen perish before her own eyes. The passengers, — they were few, — the captain and officers, found refuge in her father's house, and were loud in their praises of Sol. Catlin. But in that grateful chorus a single gloomy voice arose, the voice of a wealthy and troubled passenger. "I will give," he said, "five thousand dollars to the man who brings me a box of securities I left in my stateroom." Every eye turned instinctively to Sol.; he answered only those of Jenny's. "Say ten thousand, and if the dod-blasted hulk holds together two hours longer I'll do it, d—n me! You hear me! My name's Sol. Catlin, and when I say a thing, by G—d, I do it." Jenny's disgust here reached its climax. The hero of a night of undoubted energy and courage had blotted it out in a single moment of native vanity and vulgar avarice.

He was gone; not only two hours, but daylight had come and they were eagerly seeking him, when he returned among them, dripping and — empty-handed. He had reached the ship, he said, with another; found the box, and trusted himself alone with it to the sea. But in the surf he had to abandon it to save himself. It had perhaps drifted ashore, and might be found; for himself, he abandoned his claim to the reward. Had he looked abashed or mortified, Jenny felt that she might have relented, but the braggart was as all-satisfied, as confident and boastful as ever. Nevertheless, as his eye seemed to seek hers, she was constrained, in mere politeness, to add her own to her father's condolences. "I suppose," she hesitated, in passing him, "that this is a mere nothing to you after all that you did last night that was really great and unselfish."

"Were you never disappointed, Miss?" he said, with exasperating abruptness.

A quick consciousness of her own thankless labor on the galleon, and a terrible idea that he might have some suspicion of, and perhaps the least suggestion that she might have been disappointed in him, brought a faint color to her cheek. But she replied with dignity: —

"I really could n't say. But certainly," she added, with a new-found pertness, "you don't look it."

"Nor do you, Miss," was his idiotic answer.

A few hours later, alarmed at what she had heard of the inroads of the sea, which had risen higher than ever known to the oldest settler, and perhaps mindful of yesterday's footprints, she sought her old secluded haunt. The wreck was still there, but the sea had reached it. The excavation between its gaunt ribs was filled with drift and the seaweed carried there by the surges and entrapped in its meshes. And there, too, caught as in a net, lay the wooden box of securities Sol. Catlin had abandoned to the sea.

This is the story as it was told to me. The singularity of coincidences has challenged some speculation. Jenny insisted at the time upon sharing the full reward with Catlin, but local critics have pointed out that from subsequent events this proved nothing. For she had married him!

OUT OF A PIONEER'S TRUNK.

It was a slightly cynical, but fairly good-humored crowd that had gathered before a warehouse on Long Wharf in San Francisco one afternoon in the summer of '51. Although the occasion was an auction, the bidders' chances more than usually hazardous, and the season and locality famous for reckless speculation, there was scarcely any excitement among the bystanders, and a lazy, half-humorous curiosity seemed to have taken the place of any zeal for gain.

It was an auction of unclaimed trunks and boxes — the personal luggage of early emigrants — which had been left on storage in hulk or warehouse at San Francisco, while the owner was seeking his fortune in the mines. The difficulty and expense of transport, often obliging the gold-seeker to make part of his journey on foot, restricted him to the smallest *impedimenta*, and that of a kind not often found in the luggage of ordinary civilization. As a consequence, during the emigration of '49, he was apt on landing to avail himself of the invitation usually displayed on some of the doors of the rude hostelries on the shore: "Rest for the Weary and Storage for Trunks." In a majority of cases he never returned to claim his stored property. Enforced absence, protracted equally by good or evil fortune, accumulated the high storage charges until they usually far exceeded the actual value of the goods; sickness, further emigration, or death also reduced the number of possible claimants, and that more wonderful human frailty — absolute forgetfulness of deposited possessions — combined together to leave the bulk of the property in the custodian's hands. Under an understood agreement they were always sold at public auction after a given time. Although the contents of some of the trunks were exposed, it was found more in keeping with the public sentiment to sell the trunks *locked* and *unopened*. The element of curiosity was kept up from time to time by the incautious disclosures of the lucky or unlucky purchaser, and general bidding thus encouraged — except when the speculator, with the true gambling instinct, gave no indication in his face of what was drawn in this lottery. Generally, however, some suggestion in the exterior of the trunk, a label or initials; some conjectural knowledge of its former owner, or the idea that he might be secretly present in the hope of getting his property back for less than the accumulated dues, kept up the bidding and interest.

A modest-looking, well-worn portmanteau had been just put up at a small opening bid, when Harry Flint joined the crowd. The young man had arrived a week before at San Francisco friendless and penniless, and had been forced to part with his own effects to procure necessary food and lodging while looking for an employment. In the irony of fate that morning the proprietors of a drygoods store, struck with his good looks and manners, had offered him a situation, if he could make himself more presentable to their fair clients. Harry Flint was gazing half abstractedly, half hopelessly, at the portmanteau without noticing the auctioneer's persuasive challenge. In his abstraction he was not aware that the auctioneer's assistant was also looking at him curiously, and that possibly his dejected and half-clad appearance had excited the attention of one of the cynical bystanders, who was exchanging a few words with the assistant. He was, however, recalled to himself a moment later when the portmanteau was knocked down at fifteen dollars, and considerably startled when the assistant placed it at his feet with a grim smile. "That's your property, Fowler, and I reckon you look as if you wanted it back bad."

"But — there's some mistake," stammered Flint. "I didn't bid."

"No, but Tom Flynn did for you. You see, I spotted you from the first, and told Flynn I reckoned you were one of those chaps who came back from the mines dead broke. And he up and bought your things for you — like a square man. That's Flynn's style, if he is a gambler."

"But," persisted Flint, "this never was my property. My name isn't Fowler, and I never left anything here."

The assistant looked at him with a grim, half-credulous, half-scornful smile. "Have it your own way," he said, "but I oughter tell ye, old man, that I'm the warehouse clerk, and I remember *you*. I'm here for that purpose. But as that thar valise is bought and paid for by somebody else and given to you, it's nothing more to me. Take it or leave it."

The ridiculousness of quarreling over the mere form of his good fortune here struck Flint, and, as his abrupt benefactor had as abruptly disappeared, he hurried off with his prize. Reaching his cheap lodging-house, he examined its contents. As he had surmised, it contained a full suit of clothing of the better sort, and suitable to his urban needs. There were a few articles of jewelry, which he put religiously aside. There were some letters, which seemed to be of a purely business character. There were a few daguerreotypes of pretty faces, one of which was singularly fascinating to him. But there was another, of a young man, which startled him with its marvelous resemblance *to himself!* In a flash of intelligence he understood it all now. It was the likeness of the former owner of the trunk, for whom the assistant had actually mistaken him! He glanced hurriedly at the envelopes of the letters. They were addressed to Shelby Fowler, the name by which the assistant had just called him. The mystery was plain now. And for the present he could fairly accept his good luck, and trust to later fortune to justify himself.

Transformed in his new garb, he left his lodgings to present himself once more to his possible employer. His way led past one of the large gambling saloons. It was yet too early to find the dry-goods trader disengaged; perhaps the consciousness of more decent, civilized garb emboldened him to mingle more freely with strangers, and he entered the saloon. He was scarcely abreast of one of the faro tables when a man suddenly leaped up with an oath and discharged a revolver full in his face. The shot missed. Before his unknown assailant could fire again the astonished Flint had closed with him, and instinctively clutched the weapon. A brief but violent struggle ensued. Flint felt his strength failing him, when suddenly a look of astonishment came into the furious eyes of his adversary, and the man's grasp mechanically relaxed. The half-freed pistol, thrown upwards by this movement, was accidentally discharged point blank into his temples, and he fell dead. No one in the crowd had stirred or interfered.

"You've done for Australian Pete this

time, Mr. Fowler," said a voice at his elbow. He turned gaspingly and recognized his strange benefactor, Flynn. "I call you all to witness, gentlemen," continued the gambler, turning dictatorially to the crowd, "that this man was *first* attacked and was *unarmed*." He lifted Flint's limp and empty hands and then pointed to the dead man, who was still grasping the weapon. "Come!" He caught the half-paralyzed arm of Flint and dragged him into the street.

"But," stammered the horrified Flint, as he was borne along, "what does it all mean? What made that man attack me?"

"I reckon it was a case of shooting on sight, Mr. Fowler; but he missed it by not waiting to see if you were armed. It wasn't the square thing, and you're all right with the crowd now, whatever he might have had agin' you."

"But," protested the unhappy Flint, "I never laid eyes on the man before, and my name isn't Fowler."

Flynn halted, and dragged him in a doorway. "Who the devil are you?" he asked roughly.

Briefly, passionately, almost hysterically,

Flint told him his scant story. An odd expression came over the gambler's face.

"Look here," he said abruptly, "I have passed my word to the crowd yonder that you are a dead-broke miner called Fowler. I allowed that you might have had some row with that Sydney duck, Australian Pete, in the mines. That satisfied them. If I go back now, and say it's a lie, that your name ain't Fowler, and you never knew who Pete was, they'll jest pass you over to the police to deal with you, and wash their hands of it altogether. You may prove to the police who you are, and how that d—— clerk mistook you, but it will give you trouble. And who is there here who knows who you really are?"

"No one," said Flint, with sudden hopelessness.

"And you say you're an orphan, and ain't got any relations livin' that you're beholden to?"

"No one."

"Then, take my advice, and *be* Fowler, and stick to it! Be Fowler until Fowler turns up, and thanks you for it; for you've saved Fowler's life, as Pete would never have funked and lost his grit over Fowler as he did with you; and you've a right to his name."

He stopped, and the same odd, superstitious look came into his dark eyes.

"Don't you see what all that means? Well, I'll tell you. You're in the biggest streak of luck a man ever had. You've got the cards in your own hand! They spell "Fowler"! Play Fowler first, last, and all the time. Good-night, and good luck, *Mr. Fowler.*"

The next morning's journal contained an account of the justifiable killing of the notorious desperado and ex-convict, Australian Pete, by a courageous young miner by the name of Fowler. "An act of firmness and daring," said the "Pioneer," "which will go far to counteract the terrorism produced by those lawless ruffians."

In his new suit of clothes, and with this paper in his hand, Flint sought the dry-goods proprietor — the latter was satisfied and convinced. That morning Harry Flint began his career as salesman and as "Shelby Fowler."

From that day Shelby Fowler's career wa one of uninterrupted prosperity. Within the year he became a partner. The same miraculous fortune followed other ventures later. He was mill owner, mine owner, bank director — a millionaire! He was popular, the reputation of his brief achievement over the desperado kept him secure from the attack of envy and rivalry. He never was confronted by the real Fowler. There was no danger of exposure by others — the one custodian of his secret, Tom Flynn, died in Nevada the year following. He had quite forgotten his youthful past, and even the more recent lucky portmanteau; remembered nothing, perhaps, but the pretty face of the daguerreotype that had fascinated him. There seemed to be no reason why he should not live and die as Shelby Fowler.

His business a year later took him to Europe. He was entering a train at one of the great railway stations of London, when the porter, who had just deposited his portmanteau in a compartment, reappeared at the window followed by a young lady in mourning.

"Beg pardon, sir, but I handed you the wrong portmanteau. That belongs to this young lady. This is yours."

Flint glanced at the portmanteau on the

seat before him. It certainly was not his, although it bore the initials "S. F." He was mechanically handing it back to the porter, when his eyes fell on the young lady's face. For an instant he stood petrified. It was the face of the daguerreotype. "I beg pardon," he stammered, "but are these your initials?" She hesitated, perhaps it was the abruptness of the question, but he saw she looked confused.

"No. A friend's."

She disappeared into another carriage, but from that moment Harry Flint knew that he had no other aim in life but to follow this clue and the beautiful girl who had dropped it. He bribed the guard at the next station, and discovered that she was going to York. On their arrival, he was ready on the platform to respectfully assist her. A few words disclosed the fact that she was a fellow-countrywoman, although residing in England, and at present on her way to join some friends at Harrogate. Her name was West. At the mention of his, he again fancied she looked disturbed.

They met again and again; the informality of his introduction was overlooked by her friends, as his assumed name was already respectably and responsibly known beyond California. He thought no more of his future. He was in love. He even dared to think it might be returned; but he felt he had no right to seek that knowledge until he had told her his real name and how he came to assume another's. He did so alone — scarcely a month after their first meeting. To his alarm, she burst into a flood of tears, and showed an agitation that seemed far beyond any apparent cause. When she had partly recovered, she said, in a low, frightened voice: —

"You are bearing *my brother's* name. But it was a name that the unhappy boy had so shamefully disgraced in Australia that he abandoned it, and, as he lay upon his death-bed, the last act of his wasted life was to write an imploring letter begging me to change mine too. For the infamous companion of his crime who had first tempted, then betrayed him, had possession of all his papers and letters, many of them from *me*, and was threatening to bring them to our Virginia home and expose him to our neighbors. Maddened by desperation, the miserable boy twice attempted the life of the scoundrel, and might have added that blood guiltiness to his other sins had he lived. I *did* change my name to my mother's maiden one, left the country, and have lived here to escape the revelations of that desperado, should he fulfill his threat."

In a flash of recollection Flint remembered the startled look that had come into his assailant's eye after they had clinched. It was the same man who had too late realized that his antagonist was not Fowler. "Thank God! you are forever safe from any exposure from that man," he said, gravely, "and the name of Fowler has never been known in San Francisco save in all respect and honor. It is for you to take back — fearlessly and alone!"

She did — but not alone, for she shared it with her husband.

THE GHOSTS OF STUKELEY CASTLE.

THERE should have been snow on the ground to make the picture seasonable and complete, but the Western Barbarian had lived long enough in England to know that, except in the pages of a holiday supplement, this was rarely the accompaniment of a Christmas landscape, and he cheerfully accepted, on the 24th of December, the background of a low, brooding sky, on which the delicate tracery of leafless sprays and blacker *chevaux de frise* of pine was faintly etched, as a consistent setting to the turrets and peacefully stacked chimneys of Stukeley Castle. Yet, even in this disastrous eclipse of color and distance, the harmonious outlines of the long, gray, irregular pile seemed to him as wonderful as ever. It still dominated the whole landscape, and, as he had often fancied, carried this subjection even to the human beings who had created it, lived in it, but which it seemed to have in some dull, senile way dozed over and forgotten. He vividly recalled the previous sunshine of an autumnal house party within its walls, where some descendants of its old castellans, encountered in long galleries or at the very door of their bedrooms, looked as alien to the house as the Barbarian himself.

For the rest it may be found described in the local guide-books, with a view of its " South Front," " West Front," and " Great Quadrangle." It was alleged to be based on an encampment of the Romans — that highly apocryphal race who seemed to have spent their time in getting up picnics on tessellated pavements, where, after hilariously emptying their pockets of their loose coin and throwing round their dishes, they instantly built a road to escape by, leaving no other record of their existence. Stow and Dugdale had recorded the date when a Norman favorite obtained the royal license to " embattle it; " it had done duty on Christmas cards with the questionable snow already referred to laid on thickly in crystal; it had been lovingly portrayed by a fair countrywoman — the vivacious correspondent of the "East Machias Sentinel" — in a combination of the most delightful feminine disregard of facts with the highest feminine respect for titles. It was rich in a real and spiritual estate of tapestries, paintings, armor, legends, and ghosts. Everything the poet could wish for, and indeed some things that decent prose might have possibly wished out of it, were there.

Yet, from the day that it had been forcibly seized by a Parliamentary General, until more recently, when it had passed by the no less desperate conveyance of marriage into the hands of a Friendly Nobleman known to the Western Barbarian, it had been supposed to suggest something or other more remarkable than itself. "Few spectators," said the guide-book, "even the most unimpassioned, can stand in the courtyard and gaze upon those historic walls without feeling a thrill of awe," etc. The Western Barbarian had stood there, gazed, and felt no thrill. "The privileged guest," said the grave historian, "passing in review the lineaments of the illustrious owners of Stukeley, as he slowly paces the sombre gallery, must be conscious of emotions of no ordinary character," etc., etc. The Barbarian had been conscious of no such emotions. And it was for this reason, and believing he *might* experience them if left there in solitude, with no distracting or extraneous humanity around him, it had been agreed between him and the Friendly Nobleman, who had fine Barbarian instincts, that as he — the Friendly Nobleman — and his family were to spend their holidays abroad, the Barbarian should be allowed, on the eve and day of Christmas, to stay at Stukeley alone. "But," added his host, "you'll find it beastly lonely, and although I've told the housekeeper to look after you — you'd better go over to dine at Audley Friars, where there's a big party, and they know you, and it will be a deuced deal more amusing. And — er — I say — you know — you're really *not* looking out for ghosts, and that sort of thing, are you? You know you fellows don't believe in them — over there." And the Barbarian, assuring him that this was a part of his deficient emotions, it was settled then and there that he should come. And that was why, on the 24th of December, the Barbarian found himself gazing hopefully on the landscape with his portmanteau at his feet, as he drove up the avenue.

The ravens did *not* croak ominously from

the battlements as he entered. And the housekeeper, although neither "stately" nor "tall," nor full of reminiscences of "his late lordship, the present Earl's father," was very sensible and practical. The Barbarian could, of course, have his choice of rooms — but — she had thought — remembering his tastes the last time, that the long blue room? Exactly! The long, low-arched room, with the faded blue tapestry, looking upon the gallery — capital! He had always liked that room. From purely negative evidence he had every reason to believe that it was the one formidable-looking room in England that Queen Elizabeth had *not* slept in.

When the footman had laid out his clothes, and his step grew fainter along the passage, until it was suddenly swallowed up with the closing of a red baize door in the turret staircase, like a trap in an *oubliette*, the whole building seemed to sink back into repose. Quiet it certainly was, but not more so, he remembered, than when the chambers on either side were filled with guests, and floating voices in the corridor were lost in those all-absorbing walls. So far, certainly, this was no new experience. It was past four. He waited for the shadows to gather. Light thickened beyond his windows; gradually the outflanking wall and part of a projecting terrace crumbled away in the darkness, as if Night were slowly reducing the castle. The figures on the tapestry in his room stood out faintly. The gallery, seen through his open door, barred with black spaces between the mullioned windows, presently became obliterated, as if invaded by a dull smoke from without. But nothing moved, nothing glimmered. Really this might become in time very stupid.

He was startled, however, while dressing, to see from his windows that the great banqueting hall was illuminated, but on coming down was amused to find his dinner served on a small table in its oaken solitude lit by the large electric chandelier — for Stukeley Castle under its present lord had all the modern improvements — shining on the tattered banners and glancing mail above him. It was evidently the housekeeper's reading of some written suggestion of her noble master. The Barbarian, in a flash of instinct, imagined the passage:—

"Humor him as a harmless lunatic; the plate is quite safe."

Declining the further offer of an illumination of the picture gallery, grand drawing-room, ball-room, and chapel, a few hours later he found himself wandering in the corridor with a single candle and a growing conviction of the hopelessness of his experiment. The castle had as yet yielded to him nothing that he had not seen before in the distraction of company and the garishness of day. It was becoming a trifle monotonous. Yet fine — exceedingly; and now that a change of wind had lifted the fog, and the full moon shone on the lower half of the pictures of the gallery, starting into the most artificial simulation of life a number of Van Dyke legs, farthingales, and fingers that would have deceived nobody, it seemed gracious, gentle, and innocent beyond expression. Wandering down the gallery, conscious of being more like a ghost than any of the painted figures, and that they might reasonably object to him, he wished he could meet the original of one of those pictured gallants and secretly compare his fingers with the copy. He remembered an embroidered pair of gloves in a cabinet and a suit of armor on the wall that, in measurement, did not seem to bear out the delicacy of the one nor the majesty of the other. It occurred to him also to satisfy a yearning he had once felt to try on a certain breastplate and steel cap that hung over an oaken settle. It will be perceived that he was getting a good deal bored. For thus caparisoned he listlessly, and, as will be seen, imprudently, allowed himself to sink back into a very modern chair, and give way to a dreamy cogitation.

What possible interest could the dead have in anything that was here? Admitting that they had any, and that it was not the *living*, whom the Barbarian had always found most inclined to haunt the past, would not a ghost of any decided convictions object to such a collection as his descendant had gathered in this gallery? Yonder idiot in silk and steel had blunderingly and cruelly persecuted his kinsman in leather and steel only a few panels distant. Would they care to meet here? And if their human weaknesses had died with them, what would bring them here at all? And if not *them* — who then? He stopped short. The door at the lower end of the gallery had opened! Not stealthily, not noiselessly, but in an ordinary fashion, and a number of figures, dressed in the habiliments of a bygone age, came trooping in. They did not glide in nor float in, but trampled in awkwardly, clumsily, and unfamiliarly, gaping about them as they walked. At the head was apparently a steward in a kind of livery, who stopped once or twice and seemed to be pointing out and explaining certain objects in the room. A flash of indignant intelligence filled the brain of the Barbarian! It seemed absurd!— impossible!— but it was true! It was a holiday excursion party of ghosts, being shown over Stukeley Castle by a ghostly Cicerone! And as his measured, monotonous voice rose on the Christmas morning air, it could be heard that he was actually showing off, not the antiquities of the Castle, but the *modern improvements!*

"This 'ere, gossips," — the Barbarian instantly detected the fallacy of all the so-called mediæval jargon he had read, — "is the Helectric Bell, which does away with our hold, hordinary 'orn blowin', and the hattendant waitin' in the 'all for the usual 'Without there, who waits?' which all of us was accustomed to in mortal flesh. You hobserve this button. I press it so, and it instantly rings a bell in the kitchen 'all, and shows in fair letters the name of this 'ere gallery — as we will see later. Will hany

good dame or gaffer press the button?
Will *you*, mistress?" said the Cicerone to a
giggling, kerchief-coifed lass.

"Oi soy, Maudlin! — look out — will yer!
— It's the soime old gag as them bloomin'
knobs you ketched hold of when yer was
'ere las' Whitsuntide," called out the mediæval 'Arry of the party.

"It is *not* the Galvanic-Magnetic machine
in 'is lordship's library," said the Cicerone,
severely, "which is a mere toy for infants,
and hold-fashioned. And we have 'ere a
much later invention. I open this little
door, I turn this 'andle — called a switch —
and, has you perceive, the gallery is hin-
stantly hilluminated."

There was a hoarse cry of astonishment
from the assemblage. The Barbarian felt
an awful thrill as this searching, insufferable
light of the nineteenth century streamed suddenly upon the up-turned, vacant-eyed, and
dull faces of those sightseers of the past.
But there was no responsive gleam in their
eyes.

"It be the sun," gasped an old woman in
a gray cloak.

"Toime to rouse out, Myryan, and make
the foire," said the mediæval 'Arry. The
custodian smiled with superior toleration.

"But what do 'ee want o' my old lanthorne," asked a yellow-jerkined stable boy, pointing to an old-fashioned horned lantern, *tempus* Edward III., "with this brave loight?"

"You know," said the custodian, with condescending familiarity, "these mortals worship what they call 'curios' and the 'antique,' and 'is lordship gave a matter of fifty pounds for that same lanthern. That's what the modern folk come 'ere to see — like as ye."

"Oi've an old three-legged stool in Whitechapel oi 'll let his lordship 'ave cheap — for five quid," suggested the humorist.

"The 'prentice wight knows not that he speaks truly. For 'ere is a braver jest than 'is. Good folks, wilt please ye to examine yon coffer?" pointing to an oaken chest.

"'T is but poor stuff, marry," said Maudlin.

"'T is a coffer — the same being made in Wardour Street last year — 'is lordship gave one hundred pounds for it. Look at these would-be worm-holes, — but they were made with an *auger*. Marry, *we* know what worm-holes are!"

A ghastly grin spread over the faces of

the spectral assembly as they gathered around the chest with silent laughter.

"Wilt walk 'ere and see the phonograph in the libry, made by Hedison, an Hamerican, which bottles up the voice and preserves it fresh for a hundred years? 'T is a rare new fancy."

"Rot," said 'Arry. Then turning to the giggling Maudlin, he whispered: "Saw it las' toime. 'Is lordship got a piece o' moy moind that oi reeled off into it about this 'ere swindle. Fawncy that old bloke there charging a tanner apiece to us for chaffin' a bit of a barrel."

"Have you no last new braveries to show us of the gallants and their mistresses, as you were wont?" said Maudlin to the Cicerone. "'T was a rare show last time — the modish silk gowns and farthingales in the closets."

"But there be no company this Christmas," said the custodian, "and 'is lordship does not entertain, unless it be the new fool 'is lordship sent down 'ere to-day, who has been mopin' and moonin' in the corridors, as is ever the way of these wittol creatures when they are not heeded. He was 'ere in a rare motley of his own choosing, with which

he thinks to raise a laugh, a moment ago.
Ye see him not — not 'avin' the gift that
belongs by right to my dread office. 'T is
a weird privilege I have — and may not be
imparted to others — save " —

"Save what, good man steward? Prithee,
speak?" said Marian earnestly.

" 'T is ever a shillin' extra."

There was no response. A few of the
more bashful ghosts thrust their hands in
their pockets and looked awkwardly another
way. The Barbarian felt a momentary relief followed by a slight pang of mortified
vanity. He was a little afraid of them.
The price was an extortion, certainly, but
surely he was worth the extra shilling!

"He has brought but little braveries of
attire into the Castle," continued the Cicerone, "but I 'ave something 'ere which was
found on the top of his portmanteau. I wot
ye know not the use of this." To the Barbarian's intense indignation, the Cicerone
produced, from under his, his (the Barbarian's) own opera hat. "Marry, what should
be this? Read me this riddle! To it —
and unyoke!"

A dozen vacant guesses were made as the
showman held it aloft. Then with a con-

juror's gesture he suddenly placed his thumbs within the rim, released the spring and extended the hat. The assembly laughed again silently as before.

"'T is a hat," said the Cicerone, with a superior air.

"Nay," said Maudlin, "give it here." She took it curiously, examined it, and then with a sudden coquettish movement lifted it towards her own coifed head, as if to try it on. The Cicerone suddenly sprang forward with a despairing gesture to prevent her. And here the Barbarian was conscious of a more startling revelation. How and why he could not tell, but he *knew* that the putting on of that article of his own dress would affect the young girl as the assumption of the steel cap and corselet had evidently affected him, and that he would instantly become as visible to her as she and her companions had been to him. He attempted to rise, but was too late; she had evaded the Cicerone by ducking, and, facing in the direction of the Barbarian, clapped the hat on her head. He saw the swift light of consciousness, of astonishment, of sudden fear spring into her eyes! She shrieked, he started, struggled, and awoke!

But what was this! He was alone in the moonlit gallery, certainly; the ghastly figures in their outlandish garb were gone; he was awake and in his senses, but, in this first flash of real consciousness, he could have sworn that something remained! Something terror-stricken, and retreating even then before him, — something of the world, modern, — and, even as he gazed, vanishing through the gallery door with the material flash and rustle of silk.

He walked quietly to the door. It was open. Ah! No doubt he had forgotten to shut it fast; a current of air or a sudden draught had opened it. That noise had awakened him. More than that, remembering the lightning flash of dream consciousness, it had been the *cause* of his dream. Yet, for a few moments he listened attentively.

What might have been the dull reverberation of a closing door in the direction of the housekeeper's room, on the lower story, was all he heard. He smiled, for even that, natural as it might be, was less distinct and real than his absurd vision.

Nevertheless the next afternoon he concluded to walk over to Audley Friars for his Christmas dinner. Its hospitable master greeted him cordially.

"But do you know, my dear fellow," he said, when they were alone for a moment, "if you had n't come by yourself I'd have sent over there for you. The fact is that A—— wrote to us that you were down at Stukeley alone, ghost-hunting or something of that sort, and I'm afraid it leaked out among the young people of our party. Two of our girls — I sha n't tell you which — stole over there last night to give you a start of some kind. They did n't see you at all, but, by Jove, it seems they got the biggest kind of a fright *themselves*, for they declare that something dreadful in armor, you know, was sitting in the gallery. Awfully good joke, was n't it? Of course *you* did n't see anything, — did you?"

"No," said the Barbarian, discreetly.

FLIP: A CALIFORNIA ROMANCE.

CONTENTS.

	PAGE
FLIP: A CALIFORNIA ROMANCE	289
FOUND AT BLAZING STAR	378

v. 23   J—Bret Harte

FLIP: A CALIFORNIA ROMANCE

CHAPTER I

Just where the track of the Los Gatos road streams on and upward like the sinuous trail of a fiery rocket until it is extinguished in the blue shadows of the Coast Range, there is an embayed terrace near the summit, hedged by dwarf firs. At every bend of the heat-laden road the eye rested upon it wistfully; all along the flank of the mountain, which seemed to pant and quiver in the oven-like air, through rising dust, the slow creaking of dragging wheels, the monotonous cry of tired springs, and the muffled beat of plunging hoofs, it held out a promise of sheltered coolness and green silences beyond. Sunburned and anxious faces yearned toward it from the dizzy, swaying tops of stagecoaches, from lagging teams far below, from the blinding white canvas covers of "mountain schooners," and from scorching saddles that seemed to weigh down the scrambling, sweating animals beneath. But it would seem that the hope was vain, the promise illusive. When the terrace was reached it appeared not only to have caught and gathered all the heat of the valley below, but to have evolved a fire of its own from some hidden crater-like source unknown. Nevertheless, instead of prostrating and enervating man and beast, it was said to have induced the wildest exaltation. The heated air was filled and stifling with resinous exhalations. The delirious spices of balm, bay, spruce, juniper, yerba buena, wild syringa, and strange aromatic herbs as yet unclassified, distilled and evaporated in that mighty heat, and seemed to fire with a midsummer madness all who breathed their fumes. They stung, smarted, stimulated, intoxicated. It was said that the most jaded and foot-sore horses became furious and ungovernable under their influence; wearied teamsters and muleteers, who had exhausted their profanity in the ascent, drank fresh draughts of inspiration in this fiery air, extended their vocabulary, and created new and startling forms of objurgation. It is recorded that one bibulous stage-driver exhausted description and condensed its virtues in a single phrase: "Gin and ginger." This felicitous epithet, flung out in a generous comparison with his favorite drink, "rum and gum," clung to it ever after.

Such was the current comment on this vale of spices. Like most human criticism it was hasty and superficial. No one yet had been known to have penetrated deeply its mysterious recesses. It was still far below the summit and its wayside inn. It had escaped the intruding foot of hunter and prospector; and the inquisitive patrol of the county surveyor had only skirted its boundary. It remained for Mr. Lance Harriott to complete its exploration. His reasons for so doing were simple. He had made the journey thither underneath the stage-coach, and clinging to its axle. He had chosen this hazardous mode of conveyance at night, as the coach crept by his place of concealment in the wayside brush, to elude the sheriff of Monterey County and his posse, who were after him.

He had not made himself known to his fellow-passengers as they already knew him as a gambler, an outlaw, and a desperado; he deemed it unwise to present himself in a newer reputation of a man who had just slain a brother gambler in a quarrel, and for whom a reward was offered. He slipped from the axle as the stage-coach swirled past the brushing branches of fir, and for an instant lay unnoticed, a scarcely distinguishable mound of dust in the broken furrows of the road. Then, more like a beast than a man, he crept on his hands and knees into the steaming underbrush. Here he lay still until the clatter of harness and the sound of voices faded in the distance. Had he been followed, it would have been difficult to detect in that inert mass of rags any semblance to a known form or figure. A hideous reddish mask of dust and clay obliterated his face; his hands were shapeless stumps exaggerated in his trailing sleeves. And when he rose, staggering like a drunken man, and plunged wildly into the recesses of the wood, a cloud of dust followed him, and pieces and patches of his frayed and rotten garments clung to the impeding branches. Twice he fell, but, maddened and upheld by the smarting spices and stimulating aroma of the air, he kept on his course.

Gradually the heat became less oppressive; once when he stopped and leaned exhaustedly against a sapling, he fancied he saw the zephyr he could not yet feel in the glittering and trembling of leaves in the distance before him. Again the deep stillness was moved with a faint sighing rustle, and he knew he must be nearing the edge of the thicket. The spell of silence thus broken was followed by a fainter, more musical interruption—the glassy tinkle of water! A step further his foot trembled on the verge of a slight ravine, still closely canopied by the interlacing boughs overhead. A tiny stream that he could have dammed with his hand yet lingered in this parched red gash in the hillside and trickled into a deep, irregular, well-like cavity, that again overflowed and sent its slight surplus on. It had been the luxurious retreat of many a spotted trout; it was to be the bath of Lance Harriott. Without a moment's hesitation, without removing a single garment, he slipped cautiously into it, as if fearful of losing a single drop. His head disappeared from the level of the bank; the solitude was again unbroken. Only two objects remained upon the edge of the ravine, —his revolver and tobacco pouch.

A few minutes elapsed. A fearless blue jay alighted on the bank and made a prospecting peck at the tobacco pouch. It yielded in favor of a gopher, who endeavored to draw it toward his hole, but in turn gave way to a red squirrel, whose attention was divided, however, between the pouch and the revolver, which he regarded with mischievous fascination. Then there was a splash, a grunt, a sudden dispersion of animated nature, and the head of Mr. Lance Harriott appeared above the bank. It was a startling transformation. Not only that he had, by this wholesale process, washed himself and his light "drill" garments entirely clean, but that he had, apparently by the same operation, morally cleansed *himself,* and left every stain and ugly blot of his late misdeeds and reputation in his bath. His face, albeit scratched here and there, was rosy, round, shining with irrepressible good humor and youthful levity. His large blue eyes were infantine in their innocent surprise and thoughtlessness. Dripping yet with water, and panting, he rested his elbows lazily on the bank, and became instantly absorbed with a boy's delight in the movements of the gopher, who, after the first alarm, returned cautiously to abduct the tobacco pouch. If any familiar had failed to detect Lance Harriott in this hideous masquerade of dust and grime and tatters, still less would any passing stranger have recognized in this blond faun the possible outcast and murderer. And, when with a swirl of his spattering sleeve, he drove back the gopher in a shower of spray and leaped to the bank, he seemed to have accepted his felonious hiding-place as a mere picnicking bower.

A slight breeze was unmistakably permeating the wood from the west. Looking in that direction, Lance imagined that the shadow was less dark, and although the undergrowth was denser, he struck off carelessly toward it. As he went on, the wood became lighter and lighter; branches, and presently leaves, were painted against the vivid blue of the sky. He knew he must be near the summit, stopped, felt for his revolver, and then lightly put the few remaining branches aside.

The full glare of the noonday sun at first blinded him. When he could see more clearly, he found himself on the open western slope of the mountain, which in the Coast Range was seldom wooded. The spiced thicket stretched between him and the summit, and again between him and the stage road that plunges from the terrace, like forked lightning into the valley below. He could command all the approaches without being seen. Not that this seemed to occupy his thoughts or cause him any anxiety. His first act was to disencumber himself of his tattered coat; he then filled and lighted his pipe, and stretched himself full-length on the open hillside, as if to bleach in the fierce sun. While smoking he carelessly perused the fragment of a newspaper which had enveloped his tobacco, and being struck with some amusing paragraph, read it half aloud again to some imaginary auditor, emphasizing its humor with an hilarious slap upon his leg.

Possibly from the relaxation of fatigue and the bath, which had become a vapor one as he alternately rolled and dried himself in the baking grass, his eyes closed dreamily. He was awakened by the sound of voices. They were distant; they were vague; they approached no nearer. He rolled himself to the verge of the first precipitous grassy descent. There was another bank or plateau below him, and then a confused depth of olive shadows, pierced here and there by the spiked helmets of pines.

There was no trace of habitation, yet the voices were those of some monotonous occupation, and Lance distinctly heard through them the click of crockery and the ring of some household utensil. It appeared to be the interjectional, half listless, half perfunctory, domestic dialogue of an old man and a girl, of which the words were unintelligible. Their voices indicated the solitude of the mountain, but without sadness; they were mysterious without being awe-inspiring. They might have uttered the dreariest commonplaces, but, in their vast isolation, they seemed musical and eloquent. Lance drew his first sigh,—they had suggested dinner.

Careless as his nature was, he was too cautious to risk detection in broad daylight. He contented himself for the present with endeavoring to locate that particular part of the depths from which the voices seemed to rise. It was more difficult, however, to select some other way of penetrating it than by the stage road. "They're bound to have a fire or show a light when it's dark," he reasoned, and, satisfied with that reflection, lay down again. Presently he began to amuse himself by tossing some silver coins in the air. Then his attention was directed to a spur of the Coast Range which had been sharply silhouetted against the cloudless western sky. Something intensely white, something so small that it was scarcely larger than the silver coin in his hand, was appearing in a slight cleft of the range.

While he looked it gradually filled and obliterated the cleft. In another moment the whole serrated line of mountain had disappeared. The dense, dazzling white, encompassing host began to pour over and down every ravine and pass of the coast.

Lance recognized the sea-fog, and knew that scarcely twenty miles away lay the ocean—and safety! The drooping sun was now caught and hidden in its soft embraces. A sudden chill breathed over the mountain. He shivered, rose, and plunged again for very warmth into the spice-laden thicket. The heated balsamic air began to affect him like a powerful sedative; his hunger was forgotten in the languor of fatigue; he slumbered. When he awoke it was dark. He groped his way through the thicket. A few stars were shining directly above him, but beyond and below, everything was lost in the soft, white, fleecy veil of fog. Whatever light or fire might have betokened human habitation was hidden. To push on blindly would be madness; he could only wait for morning. It suited the outcast's lazy philosophy. He crept back again to his bed in the hollow and slept. In that profound silence and shadow, shut out from human association and sympathy by the ghostly fog, what torturing visions conjured up by remorse and fear should have pursued him? What spirit passed before him, or slowly shaped itself out of the infinite blackness of the wood? None. As he slipped gently into that blackness he remembered with a slight regret, some biscuits that were dropped from the coach by a careless luncheon-consuming passenger. That pang over, he slept as sweetly, as profoundly, as divinely, as a child.

CHAPTER II.

He awoke with the aroma of the woods still steeping his senses. His first instinct was that of all young animals; he seized a few of the young, tender green leaves of the yerba buena vine that crept over his mossy pillow and ate them, being rewarded by a half berry-like flavor that seemed to soothe the cravings of his appetite. The languor of sleep being still upon him, he lazily watched the quivering of a sunbeam that was caught in the canopying boughs above. Then he dozed again. Hovering between sleeping and waking, he became conscious of a slight movement among the dead leaves on the bank beside the hollow in which he lay. The movement appeared to be intelligent, and directed toward his revolver, which glittered on the bank. Amused at this evident return of his larcenous friend of the previous day, he lay perfectly still. The movement and rustle continued, but it now seemed long and undulating. Lance's eyes suddenly became set; he was intensely, keenly awake. It was not a snake, but the hand of a human arm, half hidden in the moss, groping for the weapon. In that flash of perception he saw that it was small, bare, and deeply freckled. In an instant he grasped it firmly, and rose to his feet, dragging to his own level as he did so, the struggling figure of a young girl.

"Leave me go!" she said, more ashamed than frightened.

Lance looked at her. She was scarcely more than fifteen, slight and lithe, with a boyish flatness of breast and back. Her flushed face and bare throat were absolutely peppered with minute brown freckles, like grains of spent gunpowder. Her eyes, which were large and gray, presented the singular spectacle of being also freckled,—at least they were shot through in pupil and cornea with tiny spots like powdered allspice. Her hair was even more remarkable in its tawny, deer-skin color, full of lighter shades, and bleached to the faintest of blondes on the crown of her head, as if by the action of the sun. She had evidently outgrown her dress, which was made for a smaller child, and the too brief skirt disclosed a bare, freckled, and sandy desert of shapely limb, for which the darned stockings were equally too scant. Lance let his grasp slip from her thin wrist to her hand, and then with a good-humored gesture tossed it lightly back to her.

She did not retreat, but continued looking at him in a half-surly embarrassment.

"I ain't a bit frightened," she said; "I'm not going to run away,—don't you fear."

"Glad to hear it," said Lance, with unmistakable satisfaction, "but why did you go for my revolver?"

She flushed again and was silent. Presently she began to kick the earth at the roots of the tree, and said, as if confidentially to her foot,—

"I wanted to get hold of it before you did."

"You did?—and why?"

"Oh, you know why."

Every tooth in Lance's head showed that he did, perfectly. But he was discreetly silent.

"I didn't know what you were hiding there for," she went on, still addressing the tree, "and," looking at him sideways under her white lashes, "I didn't see your face."

This subtle compliment was the first suggestion of her artful sex. It actually sent the blood into the careless rascal's face, and for a moment confused him. He coughed. "So you thought you'd freeze on to that six-shooter of mine until you saw my hand?"

She nodded. Then she picked up a broken hazel branch, fitted it into the small of her back, threw her tanned bare arms over the ends of it, and expanded her chest and her biceps at the same moment. This simple action was supposed to convey an impression at once of ease and muscular force.

"Perhaps you'd like to take it now," said Lance, handing her the pistol.

"I've seen six-shooters before now," said the girl, evading the proffered weapon and its suggestion. "Dad has one, and my brother had two derringers before he was half as big as me."

She stopped to observe in her companion

the effect of this capacity of her family to bear arms. Lance only regarded her amusedly. Presently she again spoke abruptly:—

"What made you eat that grass, just now?"

"Grass!" echoed Lance.

"Yes, there," pointing to the yerba buena.

Lance laughed. "I was hungry. Look!" he said, gayly tossing some silver into the air. "Do you think you could get me some breakfast for that, and have enough left to buy something for yourself?"

The girl eyed the money and the man with half-bashful curiosity.

"I reckon Dad might give ye suthing if he had a mind ter, though ez a rule he's down on tramps ever since they run off his chickens. Ye might try."

"But I want *you* to try. You can bring it to me here."

The girl retreated a step, dropped her eyes, and, with a smile that was a charming hesitation between bashfulness and impudence, said: "So you *are* hidin', are ye?"

"That's just it. Your head's level. I am," laughed Lance unconcernedly.

"Yur ain't one o' the McCarty gang—are ye?"

Mr. Lance Harriott felt a momentary moral exaltation in declaring truthfully that he was not one of a notorious band of mountain freebooters known in the district under that name.

"Nor ye ain't one of them chicken lifters that raided Henderson's ranch? We don't go much on that kind o' cattle yer."

"No," said Lance, cheerfully.

"Nor ye ain't that chap ez beat his wife unto death at Santa Clara?"

Lance honestly scorned the imputation. Such conjugal ill treatment as he had indulged in had not been physical, and had been with other men's wives.

There was a moment's further hesitation on the part of the girl. Then she said shortly:

"Well, then, I reckon you kin come along with me."

"Where?" asked Lance.

"To the ranch," she replied simply.

"Then you won't bring me anything to eat here?"

"What for? You kin get it down

there." Lance hesitated. "I tell you it's all right," she continued. "I'll make it all right with Dad."

"But suppose I reckon I'd rather stay here," persisted Lance, with a perfect consciousness, however, of affectation in his caution.

"Stay away then," said the girl coolly; "only as Dad perempted this yer woods"—

"*Pre*-empted," suggested Lance.

"Per-empted or pre-emp-ted, as you like," continued the girl scornfully,—"ez he's got a holt on this yer woods, ye might ez well see him down thar ez here. For here he's like to come any minit. You can bet your life on that."

She must have read Lance's amusement in his eyes, for she again dropped her own with a frown of brusque embarrassment. "Come along, then; I'm your man," said Lance, gayly, extending his hand.

She would not accept it, eying it, however, furtively, like a horse about to shy. "Hand me your pistol first," she said.

He handed it to her with an assumption of gayety. She received it on her part with unfeigned seriousness, and threw it over her shoulder like a gun. This combined action of the child and heroine, it is quite unnecessary to say, afforded Lance undiluted joy.

"You go first," she said.

Lance stepped promptly out, with a broad grin. "Looks kinder as if I was a prisoner, don't it?" he suggested.

"Go on, and don't fool," she replied.

The two fared onward through the wood. For one moment he entertained the facetious idea of appearing to rush frantically away, "just to see what the girl would do," but abandoned it. "It's an even thing if she wouldn't spot me the first pop," he reflected admiringly.

When they had reached the open hillside, Lance stopped inquiringly. "This way," she said, pointing toward the summit, and in quite an opposite direction to the valley where he had heard the voices, one of which he now recognized as hers. They skirted the thicket for a few moments, and then turned sharply into a trail which began to dip toward a ravine leading to the valley.

"Why do you have to go all the way round?" he asked.

"*We* don't," the girl replied with emphasis; "there's a shorter cut."

"Where?"

"That's telling," she answered shortly.

"What's your name?" asked Lance, after a steep scramble and a drop into the ravine.

"Flip."

"What?"

"Flip."

"I mean your first name,—your front name."

"Flip."

"Flip! Oh, short for Felipa!"

"It ain't Flipper,—it's Flip." And she relapsed into silence.

"You don't ask me mine?" suggested Lance.

She did not vouchsafe a reply.

"Then you don't want to know?"

"Maybe Dad will. You can lie to *him*."

This direct answer apparently sustained the agreeable homicide for some moments. He moved onward, silently exuding admiration.

"Only," added Flip, with a sudden caution, "you'd better agree with me."

The trail here turned again abruptly

and reëntered the cañon. Lance looked up, and noticed they were almost directly beneath the bay thicket and the plateau that towered far above them. The trail here showed signs of clearing, and the way was marked by felled trees and stumps of pines.

"What does your father do here?" he finally asked. Flip remained silent, swinging the revolver. Lance repeated his question.

"Burns charcoal and makes diamonds," said Flip, looking at him from the corners of her eyes.

"Makes diamonds?" echoed Lance.

Flip nodded her head.

"Many of 'em?" he continued carelessly.

"Lots. But they're not big," she returned, with a sidelong glance.

"Oh, they're not big?" said Lance gravely.

They had by this time reached a small staked inclosure, whence the sudden fluttering and cackle of poultry welcomed the return of the evident mistress of this sylvan retreat. It was scarcely imposing. Further on, a cooking stove under a tree, a saddle and bridle, a few household implements, scattered about, indicated the "ranch." Like most pioneer clearings, it was simply a disorganized raid upon nature that had left behind a desolate battlefield strewn with waste and decay. The fallen trees, the crushed thicket, the splintered limbs, the rudely torn-up soil, were made hideous by their grotesque juxtaposition with the wrecked fragments of civilization, in empty cans, broken bottles, battered hats, soleless boots, frayed stockings, cast-off rags, and the crowning absurdity of the twisted-wire skeleton of a hooped skirt hanging from a branch. The wildest defile, the densest thicket, the most virgin solitude, was less dreary and forlorn than this first footprint of man. The only redeeming feature of this prolonged bivouac was the cabin itself. Built of the half-cylindrical strips of pine bark, and thatched with the same material, it had a certain picturesque rusticity. But this was an accident of economy rather than taste, for which Flip apologized by saying that the bark of the pine was "no good" for charcoal.

"I reckon Dad's in the woods," she added, pausing before the open door of the cabin. "Oh, Dad!" Her voice, clear and high, seemed to fill the whole long cañon, and echoed from the green plateau above. The monotonous strokes of an axe were suddenly pretermitted, and somewhere from the depths of the close-set pines a voice answered "Flip." There was a pause of a few moments, with some muttering, stumbling, and crackling in the underbrush, and then the sudden appearance of "Dad."

Had Lance first met him in the thicket, he would have been puzzled to assign his race to Mongolian, Indian, or Ethiopian origin. Perfunctory but incomplete washings of his hands and face, after charcoal burning, had gradually ground into his skin a grayish slate-pencil pallor, grotesquely relieved at the edges, where the washing had left off, with a border of a darker color. He looked like an overworked Christy minstrel with the briefest of intervals between his performances. There were black rims in the orbits of his eyes, as if he gazed feebly out of unglazed spectacles, which heightened his simian resemblance, already grotesquely exaggerated by what appeared to be repeated and spasmodic experiments in dyeing his gray hair. Without the slightest notice of Lance, he inflicted his protesting and querulous presence entirely on his daughter.

"Well, what's up now? Yer ye are calling me from work an hour before noon. Dog my skin, ef I ever get fairly limbered up afore it's 'Dad!' and 'Oh, Dad!'"

To Lance's intense satisfaction the girl received this harangue with an air of supreme indifference, and when "Dad" had relapsed into an unintelligible, and, as it seemed to Lance, a half-frightened muttering, she said coolly,—

"Ye'd better drop that axe and scoot round getten' this stranger some breakfast and some grub to take with him. He's one of them San Francisco sports out here trout fishing in the branch. He's got adrift from his party, has lost his rod and fixins, and had to camp out last night in the Gin and Ginger Woods."

"That's just it; it's allers suthin like that," screamed the old man, dashing his fist on his leg in a feeble, impotent passion, but without looking at Lance. "Why in blazes don't he go up to that there blamed hotel on the summit? Why in thunder—" But here he caught his daughter's large, freckled eyes full in his own. He blinked feebly, his voice fell into a tone of whining entreaty. "Now, look yer, Flip, it's playing it rather low down on the old man, this yer running' in o' tramps and desarted emigrants and castashore sailors and forlorn widders and ravin' lunatics, on this yer ranch. I put it to you, Mister," he said abruptly, turning to Lance for the first time, but as if he had already taken an active part in the conversation,—"I put it as a gentleman yourself, and a fair-minded sportin' man, if this is the square thing?"

Before Lance could reply, Flip had already begun. "That's just it! D'ye reckon, being a sportin' man and an A 1 feller, he's goin' to waltz down inter that hotel, rigged out ez he is? D'ye reckon he's goin' to let his partners get the laugh onter him? D' ye reckon he's goin' to show his head outer this yer ranch till he can do it square? Not much! Go 'long. Dad, you're talking silly!"

The old man weakened. He feebly trailed his axe between his legs to a stump and sat down, wiping his forehead with his sleeve, and imparting to it the appearance of a slate with a difficult sum partly rubbed out. He looked despairingly at Lance. "In course," he said, with a deep sigh, "you naturally ain't got any money. In course you left your pocketbook, containing fifty dollars, under a stone, and can't find it. In course," he continued, as he observed Lance put his hand to his pocket, "you've only got a blank check on Wells, Fargo & Co. for a hundred dollars, and you'd like me to give you the difference?"

Amused as Lance evidently was at this, his absolute admiration for Flip absorbed everything else. With his eyes fixed upon the girl, he briefly assured the old man that he would pay for everything he wanted. He did this with a manner quite different from the careless, easy attitude he had assumed toward Flip; at least the quick-witted girl noticed it, and wondered if he was angry. It was quite true that ever since his eye had fallen upon another of his own sex, its glance had been less frank and careless. Certain traits of possible impatience, which might develop into man-slaying, were coming to the fore. Yet a word or a gesture of Flip's was sufficient to change that manner, and when, with the fretful assistance of her father, she had prepared a somewhat sketchy and primitive repast, he questioned the old man about diamond-making. The eye of Dad kindled.

"I want ter know how ye knew I was making diamonds," he asked, with a certain bashful pettishness not unlike his daughter's.

"Heard it in 'Frisco," replied Lance, with glib mendacity, glancing at the girl.

"I reckon they're gettin' sort of skeert down there—them jewelers," chuckled Dad, "yet it's in nater that their figgers will have to come down. It's only a question of the price of charcoal. I suppose they didn't tell you how I made the discovery?"

Lance would have stopped the old man's narrative by saying that he knew the story, but he wished to see how far Flip lent herself to her father's delusion.

"Ye see, one night about two years ago I had a pit o' charcoal burning out there, and tho' it had been a smouldering and a smoking and a blazing for nigh unto a month, somehow it didn't charcoal worth a cent. And yet, dog my skin, but the heat o' that er pit was suthin hidyus and frightful; ye couldn't stand within a hundred yards of it, and they could feel it on the stage road three miles over yon, t'other side the mountain. There was nights when me and Flip had to take our blankets up the ravine and camp out all night, and the back of this yer hut shriveled up like that bacon. It was about as nigh on to hell as any sample ye kin get here. Now, mebbe you think I built that air fire? Mebbe you'll allow the heat was just the nat'ral burning of that pit?"

"Certainly," said Lance, trying to see Flip's eyes, which were resolutely averted.

"Thet's whar you'd be lyin'! That yar heat kem out of the bowels of the yearth,— kem up like out of a chimbley or a blast, and kep up that yar fire. And when she cools down a month after, and I got to strip her, there was a hole in the yearth, and a spring o' bilin', scaldin' water pourin' out of it ez big as your waist. And right in the middle of it was this yer." He rose with the instinct of a skillful *raconteur,* and whisked from under his bunk a chamois leather bag, which he emptied on the table before them. It contained a small fragment of native rock crystal, half-fused upon a petrified bit of pine. It was so glaringly truthful, so really what it purported to be, that the most unscientific woodman or pioneer would have understood it at a glance. Lance raised his mirthful eyes to Flip.

"It was cooled suddint,—stunted by the water," said the girl, eagerly. She stopped, and as abruptly turned away her eyes and her reddened face.

"That's it, that's just it," continued the old man. "Thar's Flip, thar, knows it; she ain't no fool!" Lance did not speak, but turned a hard, unsympathizing look upon the old man, and rose almost roughly. The old man clutched his coat. "That's it, ye see. The carbon's just turning to di'mens. And stunted. And why? 'Cos the heat wasn't kep up long enough. Mebbe yer think I stopped thar? That ain't me. Thar's a pit out yar in the woods ez hez been burning six months; it hain't, in course, got the advantages o' the old one, for it's nat'ral heat. But I'm keeping that heat up. I've got a hole where I kin watch it every four hours. When the time comes, I'm thar! Don't you see? That's me! that's David Fairley,—that's the old man,—you bet!"

"That's so," said Lance, curtly. "And now, Mr. Fairley, if you'll hand me over a coat or a jacket till I can get past these fogs on the Monterey road, I won't keep you from your diamond pit." He threw down a handful of silver on the table.

"Ther's a deerskin jacket yer," said the old man, "that one o' them vaqueros left for the price of a bottle of whiskey."

"I reckon it wouldn't suit the stranger," said Flip, dubiously producing a much-worn, slashed, and braided vaquero's jacket. But it did suit Lance, who found it warm, and also had suddenly found a certain satisfaction in opposing Flip. When he had put it on, and nodded coldly to the old man, and carelessly to Flip, he walked to the door.

"If you're going to take the Monterey road, I can show you a short cut to it," said Flip, with a certain kind of shy civility.

The paternal Fairley groaned. "That's it; let the chickens and the ranch go to thunder, as long as there's a stranger to trapse round with; go on!"

Lance would have made some savage reply, but Flip interrupted. "You know yourself, Dad, it's a blind trail, and as that 'ere constable that kem out here hunting French Pete, couldn't find it, and had to go round by the cañon, like ez not the stranger would lose his way, and have to come back!" This dangerous prospect silenced the old man, and Flip and Lance stepped into the road together. They walked on for some moments without speaking. Suddenly Lance turned upon his companion.

"You didn't swallow all that rot about the diamond, did you?" he asked, crossly.

Flip ran a little ahead, as if to avoid a reply.

"You don't mean to say that's the sort of hog wash the old man serves out to you regularly?" continued Lance, becoming more slangy in his ill temper.

"I don't know that it's any consarn o' yours what I think," replied Flip, hopping from boulder to boulder, as they crossed the bed of a dry watercourse.

"And I suppose you've piloted round

and dry-nussed every tramp and dead beat you've met since you came here," continued Lance, with unmistakable ill humor. "How many have you helped over this road?"

"It's a year since there was a Chinaman chased by some Irishmen from the Crossing into the brush about yer, and he was too afeered to come out, and nigh most starved to death in thar. I had to drag him out and start him on the mountain, for you couldn't get him back to the road. He was the last one but *you*."

"Do you reckon it's the right thing for a girl like you to run about with trash of this kind, and mix herself up with all sorts of rough and bad company?" said Lance.

Flip stopped short. "Look! if you're goin' to talk like Dad, I'll go back."

The ridiculousness of such a resemblance struck him more keenly than a consciousness of his own ingratitude. He hastened to assure Flip that he was joking. When he had made his peace they fell into talk again, Lance becoming unselfish enough to inquire into one or two facts concerning her life which did not immediately affect him. Her mother had died on the plains when she was a baby, and her brother had run away from home at twelve. She fully expected to see him again, and thought he might sometime stray into their cañon. "That is why, then, you take so much stock in tramps," said Lance. "You expect to recognize *him?*"

"Well," replied Flip, gravely, "there is suthin in *that,* and there's suthin in *this:* some o' these chaps might run across brother and do him a good turn for the sake of me."

"Like me, for instance?" suggested Lance.

"Like you. You'd do him a good turn, wouldn't you?"

"You bet!" said Lance, with a sudden emotion that quite startled him; "only don't you go to throwing yourself round promiscuously." He was half-conscious of an irritating sense of jealousy, as he asked if any of her *protégés* had ever returned.

"No," said Flip, "no one ever did. It shows," she added with sublime simplicity, "I had done 'em good, and they could get on alone. Don't it?"

"It does," responded Lance grimly. "Have you any other friends that come?"

"Only the Postmaster at the Crossing."

"The Postmaster?"

"Yes; he's reckonin' to marry me next year, if I'm big enough."

"And what do you reckon?" asked Lance earnestly.

Flip began a series of distortions with her shoulders, ran on ahead, picked up a few pebbles and threw them into the wood, glanced back at Lance with swimming mottled eyes, that seemed a piquant incarnation of everything suggestive and tantalizing, and said,

"That's telling."

They had by this time reached the spot where they were to separate. "Look," said Flip, pointing to a faint deflection of their path, which seemed, however, to lose itself in the underbrush a dozen yards away, "ther's your trail. It gets plainer and broader the further you get on, but you must use your eyes here, and get to know it well afore you get into the fog. Good-by."

"Good-by." Lance took her hand and drew her beside him. She was still redolent of the spices of the thicket, and to the young man's excited fancy seemed at that moment to personify the perfume and intoxication of her native woods. Half laughingly, half earnestly, he tried to kiss her; she struggled for some time strongly, but at the last moment yielded, with a slight return and the exchange of a subtle fire that thrilled him, and left him standing confused and astounded as she ran away. He watched her lithe, nymph-like figure disappear in the checkered shadows of the wood, and then he turned briskly down the half-hidden trail. His eyesight was keen, he made good progress, and was soon well on his way toward the distant ridge.

But Flip's return had not been as rapid. When she reached the wood she crept to its beetling verge, and, looking across the cañon, watched Lance's figure as it vanished and reappeared in the shadows and sinuosities of the ascent. When he reached the ridge the outlying fog crept across the summit, caught him in its embrace, and wrapped him from her gaze. Flip sighed, raised herself, put her alternate foot on a stump, and took a long pull at her too-brief stockings. When she had pulled down her skirt and endeavored once more to renew the intimacy that had existed in previous years between the edge of her petticoat and the top of her stockings, she sighed again, and went home.

CHAPTER III.

For six months the sea fogs monotonously came and went along the Monterey coast; for six months they beleaguered the Coast Range with afternoon sorties of white hosts that regularly swept over the mountain crest, and were as regularly beaten back again by the leveled lances of the morning sun. For six months that white veil which had once hidden Lance Harriott in its folds returned without him. For that amiable outlaw no longer needed disguise or hiding-place. The swift wave of pursuit that had dashed him on the summit had fallen back, and the next day was broken and scattered. Before the week had passed, a regular judicial inquiry relieved his crime of premeditation, and showed it to be a rude duel of two armed and equally desperate men. From a secure vantage in a seacoast town Lance challenged a trial by his peers, and, as an already prejudged man escaping from his executioners, obtained a change of venue. Regular justice, seated by the calm Pacific, found the action of an interior, irregular jury rash and hasty. Lance was liberated on bail.

The Postmaster at Fisher's Crossing had just received the weekly mail and express from San Francisco, and was engaged in examining it. It consisted of five letters and two parcels. Of these, three of the letters and the two parcels were directed to Flip. It was not the first time during the last six months that this extraordinary event had occurred, and the curiosity of the Crossing was duly excited. As Flip had never called personally for the letters or parcels, but had sent one of her wild, irregular scouts or henchmen to bring them, and as she was seldom seen at the Crossing or on the stage road, that curiosity was never satisfied. The disappointment to the Postmaster—a man past the middle age—partook of a sentimental nature. He looked at the letters and parcels; he looked at his watch; it was yet early, he could return by noon. He again examined the addresses; they were

in the same handwriting as the previous
letters. His mind was made up, he would
deliver them himself. The poetic, soulful
side of his mission was delicately indicated
by a pale blue necktie, a clean shirt, and
a small package of gingernuts, of which
Flip was extravagantly fond.

The common road to Fairley's Ranch
was by the stage turnpike to a point below
the Gin and Ginger Woods, where the
prudent horseman usually left his beast
and followed the intersecting trail afoot.
It was here that the Postmaster suddenly
observed on the edge of the wood the figure of an elegantly-dressed woman; she
was walking slowly, and apparently at her
ease; one hand held her skirts lightly
gathered between her gloved fingers, the
other slowly swung a riding whip. Was
it a picnic of some people from Monterey
or Santa Cruz? The spectacle was novel
enough to justify his coming nearer. Suddenly she withdrew into the wood; he lost
sight of her; she was gone. He remembered, however, that Flip was still to be
seen, and as the steep trail was beginning
to tax all his energies, he was fain to hurry
forward. The sun was nearly vertical

when he turned into the cañon, and saw the bark roof of the cabin beyond. At almost the same moment Flip appeared, flushed and panting, in the road before him.

"You've got something for me," she said, pointing to the parcel and letters. Completely taken by surprise, the Postmaster mechanically yielded them up, and as instantly regretted it. "They're paid for," continued Flip, observing his hesitation.

"That's so," stammered the official of the Crossing, seeing his last chance of knowing the contents of the parcel vanish; "but I thought ez it's a valooable package, maybe ye might want to examine it to see that it was all right afore ye receipted for it."

"I'll risk it," said Flip, coolly, "and if it ain't right I'll let ye know."

As the girl seemed inclined to retire with her property, the Postmaster was driven to other conversation. "We ain't had the pleasure of seeing you down at the Crossing for a month o' Sundays," he began, with airy yet pronounced gallantry. "Some folks let on you was keepin' company with some feller like Bijah Brown, and you were getting a little too set up for the Crossing." The individual here mentioned being the county butcher, and supposed to exhibit his hopeless affection for Flip by making a long and useless divergence from his weekly route to enter the cañon for "orders," Flip did not deem it necessary to reply. "Then I allowed how ez you might have company," he continued; "I reckon there's some city folks up at the summit. I saw a mighty smart, fash'n'ble gal cavorting round. Hed no end o' style and fancy fixin's. That's my kind, I tell you. I just weaken on that sort o' gal," he continued, in the firm belief that he had awakened Flip's jealousy, as he glanced at her well-worn homespun frock, and found her eyes suddenly fixed on his own.

"Strange I ain't got to see her yet," she replied coolly, shouldering her parcel, and quite ignoring any sense of obligation to him for his extra-official act.

"But you might get to see her at the edge of the Gin and Ginger Woods," he persisted feebly, in a last effort to detain her; "if you'll take a *pasear* there with me." Flip's only response was to walk on toward the cabin, whence, with a vague complimentary suggestion of "droppin' in to pass the time o' day" with her father, the Postmaster meekly followed.

The paternal Fairley, once convinced that his daughter's new companion required no pecuniary or material assistance from his hands, relaxed to the extent of entering into a querulous confidence with him, during which Flip took the opportunity of slipping away. As Fairley had that infelicitous tendency of most weak natures, to unconsciously exaggerate unimportant details in their talk, the Postmaster presently became convinced that the butcher was a constant and assiduous suitor of Flip's. The absurdity of his sending parcels and letters by post when he might bring them himself did not strike the official. On the contrary, he believed it to be a master stroke of cunning. Fired by jealousy and Flip's indifference, he "deemed it his duty"—using that facile form of cowardly offensiveness—to betray Flip.

Of which she was happily oblivious. Once away from the cabin, she plunged into the woods, with the parcel swung behind her like a knapsack. Leaving the trail, she presently struck off in a straight line through cover and underbrush with the unerring instinct of an animal, climbing hand over hand the steepest ascent, or fluttering like a bird from branch to branch down the deepest declivity. She soon reached that part of the trail where the susceptible Postmaster had seen the fascinating unknown. Assuring herself she was not followed, she crept through the thicket until she reached a little waterfall and basin that had served the fugitive Lance for a bath. The spot bore signs of later and more frequent occupancy, and when Flip carefully removed some bark and brushwood from a cavity in the rock and drew forth various folded garments, it was evident she had used it as a sylvan dressing-room. Here she opened the parcel; it contained a small and delicate shawl of yellow China crêpe. Flip instantly threw it over her shoulders and stepped hurriedly toward the edge of the wood. Then she began to pass backward and forward before the trunk of a tree. At first nothing was visible on the tree, but a closer inspection showed a large pane of ordinary window glass stuck in the fork of the branches. It was placed at such a cunning angle against the darkness of the forest opening that it made a soft and mysterious mirror, not unlike a Claude Lorraine glass, wherein not only the passing figure of the young girl was seen, but the dazzling green and gold of the hillside, and the far-off silhouetted crests of the Coast Range.

But this was evidently only a prelude to a severer rehearsal. When she returned to the waterfall she unearthed from her stores a large piece of yellow soap and some yards of rough cotton "sheeting." These she deposited beside the basin and again crept to the edge of the wood to assure herself that she was alone. Satisfied that no intruding foot had invaded that virgin bower, she returned to her bath and began to undress. A slight wind followed her, and seemed to whisper to the circumjacent trees. It appeared to waken her sister naiads and nymphs, who, joining their leafy fingers, softly drew around her a gently moving band of trembling lights and shadows, of flecked sprays and inextricably mingled branches, and involved her in a chaste sylvan obscurity, veiled alike from pursuing god or stumbling shepherd. Within these hallowed precincts was the musical ripple of laughter and falling water, and at times the glimpse of a lithe brier-caught limb, or a ray of sunlight trembling over bright flanks, or the white austere outline of a childish bosom.

When she drew again the leafy curtain, and once more stepped out of the wood, she was completely transformed. It was the figure that had appeared to the Postmaster; the slight, erect, graceful form of a young woman modishly attired. It was Flip, but Flip made taller by the lengthened skirt and clinging habiliments of fashion. Flip freckled, but, through the cunning of a relief of yellow color in her gown, her piquant brown-shot face and eyes brightened and intensified until she seemed like a spicy odor made visible. I cannot affirm that the judgment of Flip's mysterious *modiste* was infallible, or that the taste of Mr. Lance Harriott, her patron, was fastidious; enough that it was picturesque, and perhaps not more glaring and extravagant than the color in which Spring herself had once clothed the sere hillside where Flip was now seated. The phantom mirror in the tree fork caught and held her with the sky, the green leaves, the sunlight and all the graciousness of her surroundings, and the wind gently tossed her hair and the gay ribbons of her gypsy hat. Suddenly she started. Some remote sound in the trail below, inaudible to any ear less fine than hers, arrested her breathing. She rose swiftly and darted into cover.

Ten minutes passed. The sun was declining; the white fog was beginning to creep over the Coast Range. From the edge of the wood Cinderella appeared, disenchanted, and in her homespun garments. The clock had struck—the spell was past. As she disappeared down the trail even the magic mirror, moved by the wind, slipped from the tree top to the ground, and became a piece of common glass.

CHAPTER IV.

The events of the day had produced a remarkable impression on the facial aspect of the charcoal-burning Fairley. Extraordinary processes of thought, indicated by repeated rubbing of his forehead, had produced a high light in the middle and a corresponding deepening of shadow at the sides, until it bore the appearance of a perfect sphere. It was this forehead that confronted Flip reproachfully as became a deceived comrade, menacingly as became an outraged parent in the presence of a third party and—a Postmaster!

"Fine doin's this, yer receivin' clandecent bundles and letters, eh?" he began. Flip sent one swift, withering look of contempt at the Postmaster, who at once becoming invertebrate and groveling, mumbled that he must "get on" to the Crossing, and rose to go. But the old man, who had counted on his presence for moral support, and was clearly beginning to hate him for precipitating this scene with his daughter, whom he feared, violently protested.

"Sit down, can't ye? Don't you see you're a witness?" he screamed hysterically.

It was a fatal suggestion. "Witness," repeated Flip, scornfully.

"Yes, a witness! He gave ye letters and bundles."

"Weren't they directed to me?" asked Flip.

"Yes," said the Postmaster, hesitatingly; "in course, yes."

"Do *you* lay claim to them?" she said, turning to her father.

"No," responded the old man.

"Do you?" sharply, to the Postmaster.

"No," he replied.

"Then," said Flip, coolly, "if you're not claimin' 'em for yourself, and you hear father say they ain't his, I reckon the less you have to say about 'em the better."

"Thar's suthin' in that," said the old man, shamelessly abandoning the Postmaster.

"Then why don't she say who sent 'em,

and what they are like," said the Postmaster, "if there's nothin' in it?"

"Yes," echoed Dad. "Flip, why don't you?"

Without answering the direct question, Flip turned upon her father.

"Maybe you forget how you used to row and tear round here because tramps and such like came to the ranch for suthin', and I gave it to 'em? Maybe you'll quit tearin' round and letting yourself be made a fool of now by that man, just because one of those tramps gets up and sends us some presents back in turn?"

"'Twasn't me, Flip," said the old man, deprecatingly, but glaring at the astonished Postmaster. "Twasn't my doin'. I allus said if you cast your bread on the waters it would come back to you by return mail. The fact is, the Gov'ment is gettin' too high-handed! Some o' these bloated officials had better climb down before next leckshen."

"Maybe," continued Flip to her father, without looking at her discomfited visitor, "ye'd better find out whether one of those officials comes up to this yer ranch to steal away a gal about my own size, or to get points about diamond-making. I reckon he don't travel round to find out who writes all the letters that go through the Post Office."

The Postmaster had seemingly miscalculated the old man's infirm temper and the daughter's skillful use of it. He was unprepared for Flip's boldness and audacity, and when he saw that both barrels of the accusation had taken effect on the charcoal burner, who was rising with epileptic rage, he fairly turned and fled. The old man would have followed him with objurgation beyond the door, but for the restraining hand of Flip.

Baffled and beaten, nevertheless Fate was not wholly unkind to the retreating suitor. Near the Gin and Ginger Woods he picked up a letter which had fallen from Flip's pocket. He recognized the writing, and did not scruple to read it. It was not a love epistle,—at least, not such a one as he would have written,—it did not give the address nor the name of the correspondent; but he read the following with greedy eyes:—

"Perhaps it's just as well that you don't rig yourself out for the benefit of those dead beats at the Crossing, or any tramp that might hang round the ranch. Keep all your style for me when I come. I can't tell you when, it's mighty uncertain before the rainy season. But I'm coming soon. Don't go back on your promise about lettin' up on the tramps, and being a little more high-toned. And don't you give 'em so much. It's true I sent you hats *twice*. I clean forgot all about the first; but *I* wouldn't have given a ten-dollar hat to a nigger woman who had a sick baby because I had an extra hat. I'd have let that baby slide. I forgot to ask whether the skirt is worn separately; I must see the dressmaking sharp about it; but I think you'll want something on besides a jacket and skirt; at least, it looks like it up here. I don't think you could manage a piano down there without the old man knowing it, and raisin' the devil generally. I promised you I'd let up on him. Mind you keep all your promises to me. I'm glad you're gettin' on with the six-shooter; tin cans are good at fifteen yards, but try it on suthin' that *moves!* I forgot to say that I am on the track of your big brother. It's a three years' old track, and he was in Arizona. The friend who told me didn't expatiate much on what he did there, but I reckon they had a high old time. If he's above the earth I'll find him, you bet. The yerba buena and the southern wood came all right,—they smelt like you. Say, Flip, do you remember the *last*—the *very last*—thing that happened when you said 'Good-by' on the trail? Don't let me ever find out that you've let anybody else kiss—"

But here the virtuous indignation of the Postmaster found vent in an oath. He threw the letter away. He retained of it only two facts,—Flip *had* a brother who was missing; she had a lover present in the flesh.

How much of the substance of this and previous letters Flip had confided to her father I cannot say. If she suppressed anything it was probably that which affected Lance's secret alone, and it was doubtful how much of that she herself knew. In her own affairs she was frank without being communicative, and never lost her shy obstinacy even with her father. Governing the old man as completely as she did, she appeared most embarrassed when she was most dominant; she had her own way without lifting her voice or her eyes; she seemed oppressed by *mauvaise honte* when she was most triumphant; she would end a discussion with a shy murmur addressed to herself, or a single gesture of self-consciousness.

The disclosure of her strange relations with an unknown man and the exchange of presents and confidences seemed to suddenly awake Fairley to a vague, uneasy sense of some unfulfilled duties as a parent. The first effect of this on his weak nature was a peevish antagonism to the cause of it. He had long, fretful monologues on the vanity of diamond-making, if accompanied with a "pestering" by "interlopers;" on the wickedness of concealment and conspiracy, and their effects on charcoal-burning; on the nurturing of spies and "adders" in the family circle, and on the seditiousness of dark and mysterious councils in which a gray-haired father was left out. It was true that a word or look from Flip generally brought these monologues to an inglorious and abrupt termination, but they were none the less lugubrious as long as they lasted. In time they were succeeded by an affectation of contrite apology and self-depreciation. "Don't go out o' the way to ask the old man," he would say, referring to the quantity of bacon to be ordered; "it's nat'ral a young gal should have her own advisers." The state of the flour barrel would also produce a like self-abasement. "Unless ye're already in correspondence about more flour, ye might take the opinion o' the first tramp ye meet ez to whether Santa Cruz Mills is a good brand, but don't ask the old man." If Flip was in conversation with the butcher, Fairley would obtrusively retire with the hope "he wasn't intrudin' on their secrets."

These phases of her father's weakness

were not frequent enough to excite her alarm, but she could not help noticing they were accompanied with a seriousness unusual to him. He began to be tremulously watchful of her, returning often from work at an earlier hour, and lingering by the cabin in the morning. He brought absurd and useless presents for her, and presented them with a nervous anxiety, poorly concealed by an assumption of careless, paternal generosity. "Suthin' I picked up at the Crossin' for ye to-day," he would say, airily, and retire to watch the effect of a pair of shoes two sizes too large, or a fur cap in September. He would have hired a cheap parlor organ for her, but for the apparently unexpected revelation that she couldn't play. He had received the news of a clue to his long-lost son without emotion, but lately he seemed to look upon it as a foregone conclusion, and one that necessarily solved the question of companionship for Flip. "In course, when you've got your own flesh and blood with ye, ye can't go foolin' around with strangers." These autumnal blossoms of affection, I fear, came too late for any effect upon

Flip, precociously matured by her father's indifference and selfishness. But she was good humored, and, seeing him seriously concerned, gave him more of her time, even visited him in the sacred seclusion of the "diamond pit," and listened with far-off eyes to his fitful indictment of all things outside his grimy laboratory. Much of this patient indifference came with a capricious change in her own habits; she no longer indulged in the rehearsal of dress, she packed away her most treasured garments, and her leafy boudoir knew her no more. She sometimes walked on the hillside, and often followed the trail she had taken with Lance when she led him to the ranch. She once or twice extended her walk to the spot where she had parted from him, and as often came shyly away, her eyes downcast and her face warm with color. Perhaps because these experiences and some mysterious instinct of maturing womanhood had left a story in her eyes, which her two adorers, the Postmaster and the Butcher, read with passion, she became famous without knowing it. Extravagant stories of her fascinations brought strangers into the valley.

The effect upon her father may be imagined. Lance could not have desired a more effective guardian than he proved to be in this emergency. Those who had been told of this hidden pearl were surprised to find it so jealously protected.

CHAPTER V.

The long, parched summer had drawn to its dusty close. Much of it was already blown abroad and dissipated on trail and turnpike, or crackled in harsh, unelastic fibres on hillside and meadow. Some of it had disappeared in the palpable smoke by day and fiery crests by night of burning forests. The besieging fogs on the Coast Range daily thinned their hosts, and at last vanished. The wind changed from northwest to southwest. The salt breath of the sea was on the summit. And then one day the staring, unchanged sky was faintly touched with remote mysterious clouds, and grew tremulous in expression. The next morning dawned upon a newer face in the heavens, on changed woods, on altered outlines, on vanished crests, on forgotten distances. It was raining!

Four weeks of this change, with broken spaces of sunlight and intense blue aerial islands, and then a storm set in. All day the summit pines and redwoods rocked in the blast. At times the onset of the rain seemed to be held back by the fury of the gale, or was visibly seen in sharp waves on the hillside. Unknown and concealed watercourses suddenly overflowed the trails, pools became lakes and brooks rivers. Hidden from the storm, the sylvan silence of sheltered valleys was broken by the impetuous rush of waters; even the tiny streamlet that traversed Flip's retreat in the Gin and Ginger Woods became a cascade.

The storm drove Fairley from his couch early. The falling of a large tree across the trail, and the sudden overflow of a small stream beside it, hastened his steps. But he was doomed to encounter what was to him a more disagreeable object—a human figure. By the bedraggled drapery that flapped and fluttered in the wind, by the long, unkempt hair that hid the face and eyes, and by the grotesquely misplaced bonnet, the old man recognized one of his old trespassers,—an Indian squaw.

"Clear out 'er that! Come, make tracks, will ye?" the old man screamed;

but here the wind stopped his voice, and drove him against a hazel bush.

"Me heap sick," answered the squaw, shivering through her muddy shawl.

"I'll make ye a heap sicker if ye don't vamose the ranch," continued Fairley, advancing.

"Me wantee Wangee girl. Wangee girl give me heap grub," said the squaw, without moving.

"You bet your life," groaned the old man to himself. Nevertheless an idea struck him. "Ye ain't brought no presents, hev ye?" he asked cautiously. "Ye ain't got no pooty things for poor Wangee girl?" he continued, insinuatingly.

"Me got heap *cache* nuts and berries," said the squaw.

"Oh, in course! in course! That's just it," screamed Fairley; "you've got 'em *cached* only two mile from yer, and you'll go and get 'em for a half dollar, cash down."

"Me bring Wangee girl to *cache*," replied the Indian, pointing to the wood. "Honest Injin."

Another bright idea struck Mr. Fairley. But it required some elaboration. Hurrying the squaw with him through the pelting rain, he reached the shelter of the corral. Vainly the shivering aborigine drew her tightly bandaged papoose closer to her square, flat breast, and looked longingly toward the cabin; the old man backed her against the palisade. Here he cautiously imparted his dark intentions to employ her to keep watch and ward over the ranch, and especially over its young mistress—"clear out all the tramps 'ceptin' yourself, and I'll keep ye in grub and rum." Many and deliberate repetitions of this offer in various forms at last seemed to affect the squaw; she nodded violently, and echoed the last word "rum." "Now," she added. The old man hesitated; she was in possession of his secret; he groaned, and, promising an immediate installment of liquor, led her to the cabin.

The door was so securely fastened against the impact of the storm that some moments elapsed before the bar was drawn, and the old man had become impatient and profane. When it was partly opened by Flip he hastily slipped in, dragging the squaw after him, and cast one single suspicious glance around the rude apartment which served as a sitting-room. Flip had apparently been writing. A small inkstand was still on the board table, but her paper had evidently been concealed before she allowed them to enter. The squaw instantly squatted before the adobe hearth, warmed her bundled baby, and left the ceremony of introduction to her companion. Flip regarded the two with calm preoccupation and indifference. The only thing that touched her interest was the old squaw's draggled skirt and limp neckerchief. They were Flip's own, long since abandoned and cast off in the Gin and Ginger Woods. "Secrets again," whined Fairley, still eying Flip furtively. "Secrets again, in course—in course—jiss so. Secrets that must be kep from the ole man. Dark doin's by one's own flesh and blood. Go on! go on! Don't mind me." Flip did not reply. She had even lost the interest in her old dress. Perhaps it had only touched some note in unison with her revery.

"Can't ye get the poor critter some whiskey?" he queried, fretfully. "Ye used to be peart enuff before." As Flip turned to the corner to lift the demijohn,

Fairley took occasion to kick the squaw with his foot, and indicate by extravagant pantomime that the bargain was not to be alluded to before the girl. Flip poured out some whiskey in a tin cup, and, approaching the squaw, handed it to her. "It's like ez not," continued Fairley to his daughter, but looking at the squaw, "that she'll be huntin' the woods off and on, and kinder looking after the last pit near the *Madroños;* ye'll give her grub and licker ez she likes. Well, d'ye hear, Flip? Are ye moonin' agin with yer secrets? What's gone with ye?"

If the child were dreaming, it was a delicious dream. Her magnetic eyes were suffused by a strange light, as though the eye itself had blushed; her full pulse showed itself more in the rounding outline of her cheek than in any deepening of color; indeed, if there was any heightening of tint, it was in her freckles, which fairly glistened like tiny spangles. Her eyes were downcast, her shoulders slightly bent, but her voice was low and clear and thoughtful as ever.

"One o' the big pines above the *Madroño* pit has blown over into the run," she said. "It's choked up the water, and it's risin' fast. Like ez not it's pourin' over into the pit by this time."

The old man rose with a fretful cry. "And why in blazes didn't you say so first?" he screamed, catching up his axe and rushing to the door.

"Ye didn't give me a chance," said Flip, raising her eyes for the first time. With an impatient imprecation, Fairley darted by her and rushed into the wood. In an instant she had shut the door and bolted it. In the same instant the squaw arose, dashed the long hair not only from her eyes, but from her head, tore away her shawl and blanket, and revealed the square shoulders of Lance Harriott! Flip remained leaning against the door; but the young man in rising dropped the bandaged papoose, which rolled from his lap into the fire. Flip, with a cry, sprang toward it; but Lance caught her by the waist with one arm, as with the other he dragged the bundle from the flames.

"Don't be alarmed," he said, gayly, "it's only—"

"What?" said Flip, trying to disengage herself.

"My coat and trousers."

Flip laughed, which encouraged Lance to another attempt to kiss her. She evaded it by diving her head into his waistcoat, and saying, "There's father."

"But he's gone to clear away that tree?" suggested Lance.

One of Flip's significant silences followed.

"Oh, I see," he laughed. "That was a plan to get him away! Ah!" She had released herself.

"Why did you come like that?" she said, pointing to his wig and blanket.

"To see if you'd know me," he responded.

"No," said Flip, dropping her eyes. "It's to keep other people from knowing you. You're hidin' agin."

"I am," returned Lance; "but," he interrupted, "it's only the same old thing."

"But you wrote from Monterey that it was all over," she persisted.

"So it would have been," he said gloomily, "but for some dog down here who is hunting up an old scent. I'll spot him yet, and—" He stopped suddenly, with such utter abstraction of hatred in his fixed and glittering eyes that she almost feared him. She laid her hand quite unconsciously on his arm. He grasped it; his face changed.

"I couldn't wait any longer to see you, Flip, so I came here anyway," he went on. "I thought to hang round and get a chance to speak to you first, when I fell afoul of the old man. He didn't know me, and tumbled right in my little game. Why, do you believe he wants to hire me for my grub and liquor, to act as a sort of sentry over you and the ranch?" And here he related with great gusto the substance of his interview. "I reckon as he's that suspicious," he concluded, "I'd better play it out now as I've begun, only it's mighty hard I can't see you here before the fire in your fancy toggery, Flip, but must dodge in and out of the wet underbrush in these yer duds of yours that I picked up in the old place in the Gin and Ginger Woods."

"Then you came here just to see me?" asked Flip.

"I did."

"For only that?"

"Only that."

Flip dropped her eyes. Lance had got

his other arm around her waist, but her resisting little hand was still potent.

"Listen," she said at last without looking up, but apparently talking to the intruding arm, "when Dad comes I'll get him to send you to watch the diamond pit. It isn't far; it's warm, and"—

"What?"

"I'll come, after a bit, and see you. Quit foolin' now. If you'd only have come here like yourself—like—like—a white man."

"The old man," interrupted Lance, "would have just passed me on to the summit. I couldn't have played the lost fisherman on him at this time of year."

"Ye could have been stopped at the Crossing by high water, you silly," said the girl. "It was." This grammatical obscurity referred to the stage coach.

"Yes, but I might have been tracked to this cabin. And look here, Flip," he said, suddenly straightening himself, and lifting the girl's face to a level with his own, "I don't want you to lie any more for me. It ain't right."

"All right. Ye needn't go to the pit, then, and I won't come."

"Flip!"

"And here's Dad coming. Quick!"

Lance chose to put his own interpretation on this last adjuration. The resisting little hand was now lying quite limp on his shoulder. He drew her brown, bright face near his own, felt her spiced breath on his lips, his cheeks, his hot eyelids, his swimming eyes, kissed her, hurriedly replaced his wig and blanket, and dropped beside the fire with the tremulous laugh of youth and innocent first passion. Flip had withdrawn to the window, and was looking out upon the rocking pines.

"He don't seem to be coming," said Lance, with a half-shy laugh.

"No," responded Flip demurely, pressing her hot oval cheek against the wet panes; "I reckon I was mistaken. You're sure," she added, looking resolutely another way, but still trembling like a magnetic needle toward Lance, as he moved slightly before the fire, "you're *sure* you'd like me to come to you?"

"Sure, Flip?"

"Hush!" said Flip, as this reassuring query of reproachful astonishment appeared about to be emphasized by a forward amatory dash of Lance's; "hush! he's coming this time, sure."

It was, indeed, Fairley, exceedingly wet, exceedingly bedraggled, exceedingly sponged out as to color, and exceedingly profane. It appeared that there was, indeed, a tree that had fallen in the "run," but that, far from diverting the overflow into the pit, it had established "back water," which had forced another outlet. All this might have been detected at once by any human intellect not distracted by correspondence with strangers, and enfeebled by habitually scorning the intellect of its own progenitor. This reckless selfishness had further only resulted in giving "rheumatics" to that progenitor, who now required the external administration of opodeldoc to his limbs, and the internal administration of whiskey. Having thus spoken, Mr. Fairley, with great promptitude and infantine simplicity, at once bared two legs of entirely different colors and mutely waited for his daughter to rub them. If Flip did this all unconsciously, and with the mechanical dexterity of previous habit, it was because she did not quite understand the savage eyes and impatient gestures of Lance in his encompassing wig and blanket, and because it helped her to voice her thought.

"Ye'll never be able to take yer watch at the diamond pit to-night, Dad," she said; "and I've been reck'nin' you might set the squaw there instead. I can show her what to do."

But to Flip's momentary discomfiture, her father promptly objected. "Mebbee I've got suthin' else for her to do. Mebbee I may have my secrets, too—eh?" he said, with dark significance, at the same time administering a significant nudge to Lance, which kept up the young man's exasperation. "No, she'll rest yer a bit just now. I'll set her to watchin' suthin' else, like as not, when I want her." Flip fell into one of her suggestive silences. Lance watched her earnestly, mollified by a single furtive glance from her significant eyes; the rain dashed against the windows, and occasionally spattered and hissed in the hearth of the broad chimney, and Mr. David Fairley, somewhat assuaged by the internal administration of whiskey, grew more loquacious. The genius of incongruity and inconsistency which generally ruled his conduct came out with freshened vigor under the gentle stimulation of spirit. "On an evening like this," he began, comfortably settling himself on the floor beside the chimney, "ye might rig yerself out in them new duds and fancy fixin's that that Sacramento shrimp sent ye, and let your own flesh and blood see ye. If that's too much to do for your old dad, ye might do it to please that digger squaw as a Christian act." Whether in the hidden depths of the old man's consciousness there was a feeling of paternal vanity in showing this wretched aborigine the value and importance of the treasure she was about to guard, I cannot say. Flip darted an interrogatory look at Lance, who nodded a quiet assent, and she flew into the inner room. She did not linger on the details of her toilet, but reappeared almost the next moment in her new finery; buttoning the neck of her gown as she entered the room, and chastely stopping at the window to characteristically pull up her stocking. The peculiarity of her situation increased her usual shyness; she played with the black and gold beads of a handsome necklace,—Lance's last gift,—as the merest child might; her unbuckled shoe gave the squaw a natural opportunity of showing her admiration and devotion by insisting upon buckling it, and gave Lance, under that disguise, an opportunity of covertly kissing the little foot and ankle in the shadow of the chimney; an event which provoked slight hysterical symptoms in Flip, and caused her to sit suddenly down in spite of the remonstrances of her parent. "Ef you can't quit gigglin' and squirmin' like an Injin baby yourself, ye'd better git rid o' them duds," he ejaculated with peevish scorn.

Yet, under this perfunctory rebuke, his weak vanity could not be hidden, and he enjoyed the evident admiration of a creature whom he believed to be half-witted and degraded all the more keenly because it did not make him jealous. She could not take Flip from him. Rendered garrulous by liquor, he went to voice his contempt for those who might attempt it. Taking advantage of his daughter's absence to resume her homely garments, he whispered confidentially to Lance,—

"Ye see these yer fine dresses, ye might think is presents. Pr'aps Flip lets on they are? Pr'aps she don't know any better. But they ain't presents. They're only samples o' dressmaking and jewelry that a vain, conceited shrimp of a feller up in Sacramento sends down here to get customers for. In course I'm to pay for 'em. In course he reckons I'm to do it. In course I calkilate to do it; but he needn't try to play 'em off as presents. He talks suthin' o' coming down here, sportin' hisself off on Flip as a fancy buck! Not ez long ez the old man's here, you bet." Thoroughly carried away by his fancied wrongs, it was perhaps fortunate that he did not observe the flashing eyes of Lance behind his lank and lustreless wig; but seeing only the figure of Lance, as he had conjured him, he went on: "That's why I want you to hang around her. Hang around her ontil my boy,—him that's comin' home on a visit,—gets here, and I reckon he'll clear out that yar Sacramento counter-jumper. Only let me get a sight o' him afore Flip does. Eh? D'ye hear? Dog my skin if I don't believe the d——d Injin's drunk." It was fortunate that at that moment Flip reappeared, and, dropping on the hearth between her father and the infuriated

Lance, let her hand slip in his with a warning pressure. The light touch momentarily recalled him to himself and her, but not until the quick-witted girl had had revealed to her in one startled wave of consciousness, the full extent of Lance's infirmity of temper. With the instinct of awakened tenderness came a sense of responsibility, and a vague premonition of danger. The coy blossom of her heart was scarce unfolded before it was chilled by approaching shadows. Fearful of, she knew not what, she hesitated. Every moment of Lance's stay was imperiled by a single word that might spring from his suppressed white lips; beyond and above the suspicions his sudden withdrawal might awaken in her father's breast, she was dimly conscious of some mysterious terror without that awaited him. She listened to the furious onslaught of the wind upon the sycamores beside their cabin, and thought she heard it there; she listened to the sharp fusillade of rain upon roof and pane, and the turbulent roar and rush of leaping mountain torrents at their very feet, and fancied it was there. She suddenly sprang to the window, and, pressing her eyes to the pane, saw through the misty turmoil of tossing boughs and swaying branches the scintillating intermittent flames of torches moving on the trail above, and *knew* it was there!

In an instant she was collected and calm. "Dad," she said, in her ordinary indifferent tone, "there's torches movin' up toward the diamond pit. Likely it's tramps. I'll take the squaw and see." And before the old man could stagger to his feet she had dragged Lance with her into the road.

CHAPTER VI.

The wind charged down upon them, slamming the door at their backs, extinguishing the broad shaft of light that had momentarily shot out into the darkness, and swept them a dozen yards away. Gaining the lee of a madroño tree, Lance opened his blanketed arms, enfolded the girl, and felt her for one brief moment tremble and nestle in his bosom like some frightened animal. "Well," he said, gayly, "what next?" Flip recovered herself. "You're safe now anywhere outside the house. But did you expect them tonight?" Lance shrugged his shoulders. "Why not?" "Hush!" returned the girl; "they're coming this way."

The four flickering, scattered lights presently dropped into line. The trail had been found; they were coming nearer. Flip breathed quickly; the spiced aroma of her presence filled the blanket as he drew her tightly beside him. He had forgotten the storm that raged around them, the mysterious foe that was approaching, until Flip caught his sleeve with a slight laugh. "Why, it's Kennedy and Bijah?"

"Who's Kennedy and Bijah?" asked Lance, curtly.

"Kennedy's the Postmaster and Bijah's the Butcher."

"What do they want?" continued Lance.

"Me," said Flip, coyly.

"You?"

"Yes; let's run away."

Half leading, half dragging her friend, Flip made her way with unerring woodcraft down the ravine. The sound of voices and even the tumult of the storm became fainter, an acrid smell of burning green wood smarted Lance's lips and eyes; in the midst of the darkness beneath him gradually a faint, gigantic nimbus like a lurid eye glowed and sank, quivered and faded with the spent breath of the gale as it penetrated their retreat. "The pit," whispered Flip; "it's safe on the other side," she added, cautiously skirting the orbit of the great eye, and leading him to a sheltered nest of bark and sawdust. It was warm and odorous. Nevertheless, they both deemed it necessary to enwrap themselves in the single blanket. The eye beamed fitfully upon them, occasionally a wave of lambent tremulousness passed across it; its weirdness was an excuse for their drawing nearer each other in playful terror.

"Flip."

"Well?"

"What did the other two want? To see you, *too?*"

"Likely," said Flip, without the least trace of coquetry. "There's been a lot of strangers yer, off and on."

"Perhaps you'd like to go back and see them?"

"Do you want me to?"

Lance's reply was a kiss. Nevertheless he was vaguely uneasy. "Looks a little as if I were running away, don't it?" he suggested.

"No," said Flip; "they think you're only a squaw; it's me they're after." Lance smarted a little at this infelicitous speech. A strange and irritating sensation had been creeping over him—it was his first experience of shame and remorse.

"I reckon I'll go back and see," he said, rising abruptly.

Flip was silent. She was thinking. Believing that the men were seeking her only, she knew that their attention would be directed from her companion when it was found out he was no longer with her, and she dreaded to meet them in his irritable presence.

"Go," she said, "tell Dad something's gone wrong in the diamond pit, and say I'm watching it for him here."

"And you?"

"I'll go there and wait for him. If he can't get rid of them, and they follow him there, I'll come back here and meet you. Anyhow, I'll manage to have Dad wait there a spell."

She took his hand and led him back by a different path to the trail. He was surprised to find that the cabin, its window glowing from the fire, was only a hundred yards away. "Go in the back way, by the shed. Don't go in the room, nor near the light, if you can. Don't talk inside, but call or beckon to Dad. Remember," she said, with a laugh, "you're keeping watch of me for him. Pull your hair down on

368 *FLIP: A CALIFORNIA ROMANCE.*

your eyes so." This operation, like most feminine embellishments of the masculine toilet was attended by a kiss, and Flip, stepping back into the shadow, vanished in the storm.

Lance's first movements were inconsistent with his assumed sex. He picked up his draggled skirt, and drew a bowie knife from his boot. From his bosom he took a revolver, turning the chambers noiselessly as he felt the caps. He then crept toward the cabin softly and gained the shed. It was quite dark but for a pencil of light piercing a crack of the rude, ill-fitting door that opened on the sitting-room. A single voice not unfamiliar to him, raised in half-brutal triumph, greeted his ears.

A name was mentioned—his own! His angry hand was on the latch. One moment more and he would have burst the door, but in that instant another name was uttered—a name that dropped his hand from the latch and the blood from his cheeks. He staggered backward, passed his hand swiftly across his forehead, recovered himself with a gesture of mingled rage and despair, and, sinking on his knees beside the door, pressed his hot temples against the crack.

"Do I know Lance Harriott?" said the voice. "Do I know the d——d ruffian? Didn't I hunt him a year ago into the brush three miles from the Crossing? Didn't we lose sight of him the very day he turned up yer at this ranch, and got smuggled over into Monterey? Ain't it the same man as killed Arkansaw Bob—Bob Ridley—the name he went by in Sonora? And who was Bob Ridley, eh? Who? Why, you d——d old fool, it was Bob Fairley—YOUR SON!"

The old man's voice rose querulous and indistinct.

"What are ye talkin' about?" interrupted the first speaker. "I tell you I *know*. Look at these pictures. I found 'em on his body. Look at 'em. Pictures of you and your girl. Pr'aps you'll deny them. Pr'aps you'll tell me I lie when I tell you *he* told me he was your son; told me how he ran away from you; how you were livin' somewhere in the mountains makin' gold, or suthin' else, outer charcoal. He told me who he was as a secret. He never let on he told it to any one else.

And when I found that the man who killed him, Lance Harriott, had been hidin' here, had been sendin' spies all around to find out all about your son, had been foolin' you and tryin' to ruin your gal as he had killed your boy, I knew that *he* knew it, too."

"Liar!"

The door fell in with a crash. There was the sudden apparition of a demoniac face, still half hidden by the long trailing black locks of hair that curled like Medusa's around it. A cry of terror filled the room. Three of the men dashed from the door and fled precipitately. The man who had spoken sprang toward his rifle in the chimney corner. But the movement was his last; a blinding flash and shattering report interposed between him and his weapon.

The impulse carried him forward headlong into the fire, that hissed and spluttered with his blood, and Lance Harriott with his smoking pistol, strode past him to the door. Already far down the trail there were hurried voices, the crack and crackling of impending branches growing fainter and fainter in the distance. Lance turned back to the solitary living figure—the old man.

Yet he might have been dead, too, he sat so rigid and motionless, his fixed eyes staring vacantly at the body on the hearth. Before him on the table lay the cheap photographs, one evidently of himself, taken in some remote epoch of complexion, one of a child which Lance recognized as Flip.

"Tell me," said Lance hoarsely, laying his quivering hand on the table, "was Bob Ridley your son?"

"My son," echoed the old man in a strange, far-off voice, without turning his eyes from the corpse—"My son—is—is— is there!" pointing to the dead man. "Hush! Didn't he tell you so? Didn't you hear him say it? Dead—dead— shot—shot!"

"Silence! are you crazy, man?" repeated Lance, tremblingly; "that is not Bob Ridley, but a dog, a coward, a liar gone to his reckoning. Hear me! If your son *was* Bob Ridley, I swear to God I never knew it, now or—or—*then*. Do you hear me? Tell me! Do you believe me? Speak! You shall speak."

He laid his hand almost menacingly on the old man's shoulder. Fairley slowly raised his head. Lance fell back with a groan of horror. The weak lips were wreathed with a feeble imploring smile, but the eyes wherein the fretful, peevish, suspicious spirit had dwelt were blank and tenantless; the flickering intellect that had lit them was blown out and vanished.

Lance walked toward the door and remained motionless for a moment, gazing into the night. When he turned back again toward the fire his face was as colorless as the dead man's on the hearth; the fire of passion was gone from his beaten eyes; his step was hesitating and slow. He went up to the table.

"I say, old man," he said, with a strange smile and an odd, premature suggestion of the infinite weariness of death in his voice, "you wouldn't mind giving me this, would you?" and he took up the picture of Flip. The old man nodded repeatedly. "Thank you," said Lance. He went to the door, paused a moment, and returned. "Good-by, old man," he said, holding out his hand. Fairley took it with a childish smile. "He's dead," said the old man softly, holding Lance's hand, but pointing to the hearth. "Yes," said Lance, with the faintest of smiles on the palest of faces. "You feel sorry for any one that's dead, don't you?" Fairley nodded again. Lance looked at him with eyes as remote as his own, shook his head, and turned away. When he reached the door he laid his revolver carefully, and, indeed, somewhat ostentatiously, upon a chair. But when he stepped from the threshold he stopped a moment in the light of the open door to examine the lock of a small derringer which he drew from his pocket. He then shut the door carefully, and with the same slow, hesitating step, felt his way into the night.

He had but one idea in his mind, to find some lonely spot; some spot where the footsteps of man would never penetrate, some spot that would yield him rest, sleep, obliteration, forgetfulness, and, above all, where *he* would be forgotten. He had seen such places; surely there were many, —where bones were picked up of dead men who had faded from the earth and had left no other record. If he could only keep his senses now he might find such a spot, but he must be careful, for her little feet went everywhere, and she must never see him again alive or dead. And in the midst of his thoughts, and the darkness, and the storm, he heard a voice at his side, "Lance, how long you have been!"

. . . .

Left to himself, the old man again fell into a vacant contemplation of the dead body before him, until a stronger blast swept down like an avalanche upon the cabin, burst through the ill-fastened door and broken chimney, and, dashing the ashes and living embers over the floor, filled the room with blinding smoke and flame. Fairley rose with a feeble cry, and then, as if acted upon by some dominant memory, groped under the bed until he found his buckskin bag and his precious crystal, and fled precipitately from the room. Lifted by this second shock from his apathy, he returned to the fixed idea of his life,—the discovery and creation of the diamond,—and forgot all else. The feeble grasp that his shaken intellect kept of the events of the night relaxed, the disguised Lance, the story of his son, the murder, slipped into nothingness; there remained only the one idea, his nightly watch by the diamond pit. The instinct of long habit was stronger than the darkness or the onset of the storm, and he kept his tottering way over stream and fallen timber until he reached the spot. A sudden tremor seemed to shake the lambent flame that had lured him on. He thought he heard the sound of voices; there were signs of recent disturbance,—footprints in the sawdust! With a cry of rage and suspicion, Fairley slipped into the pit and sprang toward the nearest opening. To his frenzied fancy it had been tampered with, his secret discovered, the fruit of his long labors stolen from him that very night. With superhuman strength he began to open the pit, scattering the half-charred logs right and left, and giving vent to the suffocating gases that rose from the now incandescent charcoal. At times the fury of the gale would drive it back and hold it against the sides of the pit, leaving the opening free; at times, following the blind instinct of habit, the demented man would fall upon his face and bury his nose and mouth in the wet bark and sawdust. At last, the paroxysm past, he sank back again in his old apathetic attitude of watching, the attitude he had so often kept beside his sylvan crucible. In this attitude and in silence he waited for the dawn.

It came with a hush in the storm; it came with blue openings in the broken up and tumbled heavens; it came with stars that glistened first, and then paled, and at last sank drowning in those deep cerulean lakes; it came with those cerulean lakes broadening into vaster seas, whose shores expanded at last into one illimitable ocean, cerulean no more, but flecked with crimson and opal dyes; it came with the lightly lifted misty curtain of the day, torn and rent on crag and pine top, but always lifting, lifting. It came with the sparkle of emerald in the grasses, and the flash of diamonds in every spray, with a whisper in the awakening woods, and voices in the traveled roads and trails.

The sound of these voices stopped before the pit, and seemed to interrogate the old man. He came, and, putting his finger on his lips, made a sign of caution. When three or four men had descended he bade them follow him, saying, weakly and disjointedly, but persistently: "My boy—my son Robert—came home—came home at last—here with Flip—both of them—come and see!"

He had reached a little niche or nest in the hillside, and stopped and suddenly drew aside a blanket. Beneath it, side by side, lay Flip and Lance, dead, with their cold hands clasped in each other's.

"Suffocated!" said two or three, turning with horror toward the broken up and still smouldering pit.

"Asleep!" said the old man. "Asleep! I've seen 'em lying that way when they were babies together. Don't tell me! Don't say I don't know my own flesh and blood! So! so! So, my pretty ones!" He stooped and kissed them. Then, drawing the blanket over them gently, he rose and said softly, "Good night!"

FOUND AT BLAZING STAR.

The rain had only ceased with the gray streaks of morning at Blazing Star, and the settlement awoke to a moral sense of cleanliness, and the finding of forgotten knives, tin cups, and smaller camp utensils, where the heavy showers had washed away the débris and dust heaps before the cabin doors. Indeed, it was recorded in Blazing Star that a fortunate early riser had once picked up on the highway a solid chunk of gold quartz which the rain had freed from its incumbering soil, and washed into immediate and glittering popularity. Possibly this may have been the reason why early risers in that locality, during the rainy season, adopted a thoughtful habit of body, and seldom lifted their eyes to the rifted or india-ink washed skies above them.

"Cass" Beard had risen early that morning, but not with a view to discovery. A leak in his cabin roof,—quite consistent with his careless, improvident habits,—had roused him at 4 A. M., with a flooded "bunk" and wet blankets. The chips from his wood pile refused to kindle a fire to dry his bed-clothes, and he had recourse to a more provident neighbor's to supply the deficiency. This was nearly opposite. Mr. Cassius crossed the highway, and stopped suddenly. Something glittered in the nearest red pool before him. Gold, surely! But, wonderful to relate, not an irregular, shapeless fragment of crude ore, fresh from Nature's crucible, but a bit of jeweler's handicraft in the form of a plain gold ring. Looking at it more attentively, he saw that it bore the inscription, "May to Cass."

Like most of his fellow gold-seekers, Cass was superstitious. "Cass!" His own name! He tried the ring. It fitted his little finger closely. It was evidently a woman's ring. He looked up and down the highway. No one was yet stirring. Little pools of water in the red road were beginning to glitter and grow rosy from the far-flushing east, but there was no trace of the owner of the shining waif. He knew that there was no woman in camp, and among his few comrades in the settlement he remembered to have seen none wearing an ornament like that. Again, the coincidence of the inscription to his rather peculiar nickname would have been a perennial source of playful comment in a camp that made no allowance for sentimental memories. He slipped the glittering little hoop into his pocket, and thoughtfully returned to his cabin.

Two hours later, when the long, straggling procession, which every morning wended its way to Blazing Star Gulch,— the seat of mining operations in the settlement,—began to move, Cass saw fit to interrogate his fellows. "Ye didn't none on ye happen to drop anything round yer last night?" he asked, cautiously.

"I dropped a pocketbook containing government bonds and some other securities, with between fifty and sixty thousand dollars," responded Peter Drummond, carelessly; "but no matter, if any man will return a few autograph letters from foreign potentates that happened to be in it,—of no value to anybody but the owner,—he can keep the money. Thar's nothin' mean about me," he concluded, languidly.

This statement, bearing every evidence of the grossest mendacity, was lightly passed over, and the men walked on with the deepest gravity.

"But hev you?" Cass presently asked of another.

"I lost my pile to Jack Hamlin at draw-poker, over at Wingdam last night," returned the other, pensively, "but I don't calkilate to find it lying round loose."

Forced at last by this kind of irony into more detailed explanation, Cass confided to them his discovery, and produced his treasure. The result was a dozen vague surmises,—only one of which seemed to be popular, and to suit the dyspeptic despondency of the party,—a despondency born of hastily masticated fried pork and flapjacks. The ring was believed to have been dropped by some passing "road agent" laden with guilty spoil.

"Ef I was you," said Drummond, gloomily, "I wouldn't flourish that yer ring around much afore folks. I've seen better men nor you strung up a tree by

Vigilantés for having even less than that in their possession."

"And I wouldn't say much about bein' up so d—d early this morning," added an even more pessimistic comrade; "it might look bad before a jury."

With this the men sadly dispersed, leaving the innocent Cass with the ring in his hand, and a general impression on his mind that he was already an object of suspicion to his comrades,—an impression, it is hardly necessary to say, they fully intended should be left to rankle in his guileless bosom.

Notwithstanding Cass's first hopeful superstition the ring did not seem to bring him nor the camp any luck. Daily the "clean up" brought the same scant rewards to their labors, and deepened the sardonic gravity of Blazing Star. But, if Cass found no material result from his treasure, it stimulated his lazy imagination, and, albeit a dangerous and seductive stimulant, at least lifted him out of the monotonous grooves of his half-careless, half-slovenly, but always self-contented camp life. Heeding the wise caution of his comrades, he took the habit of wearing the ring only at night. Wrapped in his blanket, he stealthily slipped the golden circlet over his little finger, and, as he averred, "slept all the better for it." Whether it ever evoked any warmer dream or vision during those calm, cold, virgin-like spring nights, when even the moon and the greater planets retreated into the icy blue, steel-like firmament, I cannot say. Enough that this superstition began to be colored a little by fancy, and his fatalism somewhat mitigated by hope. Dreams of this kind did not tend to promote his efficiency in the communistic labors of the camp, and brought him a self-isolation that, however gratifying at first, soon debarred him the benefits of that hard practical wisdom which underlaid the grumbling of his fellow workers.

"I'm dog-goned," said one commentator, "ef I don't believe that Cass is looney over that yer ring he found. Wears it on a string under his shirt."

Meantime, the seasons did not wait the discovery of the secret. The red pools in Blazing Star highway were soon dried up in the fervent June sun and riotous night winds of those altitudes. The ephemeral grasses that had quickly supplanted these pools and the chocolate-colored mud, were as quickly parched and withered. The footprints of spring became vague and indefinite, and were finally lost in the impalpable dust of the summer highway.

In one of his long, aimless excursions, Cass had penetrated a thick undergrowth of buckeye and hazel, and found himself quite unexpectedly upon the high road to Red Chief's Crossing. Cass knew by the lurid cloud of dust that hid the distance, that the up coach had passed. He had already reached that stage of superstition when the most trivial occurrence seemed to point in some way to an elucidation of the mystery of his treasure. His eyes had mechanically fallen to the ground again, as if he half expected to find in some other waif a hint or corroboration of his imaginings. Thus abstracted, the figure of a young girl on horseback, in the road directly before the bushes he emerged from, appeared to have sprung directly from the ground.

"Oh, come here, please do; quick!"

Cass stared, and then moved hesitatingly toward her.

"I heard some one coming through the bushes, and I waited," she went on. "Come quick. It's something too awful for anything."

In spite of this appalling introduction, Cass could not but notice that the voice, although hurried and excited, was by no means agitated or frightened; that the eyes which looked into his sparkled with a certain kind of pleased curiosity.

"It was just here," she went on vivaciously, "just here that I went into the bush and cut a switch for my mare,—and,"—leading him along at a brisk trot by her side,—"just here, look, see! this is what I found."

It was scarcely thirty feet from the road. The only object that met Cass's eye was a man's stiff, tall hat, lying emptily and vacantly in the grass. It was new, shiny, and of modish shape. But it was so incongruous, so perkily smart, and yet so feeble and helpless lying there, so ghastly ludicrous in its very appropriateness and incapacity to adjust itself to the surrounding landscape, that it affected him with something more than a sense of its grotesqueness, and he could only stare at it blankly.

"But you're not looking the right way," the girl went on sharply; "look there!"

Cass followed the direction of her whip. At last, what might have seemed a coat thrown carelessly on the ground met his eye, but presently he became aware of a white, rigid, aimlessly-clinched hand protruding from the flaccid sleeve; mingled with it in some absurd way and half hidden by the grass, lay what might have been a pair of cast-off trousers but for two rigid boots that pointed in opposite angles to the sky. It was a dead man. So palpably dead that life seemed to have taken flight from his very clothes. So impotent, feeble, and degraded by them that the naked subject of a dissecting table would have been less insulting to humanity. The head had fallen back, and was partly hidden in a gopher burrow, but the white, upturned face and closed eyes had less of helpless death in them than those wretched enwrappings. Indeed, one limp hand that lay across the swollen abdomen lent itself to the grotesquely hideous suggestion of a gentleman sleeping off the excesses of a hearty dinner.

"Ain't he horrid?" continued the girl; "but what killed him?"

Struggling between a certain fascination at the girl's cold-blooded curiosity and horror of the murdered man, Cass hesitatingly lifted the helpless head. A bluish hole above the right temple, and a few brown paint-like spots on the forehead, shirt collar, and matted hair proved the only record.

"Turn him over again," said the girl, impatiently, as Cass was about to relinquish his burden. "May be you'll find another wound."

But Cass was dimly remembering certain formalities that in older civilizations attend the discovery of dead bodies, and postponed a present inquest.

"Perhaps you'd better ride on, Miss, afore you get summoned as a witness. I'll give warning at Red Chief's Crossing, and send the coroner down here."

"Let me go with you," she said, earnestly, "it would be such fun. I don't mind being a witness. Or," she added, without heeding Cass's look of astonishment, "I'll wait here till you come back."

"But you see, Miss, it wouldn't seem right—" began Cass.

"But I found him first," interrupted the girl, with a pout.

Staggered by this preëmptive right, sacred to all miners, Cass stopped.

"Who is the coroner?" she asked.

"Joe Hornsby."

"The tall, lame man, who was half eaten by a grizzly?"

"Yes."

"Well, look now! I'll ride on and bring him back in half an hour. There!"

"But, Miss—!"

"Oh, don't mind *me*. I never saw anything of this kind before, and I want to see it *all*."

"Do you know Hornsby?" asked Cass, unconsciously a trifle irritated.

"No, but I'll bring him." She wheeled her horse into the road.

In the presence of this living energy Cass quite forgot the helpless dead. "Have you been long in these parts, Miss?" he asked.

"About two weeks," she answered,

shortly. "Good-by, just now. Look around for the pistol or anything else you can find, although *I* have been over the whole ground twice already."

A little puff of dust as the horse sprang into the road, a muffled shuffle, struggle, then the regular beat of hoofs, and she was gone.

After five minutes had passed, Cass regretted that he had not accompanied her; waiting in such a spot was an irksome task. Not that there was anything in the scene itself to awaken gloomy imaginings; the bright, truthful Californian sunshine scoffed at any illusion of creeping shadows or waving branches. Once, in the rising wind, the empty hat rolled over—but only in a ludicrous, drunken way. A search for any further sign or token had proved futile, and Cass grew impatient. He began to hate himself for having stayed; he would have fled but for shame. Nor was his good humor restored when at the close of a weary half hour two galloping figures emerged from the dusty horizon—Hornsby and the young girl.

His vague annoyance increased as he fancied that both seemed to ignore him, the coroner barely acknowledging his presence with a nod. Assisted by the young girl, whose energy and enthusiasm evidently delighted him, Hornsby raised the body for a more careful examination. The dead man's pockets were carefully searched. A few coins, a silver pencil, knife, and tobacco-box were all they found. It gave no clew to his identity. Suddenly the young girl, who had, with unabashed curiosity, knelt beside the exploring official hands of the Red Chief, uttered a cry of gratification.

"Here's something! It dropped from the bosom of his shirt on the ground. Look!"

She was holding in the air, between her thumb and forefinger, a folded bit of well-worn newspaper. Her eyes sparkled.

"Shall I open it?" she asked.

"Yes."

"It's a little ring" she said; "looks like an engagement ring. Something is written on it. Look! 'May to Cass.'"

Cass darted forward. "It's mine," he stammered, "mine! I dropped it. It's nothing—nothing," he went on, after a pause, embarrassed and blushing, as the

girl and her companion both stared at him
—"a mere trifle. I'll take it."

But the coroner opposed his outstretched
hand. "Not much," he said, significantly.

"But it's *mine*," continued Cass, indignation taking the place of shame at his discovered secret. "I found it six months ago in the road. I—picked it up."

"With your name already written on it!
How handy!" said the coroner, grimly.

"It's an old story" said Cass, blushing
again under the half-mischievous, half-searching eyes of the girl. "All Blazing
Star knows I found it."

"Then ye'll have no difficulty in provin'
it," said Hornsby, coolly. "Just now,
however, *we've* found it, and we propose
to keep it for the inquest."

Cass shrugged his shoulders. Further
altercation would have only heightened his
ludicrous situation in the girl's eyes. He
turned away, leaving his treasure in the
coroner's hands.

The inquest, a day or two later, was
prompt and final. No clew to the dead
man's identity; no evidence sufficiently
strong to prove murder or suicide; no trace
of any kind, inculpating any party, known

or unknown, were found. But much publicity and interest were given to the proceedings by the presence of the principal witness, a handsome girl. "To the pluck, persistency, and intellect of Miss Porter," said the "Red Chief Recorder," "Tuolumne County owes the recovery of the body."

No one who was present at the inquest failed to be charmed with the appearance and conduct of this beautiful young lady.

"Miss Porter has but lately arrived in this district, in which, it is hoped, she will become an honored resident, and continue to set an example to all lackadaisical and sentimental members of the so-called 'sterner sex.'" After this universally recognized allusion to Cass Beard, the "Recorder" returned to its record: "Some interest was excited by what appeared to be a clew to the mystery in the discovery of a small gold engagement ring on the body. Evidence was afterward offered to show it was the property of a Mr. Cass Beard of Blazing Star, who appeared upon the scene *after* the discovery of the corpse by Miss Porter. He alleged he had dropped it in lifting the unfortunate remains of the deceased. Much amusement was created in court by the sentimental confusion of the claimant, and a certain partisan spirit shown by his fellow-miners of Blazing Star. It appearing, however, by the admission of this sighing Strephon of the Foot Hills, that he had himself *found* this pledge of affection lying in the highway six months previous, the coroner wisely placed it in the safe-keeping of the county court until the appearance of the rightful owner."

Thus on the 13th of September, 186—, the treasure found at Blazing Star passed out of the hands of its finder.

. . . .

Autumn brought an abrupt explanation of the mystery. Kanaka Joe had been arrested for horse stealing, but had with noble candor confessed to the finer offense of manslaughter. That swift and sure justice which overtook the horse stealer in these altitudes was stayed a moment and hesitated, for the victim was clearly the mysterious unknown. Curiosity got the better of an extempore judge and jury.

"It was a fair fight," said the accused, not without some human vanity, feeling that the camp hung upon his words, "and was settled by the man az was peartest and liveliest with his weapon. We had a sort of unpleasantness over at Lagrange the night afore, along of our both hevin' a monotony of four aces. We had a clinch and a stamp around, and when we was separated it was only a question of shootin' on sight. He left Lagrange at sun up the next morning, and I struck across a bit o' buckeye and underbrush and came upon him, accidental like, on the Red Chief Road. I drawed when I sighted him, and called out. He slipped from his mare and covered himself with her flanks, reaching for his holster, but she rared and backed down on him across the road and into the grass, where I got in another shot and fetched him."

"And you stole his mare?" suggested the Judge.

"I got away," said the gambler, simply.

Further questioning only elicited the fact that Joe did not know the name or condition of his victim. He was a stranger in Lagrange.

It was a breezy afternoon, with some turbulency in the camp, and much windy discussion over this unwonted delay of justice. The suggestion that Joe should be first hanged for horse stealing and then tried for murder was angrily discussed, but milder counsels were offered—that the fact of the killing should be admitted only as proof of the theft. A large party from Red Chief had come over to assist in judgment, among them the coroner.

Cass Beard had avoided these proceedings, which only recalled an unpleasant experience, and was wandering with pick, pan, and wallet far from the camp. These accoutrements, as I have before intimated, justified any form of aimless idleness under the equally aimless title of "prospecting." He had at the end of three hours' relaxation reached the highway to Red Chief, half hidden by blinding clouds of dust torn from the crumbling red road at every gust which swept down the mountain side. The spot had a familiar aspect to Cass, although some freshly-dug holes near the wayside, with scattered earth beside them, showed the presence of a recent prospector. He was struggling with his memory, when the dust was suddenly dispersed and he found himself again at the scene of the murder. He started: he had not put foot on the road since the inquest. There lacked only the helpless dead man and the contrasting figure of the alert young woman to restore the picture. The body was gone, it was true, but as he turned he beheld Miss Porter, at a few paces distant, sitting her horse as energetic and observant as on the first morning they had met. A superstitious thrill passed over him and awoke his old antagonism.

She nodded to him slightly. "I came here to refresh my memory," she said, "as Mr. Hornsby thought I might be asked to give my evidence again at Blazing Star."

Cass carelessly struck an aimless blow with his pick against the sod and did not reply.

"And you?" she queried.

"*I* stumbled upon the place just now while prospecting, or I shouldn't be here."

"Then it was *you* made these holes?"

"No," said Cass, with ill-concealed disgust. "Nobody but a stranger would go foolin' round such a spot."

He stopped, as the rude significance of his speech struck him, and added surlily, "I mean—no one would dig here."

The girl laughed and showed a set of very white teeth in her square jaw. Cass averted his face.

"Do you mean to say that every miner doesn't know that it's lucky to dig wherever human blood has been spilt?"

Cass felt a return of his superstition, but he did not look up. "I never heard it before," he said, severely.

"And you call yourself a California miner?"

"I do."

It was impossible for Miss Porter to misunderstand his curt speech and unsocial manner. She stared at him and colored slightly. Lifting her reins lightly, she said: "You certainly do not seem like most of the miners I have met."

"Nor you like any girl from the East I ever met," he responded.

"What do you mean?" she asked, checking her horse.

"What I say," he answered, doggedly. Reasonable as this reply was, it immediately struck him that it was scarcely dignified or manly. But before he could explain himself Miss Porter was gone.

He met her again that very evening.

The trial had been summarily suspended by the appearance of the Sheriff of Calaveras and his *posse,* who took Joe from that self-constituted tribunal of Blazing Star and set his face southward and toward authoritative although more cautious justice. But not before the evidence of the previous inquest had been read, and the incident of the ring again delivered to the public.

It is said the prisoner burst into an incredulous laugh and asked to see this mysterious waif. It was handed to him. Standing in the very shadow of the gallows tree—which might have been one of the pines that sheltered the billiard room in which the Vigilance Committee held their conclave—the prisoner gave way to a burst of merriment, so genuine and honest that the judge and jury joined in automatic sympathy. When silence was restored an explanation was asked by the Judge. But there was no response from the prisoner except a subdued chuckle.

"Did this ring belong to you?" asked the Judge, severely, the jury and spectators craning their ears forward with an expectant smile already on their faces. But the prisoner's eyes only sparkled maliciously as he looked around the court.

"Tell us, Joe," said a sympathetic and laughter-loving juror, under his breath. "Let it out and we'll make it easy for you."

"Prisoner," said the Judge, with a return of official dignity, "remember that your life is in peril. Do you refuse?"

Joe lazily laid his arm on the back of his chair with (to quote the words of an animated observer) "the air of having a Christian hope and a sequence flush in his hand," and said: "Well, as I reckon I'm not up yer for stealin' a ring that another man lets on to have found, and as fur as I kin see, hez nothin' to do with the case, I do!" And as it was here that the Sheriff of Calaveras made a precipitate entry into the room, the mystery remained unsolved.

The effect of this freshly-important ridicule on the sensitive mind of Cass might have been foretold by Blazing Star had it ever taken that sensitiveness into consideration. He had lost the good humor and easy pliability which had tempted him to frankness, and he had gradually become bitter and hard. He had at first affected amusement over his own vanished day dream—hiding his virgin disappointment in his own breast; but when he began to turn upon his feelings he turned upon his comrades also. Cass was for a while unpopular. There is no ingratitude so revolting to the human mind as that of the butt who refuses to be one any longer. The man who rejects that immunity which laughter generally casts upon him and demands to be seriously considered deserves no mercy.

It was under these hard conditions that Cass Beard, convicted of overt sentimentalism, aggravated by inconsistency, stepped into the Red Chief coach that evening. It was his habit usually to ride with the driver, but the presence of Hornsby and Miss Porter on the box seat changed his intention. Yet he had the satisfaction of seeing that neither had noticed him, and as there was no other passenger inside, he stretched himself on the cushion of the back seat and gave way to moody reflections. He quite determined to leave Blazing Star, to settle himself seriously to the task of money getting, and to return to his comrades, some day, a sarcastic, cynical, successful man, and so overwhelm them with confusion. For poor Cass had not yet reached that superiority of knowing that success would depend upon his ability to forego his past. Indeed, part of his boyhood had been cast among these men, and he was not old enough to have learned that success was not to be gauged by their standard. The moon lit up the dark interior of the coach with a faint poetic light. The lazy swinging of the vehicle that was bearing him away—albeit only for a night and a day— the solitude, the glimpses from the window of great distances full of vague possibilities, made the abused ring potent as that of Gyges. He dreamed with his eyes open. From an Alnaschar vision he suddenly awoke. The coach had stopped. The voices of men, one in entreaty, one in expostulation, came from the box. Cass mechanically put his hand to his pistol pocket.

"Thank you, but I *insist* upon getting down."

It was Miss Porter's voice. This was followed by a rapid, half-restrained interchange of words between Hornsby and the driver. Then the latter said, gruffly,—

"If the lady wants to ride inside, let her."

Miss Porter fluttered to the ground. She was followed by Hornsby. "Just a minit, Miss," he expostulated, half shamedly, half brusquely, "ye don't onderstand me. I only—"

But Miss Porter had jumped into the coach.

Hornsby placed his hand on the handle of the door. Miss Porter grasped it firmly from the inside. There was a slight struggle.

All of which was part of a dream to the boyish Cass. But he awoke from it—a man! "Do you," he asked, in a voice he scarcely recognized himself,—"Do you want this man inside?"

"No!"

Cass caught at Hornsby's wrist like a young tiger. But alas! what availed instinctive chivalry against main strength? He only succeeded in forcing the door open in spite of Miss Porter's superior strategy, and—I fear I must add, muscle also—and threw himself passionately at Hornsby's throat, where he hung on and calmly awaited dissolution. But he had, in the onset, driven Hornsby out into the road and the moonlight.

"Here! Somebody take my lines." The voice was "Mountain Charley's," the driver. The figure that jumped from the box and separated the struggling men belonged to this singularly direct person.

"You're riding inside?" said Charley, interrogatively, to Cass. Before he could reply Miss Porter's voice came from the window.

"He is!"

Charley promptly bundled Cass into the coach.

"And *you?*" to Hornsby, "onless you're kalkilatin' to take a little 'pasear' you're booked *outside*. Get up."

It is probable that Charley assisted Mr. Hornsby as promptly to his seat, for the next moment the coach was rolling on.

Meanwhile Cass, by reason of his forced entry, had been deposited in Miss Porter's lap, whence, freeing himself, he had attempted to climb over the middle seat, but in the starting of the coach was again thrown heavily against her hat and shoulder; all of which was inconsistent with the attitude of dignified reserve he had intended to display. Miss Porter, meanwhile, recovered her good humor.

"What a brute he was, ugh!" she said, retying the ribbons of her bonnet under her square chin, and smoothing out her linen duster.

Cass tried to look as if he had forgotten the whole affair. "Who? Oh, yes! I see!" he responded, absently.

"I suppose I ought to thank you," she went on with a smile, "but you know, really, I could have kept him out if you hadn't pulled his wrist from outside. I'll show you. Look! Put your hand on the handle there! Now, I'll hold the lock inside firmly. You see, you can't turn the catch!"

She indeed held the lock fast. It was a firm hand, yet soft—their fingers had touched over the handle—and looked white in the moonlight. He made no reply, but sank back again in his seat with a singular sensation in the fingers that had touched hers. He was in the shadow, and, without being seen, could abandon his reserve and glance at her face. It struck him that he had never really seen her before. She was not so tall as she had appeared to be. Her eyes were not large, but her pupils were black, moist, velvety, and so convex as to seem embossed on the white. She had an indistinctive nose, a rather colorless face—whiter at the angles of the mouth and nose through the relief of tiny freckles like grains of pepper. Her mouth was straight, dark, red, but moist as her eyes. She had drawn herself into the corner of the back seat, her wrist put through and hanging over the swinging strap, the easy lines of her plump figure swaying from side to side with the motion of the coach. Finally, forgetful of any presence in the dark corner opposite, she threw her head a little farther back, slipped a trifle lower, and placing two well-booted feet upon the middle seat, completed a charming and wholesome picture.

Five minutes elapsed. She was looking straight at the moon. Cass Beard felt his dignified reserve becoming very much like awkwardness. He ought to be coldly polite.

"I hope you're not flustered, Miss, by the—by the—" he began.

"I?" She straightened herself up in the seat, cast a curious glance into the dark corner, and then, letting herself down again, said: "Oh, dear, no!"

Another five minutes elapsed. She had evidently forgotten him. She might, at least, have been civil. He took refuge again in his reserve. But it was now mixed with a certain pique.

Yet how much softer her face looked in the moonlight! Even her square jaw had lost that hard, matter-of-fact, practical indication which was so distasteful to him, and always had suggested a harsh criticism of his weakness. How moist her eyes were—actually shining in the light! How that light seemed to concentrate in the corner of the lashes, and then slipped— a flash—away! Was she? Yes, she was crying.

Cass melted. He moved. Miss Porter put her head out of the window and drew it back in a moment, dry-eyed.

"One meets all sorts of folks traveling," said Cass, with what he wished to make appear a cheerful philosophy.

"I dare say. I don't know. I never before met any one who was rude to me. I have traveled all over the country alone, and with all kinds of people ever since I was so high. I have always gone my own way, without hindrance or trouble. I always do. I don't see why I shouldn't. Perhaps other people mayn't like it. I do. I like excitement. I like to see all that there is to see. Because I'm a girl I don't see why I cannot go out without a keeper, and why I cannot do what any man can do that isn't wrong, do you? Perhaps you do—perhaps you don't. Perhaps you like a girl to be always in the house dawdling or thumping a piano or reading novels. Perhaps you think I'm bold because I don't like it, and won't lie and say I do."

She spoke sharply and aggressively, and so evidently in answer to Cass's unspoken indictment against her, that he was not surprised when she became more direct.

"You know you were shocked when I went to fetch that Hornsby, the coroner, after we found the dead body."

"Hornsby wasn't shocked," said Cass, a little viciously.

"What do you mean?" she said, abruptly.

"You were good friends enough until—"

"Until he insulted me just now, is that it?"

"Until he thought," stammered Cass, "that because you were—you know—not so—so—so careful as other girls, he could be a little freer."

"And so, because I preferred to ride a mile with him to see something real that had happened, and tried to be useful instead of looking in shop windows in Main Street or promenading before the hotel—"

"And being ornamental," interrupted Cass. But this feeble and un-Cass-like attempt at playful gallantry met with a sudden check.

Miss Porter drew herself together, and looked out of the window. "Do you wish me to walk the rest of the way home?"

"No," said Cass, hurriedly, with a crimson face and a sense of gratuitous rudeness.

"Then stop that kind of talk, right there!"

There was an awkward silence. "I wish I was a man," she said, half bitterly, half earnestly. Cass Beard was not old and cynical enough to observe that this devout aspiration is usually uttered by those who have least reason to deplore their own femininity; and, but for the rebuff he had just received, would have made the usual emphatic dissent of our sex, when the wish is uttered by warm red lips and tender voices—a dissent, it may be remarked, generally withheld, however, when the masculine spinster dwells on the perfection of woman. I dare say Miss Porter was sincere, for a moment later she continued, poutingly:

"And yet I used to go to fires in Sacramento when I was only ten years old. I saw the theatre burnt down. Nobody found fault with me then."

Something made Cass ask if her father and mother objected to her boyish tastes. The reply was characteristic if not satisfactory,—

"Object? I'd like to see them do it."

The direction of the road had changed. The fickle moon now abandoned Miss Porter and sought out Cass on the front seat. It caressed the young fellow's silky moustache and long eyelashes, and took some of the sunburn from his cheek.

"What's the matter with your neck?" said the girl, suddenly.

Cass looked down, blushing to find that the collar of his smart "duck" sailor shirt was torn open. But something more than his white, soft, girlish skin was exposed; the shirt front was dyed quite red with blood from a slight cut on the shoulder. He remembered to have felt a scratch while struggling with Hornsby.

The girl's soft eyes sparkled. "Let *me*," she said, vivaciously. "Do! I'm good at wounds. Come over here. No— stay there. I'll come over to you."

She did, bestriding the back of the middle seat and dropping at his side. The magnetic fingers again touched his; he felt her warm breath on his neck as she bent toward him.

"It's nothing," he said, hastily, more agitated by the treatment than the wound.

"Give me your flask," she responded, without heeding. A stinging sensation as she bathed the edges of the cut with the spirit brought him back to common sense again. "There," she said, skillfully extemporizing a bandage from her handkerchief and a compress from his cravat. "Now, button your coat over your chest, so, and don't take cold." She insisted upon buttoning it for him; greater even than the feminine delight in a man's strength is the ministration to his weakness. Yet, when this was finished, she drew a little away from him in some embarrassment—an embarrassment she wondered at, as his skin was finer, his touch gentler, his clothes cleaner, and—not to put too fine a point upon it—he exhaled an atmosphere much sweeter than belonged to most of the men her boyish habits had brought her in contact with—not excepting her own father. Later she even exempted her mother from the possession of this divine effluence. After a moment she asked, suddenly, "What are you going to do with Hornsby?"

Cass had not thought of him. His short-lived rage was past with the occasion that provoked it. Without any fear of his adversary he would have been content and quite willing to meet him no more. He only said, "That will depend upon him."

"Oh, you won't hear from him again," said she, confidently, "but you really ought to get up a little more muscle. You've no more than a girl." She stopped, a little confused.

"What shall I do with your handkerchief?" asked the uneasy Cass, anxious to change the subject.

"Oh, keep it, if you want to, only don't show it to everybody as you did that ring you found." Seeing signs of distress in his face, she added: "Of course that was all nonsense. If you had cared so much for the ring you couldn't have talked about it, or shown it. Could you?"

It relieved him to think that this might be true; he certainly had not looked at it in that light before.

"But did you really find it?" she asked, with sudden gravity. "Really, now?"

"Yes."

"And there was no real May in the case?"

"Not that I know of," laughed Cass, secretly pleased.

But Miss Porter, after eying him critically for a moment jumped up and climbed back again to her seat. "Perhaps you had better give me that handkerchief back."

Cass began to unbutton his coat.

"No! no! Do you want to take your death of cold?" she screamed. And Cass, to avoid this direful possibility, rebuttoned his coat again over the handkerchief and a peculiarly pleasing sensation.

Very little now was said until the rattling, bounding descent of the coach denoted the approach to Red Chief. The straggling main street disclosed itself, light by light. In the flash of glittering windows and the sound of eager voices Miss Porter descended, without waiting for Cass's proffered assistance, and anticipated Mountain Charley's descent from the box. A few undistinguishable words passed between them.

"You kin freeze to me, Miss," said Charley; and Miss Porter, turning her frank laugh and frankly opened palm to Cass, half returned the pressure of his hand and slipped away.

A few days after the stage coach incident, Mountain Charley drew up beside Cass on the Blazing Star turnpike, and handed him a small packet. "I was told to give ye that by Miss Porter. Hush—listen! It's that rather old dog-goned ring o' yours that's bin in all the papers. She's bamboozled that sap-headed county judge, Boompointer, into givin' it to her. Take my advice and sling it away for some other feller to pick up and get looney over. That's all!"

"Did she say anything?" asked Cass, anxiously, as he received his lost treasure somewhat coldly.

"Well, yes! I reckon. She asked me to stand betwixt Hornsby and you. So don't *you* tackle him, and I'll see *he* don't tackle you," and with a portentous wink Mountain Charley whipped up his horses and was gone.

Cass opened the packet. It contained nothing but the ring. Unmitigated by any word of greeting, remembrance, or even raillery, it seemed almost an insult. Had she intended to flaunt his folly in his face, or had she believed he still mourned for it and deemed its recovery a sufficient reward for his slight service? For an instant he felt tempted to follow Charley's advice, and cast this symbol of folly and contempt in the dust of the mountain road.

And had she not made his humiliation complete by begging Charley's interference between him and his enemy? He would go home and send her back the handkerchief she had given him. But here the unromantic reflection that although he had washed it that very afternoon in the solitude of his own cabin, he could not possibly iron it, but must send it "rough dried," stayed his indignant feet.

Two or three days, a week, a fortnight even, of this hopeless resentment filled Cass's breast. Then the news of Kanaka Joe's acquittal in the State Court momentarily revived the story of the ring, and revamped a few stale jokes in the camp. But the interest soon flagged; the fortunes of the little community of Blazing Star had been for some months failing; and with early snows in the mountain and wasted capital in fruitless schemes on the river, there was little room for the indulgence of that lazy and original humor which belonged to their lost youth and prosperity. Blazing Star truly, in the grim figure of their slang, was "played out." Not dug out, worked out, or washed out, but dissipated in a year of speculation and chance.

Against this tide of fortune Cass struggled manfully, and even evoked the slow praise of his companions. Better still, he won a certain praise for himself, in himself, in a consciousness of increased strength, health, power, and self-reliance. He began to turn his quick imagination and perception to some practical account, and made one or two discoveries which quite startled his more experienced but more conservative companions. Nevertheless, Cass's discoveries and labors were not of a kind that produced immediate pecuniary realization, and Blazing Star, which consumed so many pounds of pork and flour daily, did not unfortunately produce the daily equivalent in gold. Blazing Star lost its credit. Blazing Star was hungry, dirty, and ragged. Blazing Star was beginning to set.

Participating in the general ill luck of the camp, Cass was not without his own individual mischances. He had resolutely determined to forget Miss Porter and all that tended to recall the unlucky ring, but, cruelly enough, she was the only thing that refused to be forgotten—whose undulating figure reclined opposite to him in the weird moonlight of his ruined cabin, whose voice mingled with the song of the river by whose banks he toiled, and whose eyes and touch thrilled him in his dreams. Partly for this reason, and partly because his clothes were beginning to be patched and torn, he avoided Red Chief and any place where he would be likely to meet her. In spite of this precaution he had once seen her driving in a pony carriage, but so smartly and fashionably dressed that he drew back in the cover of a wayside willow that she might pass without recognition. He looked down upon his red-splashed clothes and grimy, soil-streaked hands, and for a moment half hated her. His comrades seldom spoke of her—instinctively fearing some temptation that might beset his Spartan resolutions, but he heard from time to time that she had been seen at balls and parties, apparently enjoying those very frivolities of her sex she affected to condemn.

It was a Sabbath morning in early spring that he was returning from an ineffectual attempt to enlist a capitalist at the county town to redeem the fortunes of Blazing Star. He was pondering over the narrowness of that capitalist, who had evidently but illogically connected Cass's present appearance with the future of that struggling camp, when he became so footsore that he was obliged to accept a "lift" from a wayfaring teamster. As the slowly lumbering vehicle passed the new church on the outskirts of the town, the congregation were sallying forth. It was too late to jump down and run away, and Cass dared not ask his new-found friend to whip up his cattle. Conscious of his unshorn beard and ragged garments, he kept his eyes fixed upon the road. A voice that thrilled him called his name. It was Miss Porter, a resplendent vision of silk, laces, and Easter flowers—yet actually running, with something of her old dash and freedom, beside the wagon. As the astonished teamster drew up before this elegant apparition, she panted:—

"Why did you make me run so far, and why didn't you look up?"

Cass, trying to hide the patches on his knees beneath a newspaper, stammered that he had not seen her.

"And you did not hold down your head purposely?"

"No," said Cass.

"Why have you not been to Red Chief? Why didn't you answer my message about the ring?" she asked, swiftly.

"You sent nothing but the ring," said Cass, coloring, as he glanced at the teamster.

"Why, *that* was a message, you born idiot."

Cass stared. The teamster smiled. Miss Porter gazed anxiously at the wagon. "I think I'd like a ride in there; it looks awfully good." She glanced mischievously around at the lingering and curious congregation.

"May I?"

But Cass deprecated that proceeding strongly. It was dirty; he was not sure it was even *wholesome;* she would be *so* uncomfortable; he, himself, was only going a few rods farther, and in that time she might ruin her dress—

"Oh, yes," she said, a little bitterly, "certainly, my dress must be looked after. And—what else?"

"People might think it strange, and believe I had invited you," continued Cass, hesitatingly.

"When I had only invited myself? Thank you. Good-by."

She waved her hand and stepped back from the wagon. Cass would have given worlds to recall her, but he sat still, and the vehicle moved on in moody silence. At the first cross road he jumped down. "Thank you," he said to the teamster. "You're welcome," returned that gentleman, regarding him curiously, "but the next time a gal like that asks to ride in this yer wagon, I reckon I won't take the vote of any deadhead passenger. *Adios,* young fellow. Don't stay out late; ye might be run off by some gal, and what would your mother say?" Of course the young man could only look unutterable things and walk away, but even in that dignified action he was conscious that its effect was somewhat mitigated by a large patch from a material originally used as a flour sack, which had repaired his trousers, but still bore the ironical legend, "Best Superfine."

The summer brought warmth and promise and some blossom, if not absolute fruition, to Blazing Star. The long days drew Nature into closer communion with the men, and hopefulness followed the discontent of their winter seclusion. It was easier, too, for Capital to be wooed and won into making a picnic in these mountain solitudes than when high water stayed the fords and drifting snow the Sierran trails. At the close of one of these Arcadian days Cass was smoking before the door of his lonely cabin when he was astounded by the onset of a dozen of his companions. Peter Drummond, far in the van, was waving a newspaper like a victorious banner. "All's right now, Cass, old man!" he panted as he stopped before Cass and shoved back his eager followers.

"What's all right?" asked Cass, dubiously.

"*You!* You kin rake down the pile now. You're hunky! You're on velvet. Listen!"

He opened the newspaper and read, with annoying deliberation, as follows:—

"LOST.—If the finder of a plain gold ring, bearing the engraved inscription, 'May to Cass,' alleged to have been picked up on the high road near Blazing Star on the 4th March, 186—, will apply to Bookham & Sons, bankers, 1007 Y Street, Sacramento, he will be suitably rewarded either for the recovery of the ring, or for such facts as may identify it, or the locality where it was found."

Cass rose and frowned savagely on his comrades. "No! no!" cried a dozen voices, assuringly. "It's all right! Honest Injun! True as gospel! No joke, Cass!"

"Here's the paper, Sacramento 'Union' of yesterday. Look for yourself," said Drummond, handing him the well-worn journal. "And you see," he added, "how darned lucky you are. It ain't necessary for you to produce the ring, so if that old biled owl of a Boompointer don't giv' it back to ye, it's all the same."

"And they say nobody but the finder need apply," interrupted another. "That shuts out Boompointer or Kanaka Joe, for the matter o' that."

"It's clar that it *means* you, Cass, ez much ez if they'd given your name," added a third.

For Miss Porter's sake and his own Cass had never told them of the restora-

tion of the ring, and it was evident that
Mountain Charley had also kept silent.
Cass could not speak now without violating
a secret, and he was pleased that the ring
itself no longer played an important part
in the mystery. But what was that mystery, and why was the ring secondary to
himself? Why was so much stress laid
upon his finding it?

"You see," said Drummond, as if answering his unspoken thought, "that 'ar
gal—for it is a gal in course—hez read all
about it in the papers, and hez sort o'
took a shine to ye. It don't make a bit o'
difference who in thunder Cass *is* or *waz*,
for I reckon she's kicked him over by this
time—"

"Sarved him right, too, for losing the
girl's ring and then lying low and keeping dark about it," interrupted a sympathizer.

"And she's just weakened over the romantic, high-toned way you stuck to it,"
continued Drummond, forgetting the sarcasms he had previously hurled at this romance. Indeed, the whole camp, by this
time, had become convinced that it had
fostered and developed a chivalrous devo-

tion which was now on the point of pecuniary realization. It was generally accepted that "she" was the daughter of this banker, and also felt that in the circumstances the happy father could not do less than develop the resources of Blazing Star at once. Even if there were no relationship, what opportunity could be more fit for presenting to capital a locality that even produced engagement rings, and, as Jim Fauquier put it, "the men ez knew how to keep 'em." It was this sympathetic Virginian who took Cass aside with the following generous suggestion: "If you find that you and the old gal couldn't hitch hosses, owin' to your not likin' red hair or a game leg" (it may be here recorded that Blazing Star had, for no reason whatever, attributed these unprepossessing qualities to the mysterious advertiser), "you might let *me* in. You might say ez how I used to jest worship that ring with you, and allers wanted to borrow it on Sundays. If anything comes of it— why—*we're pardners!*"

A serious question was the outfitting of Cass for what now was felt to be a diplomatic representation of the community.

His garments, it hardly need be said, were inappropriate to any wooing except that of the "maiden all forlorn," which the advertiser clearly was not. "He might," suggested Fauquier, "drop in jest as he is—kinder as if he'd got keerless of the world, being lovesick." But Cass objected strongly, and was borne out in his objection by his younger comrades. At last a pair of white duck trousers, a red shirt, a flowing black silk scarf, and a Panama hat were procured at Red Chief, on credit, after a judicious exhibition of the advertisement. A heavy wedding ring, the property of Drummond (who was not married), was also lent as a graceful suggestion, and at the last moment Fauquier affixed to Cass's scarf an enormous specimen pin of gold and quartz. "It sorter indicates the auriferous wealth o' this yer region, and the old man (the senior member of Bookham & Sons) needn't know I won it at draw poker in Frisco," said Fauquier.

"Ef you 'pass' on the gal, you kin hand it back to me and *I'll* try it on." Forty dollars for expenses was put into Cass's hands, and the entire community accompanied him to the cross roads where he was to meet the Sacramento coach, which eventually carried him away, followed by a benediction of waving hats and exploding revolvers.

That Cass did not participate in the extravagant hopes of his comrades, and that he rejected utterly their matrimonial speculations in his behalf, need not be said. Outwardly, he kept his own counsel with good-humored assent. But there was something fascinating in the situation, and while he felt he had forever abandoned his romantic dream, he was not displeased to know that it might have proved a reality. Nor was it distasteful to him to think that Miss Porter would hear of it and regret her late inability to appreciate his sentiment. If he really were the object of some opulent maiden's passion, he would show Miss Porter how he could sacrifice the most brilliant prospects for her sake. Alone, on the top of the coach, he projected one of those satisfying conversations in which imaginative people delight, but which unfortunately never come quite up to rehearsal. "Dear Miss Porter," he would say, addressing the back of the driver, "if I could remain faithful to a dream of my youth, however illusive and unreal, can you believe that for the sake of lucre I could be false to the one real passion that alone supplanted it." In the composition and delivery of this eloquent statement an hour was happily forgotten: the only drawback to its complete effect was that a misplace of epithets in rapid repetition did not seem to make the slightest difference, and Cass found himself saying "Dear Miss Porter, if I could be false to a dream of my youth, etc., etc., can you believe I could be *faithful* to the one real passion, etc., etc.," with equal and perfect satisfaction. As Miss Porter was reputed to be well off, if the unknown were poor, that might be another drawback.

The banking house of Bookham & Sons did not present an illusive nor mysterious appearance. It was eminently practical and matter of fact; it was obtrusively open and glassy; nobody would have thought of leaving a secret there that would have been inevitably circulated over the counter. Cass felt an uncomfortable sense of incongruity in himself, in his story, in his treasure, to this temple of disenchanting realism. With the awkwardness of an embarrassed man he was holding prominently in his hand an envelope containing the ring and advertisement as a voucher for his intrusion, when the nearest clerk took the envelope from his hand, opened it, took out the ring, returned it, said briskly, "T' other shop, next door, young man," and turned to another customer.

Cass stepped to the door, saw that "T'other shop" was a pawnbroker's, and returned again with a flashing eye and heightened color. "It's an advertisement I have come to answer," he began again.

The clerk cast a glance at Cass's scarf and pin. "Place taken yesterday—no room for any more," he said, abruptly.

Cass grew quite white. But his old experience in Blazing Star repartee stood him in good stead. "If it's *your* place you mean," he said coolly, "I reckon you might put a dozen men in the hole you're rattlin' round in—but it's this advertisement I'm after. If Bookham isn't in, maybe you'll send me one of the grown-up sons." The production of the advertisement and some laughter from the bystanders had its effect. The pert young clerk retired, and returned to lead the way to the bank parlor. Cass's heart sank again as he was confronted by a dark, iron-gray man—in dress, features, speech, and action—uncompromisingly opposed to Cass—his ring and his romance. When the young man had told his story and produced his treasure he paused. The banker scarcely glanced at it, but said, impatiently,—

"Well, your papers?"

"My papers?"

"Yes. Proof of your identity. You say your name is Cass Beard. Good! What have you got to prove it? How can I tell who you are?"

To a sensitive man there is no form of suspicion that is as bewildering and demoralizing at the moment as the question of his identity. Cass felt the insult in the doubt of his word, and the palpable sense of his present inability to prove it. The banker watched him keenly but not unkindly.

"Come," he said at length, "this is not my affair; if you can legally satisfy the lady for whom I am only agent, well and good. I believe you can; I only warn you that you must. And my present inquiry was to keep her from losing her time with impostors, a class I don't think you belong to. There's her card. Good day."

"Miss Mortimer." It was *not* the banker's daughter. The first illusion of Blazing Star was rudely dispelled. But the care taken by the capitalist to shield her from imposture indicated a person of wealth. Of her youth and beauty Cass no longer thought.

The address given was not distant. With a beating heart he rung the bell of a respectable-looking house, and was ushered into a private drawing-room. Instinctively he felt that the room was only temporarily inhabited; an air peculiar to the best lodgings, and when the door opened upon a tall lady in deep mourning, he was still more convinced of an incongruity between the occupant and her surroundings. With a smile that vacillated between a habit of familiarity and ease, and a recent restraint, she motioned him to a chair.

"Miss Mortimer" was still young, still handsome, still fashionably dressed, and still attractive. From her first greeting to the end of the interview Cass felt that she knew all about him. This relieved him from the onus of proving his identity, but seemed to put him vaguely at a disadvantage. It increased his sense of inexperience and youthfulness.

"I hope you will believe," she began, "that the few questions I have to ask you are to satisfy my own heart, and for no other purpose." She smiled sadly as she went on. "Had it been otherwise, I should have instituted a legal inquiry, and left this interview to some one cooler, calmer, and less interested than myself. But I think, I *know* I can trust you. Perhaps we women are weak and foolish to talk of an *instinct,* and when you know my story you may have reason to believe that but little dependence can be placed on *that;* but I am not wrong in saying,—am I?" (with a sad smile) "that *you* are not above that weakness?" She paused, closed her lips tightly, and grasped her hands before her. "You say you found that ring in the road some three months before—the —the—you know what I mean—the body —was discovered?"

"Yes."

"You thought it might have been dropped by some one in passing?"

"I thought so, yes—it belonged to no one in camp."

"Before your cabin or on the highway?"

"Before my cabin."

"You are *sure?*" There was something so very sweet and sad in her smile that it oddly made Cass color.

"But my cabin is near the road," he suggested.

"I see! And there was nothing else; no paper nor envelope?"

"Nothing."

"And you kept it because of the odd resemblance one of the names bore to yours?"

"Yes."

"For no other reason?"

"None." Yet Cass felt he was blushing.

"You'll forgive my repeating a question you have already answered, but I am *so* anxious. There was some attempt to prove at the inquest that the ring had been found on the body of—the unfortunate man. But you tell me it was not so?"

"I can swear it."

"Good God—the traitor!" She took a hurried step forward, turned to the window, and then came back to Cass with a voice broken with emotion. "I have told you I could trust you. That ring was mine!"

She stopped, and then went on hurriedly. "Years ago I gave it to a man who deceived and wronged me; a man whose life since then has been a shame and disgrace to all who knew him. A man who, once, a gentleman, sank so low as to become the associate of thieves and ruffians; sank so low, that when he died, by violence—a traitor even to them—his own confederates shrunk from him, and left him to fill a nameless grave. That man's body you found!"

Cass started. "And his name was— ?"

"Part of your surname. Cass—Henry Cass."

"You see why Providence seems to have brought that ring to you," she went on. "But you ask me why, knowing this, I am so eager to know if the ring was found by you in the road, or if it were found on his body. Listen! It is part of my mortification that the story goes that this man once showed this ring, boasted of it, staked, and lost it at a gambling table to one of his vile comrades."

"Kanaka Joe," said Cass, overcome by a vivid recollection of Joe's merriment at the trial.

"The same. Don't you see," she said, hurriedly, "if the ring had been found on him I could believe that somewhere in his heart he still kept respect for the woman he had wronged. I am a woman—a foolish woman, I know—but you have crushed that hope forever."

"But why have you sent for me?" asked Cass, touched by her emotion.

"To know it for certain," she said, almost fiercely. "Can you not understand that a woman like me must know a thing once and forever? But you *can* help me. I did not send for you only to pour my wrongs in your ears. You must take me with you to this place—to the spot where you found the ring—to the spot where you found the body—to the spot where—where *he* lies. You must do it secretly, that none shall know me."

Cass hesitated. He was thinking of his companions and the collapse of their painted bubble. How could he keep the secret from them?

"If it is money you need, let not that

stop you. I have no right to your time without recompense. Do not misunderstand me. There has been a thousand dollars awaiting my order at Bookham's when the ring should be delivered. It shall be doubled if you help me in this last moment."

It was possible. He could convey her secretly there, invent some story of a reward delayed for want of proofs, and afterward share that reward with his friends. He answered promptly, "I will take you there."

She took his hands in both of hers, raised them to her lips, and smiled. The shadow of grief and restraint seemed to have fallen from her face, and a half-mischievous, half-coquettish gleam in her dark eyes touched the susceptible Cass in so subtle a fashion that he regained the street in some confusion. He wondered what Miss Porter would have thought. But was he not returning to her, a fortunate man, with one thousand dollars in his pocket! Why should he remember he was handicapped, by a pretty woman and a pathetic episode? It did not make the proximity less pleasant as he helped her into the coach that evening, nor did the recollection of another ride with another woman obtrude itself upon those consolations which he felt it his duty, from time to time, to offer. It was arranged that he should leave her at the "Red Chief" Hotel, while he continued on to Blazing Star, returning at noon to bring her with him when he could do it without exposing her to recognition. The gray dawn came soon enough, and the coach drew up at "Red Chief" while the lights in the bar-room and dining-room of the hotel were still struggling with the far flushing east. Cass alighted, placed Miss Mortimer in the hands of the landlady, and returned to the vehicle. It was still musty, close, and frowzy, with half-awakened passengers. There was a vacated seat on the top, which Cass climbed up to, and abstractedly threw himself beside a figure muffled in shawls and rugs. There was a slight movement among the multitudinous enwrappings, and then the figure turned to him and said, dryly, "Good morning!" It was Miss Porter!

"Have you been long here?" he stammered.

"All night."

He would have given worlds to leave her at that moment. He would have jumped from the starting coach to save himself any explanation of the embarrassment he was furiously conscious of showing, without, as he believed, any adequate cause. And yet, like all inexperienced, sensitive men, he dashed blindly into that explanation; worse, he even told his secret at once, then and there, and then sat abashed and conscience stricken, with an added sense of its utter futility.

"And this," summed up the young girl, with a slight shrug of her pretty shoulders, "is *your May?*"

Cass would have recommenced his story.

"No, don't, pray! It isn't interesting, nor original. Do *you* believe it?"

"I do," said Cass, indignantly.

"How lucky! Then let me go to sleep."

Cass, still furious, but uneasy, did not again address her. When the coach stopped at Blazing Star she asked him, indifferently: "When does this sentimental pilgrimage begin?"

"I return for her at one o'clock," replied Cass, stiffly.

He kept his word. He appeased his

eager companions with a promise of future fortune, and exhibited the present and tangible reward. By a circuitous route known only to himself, he led Miss Mortimer to the road before the cabin. There was a pink flush of excitement on her somewhat faded cheek.

"And it was here?" she asked, eagerly.

"I found it here."

"And the body?"

"That was afterward. Over in that direction, beyond the clump of buckeyes, on the Red Chief turnpike."

"And any one coming from the road we left just now and going to—to—that place, would have to cross just here? Tell me," she said, with a strange laugh, laying her cold nervous hand on his, "wouldn't they?"

"They would."

"Let us go to that place."

Cass stepped out briskly to avoid observation and gain the woods beyond the highway. "You have crossed here before," she said. "There seems to be a trail."

"I may have made it: it's a short cut to the buckeyes."

"You never found anything else on the trail?"

"You remember, I told you before, the ring was all I found."

"Ah, true!" she smiled sweetly; "it was *that* which made it seem so odd to you. I forgot."

In half an hour they reached the buckeyes. During the walk she had taken rapid recognizance of everything in her path. When they crossed the road and Cass had pointed out the scene of the murder, she looked anxiously around. "You are sure we are not seen?"

"Quite."

"You will not think me foolish if I ask you to wait here while I go in there"—she pointed to the ominous thicket near them—"alone?"

She was quite white.

Cass's heart, which had grown somewhat cold since his interview with Miss Porter, melted at once.

"Go; I will stay here."

He waited five minutes. She did not return.

What if the poor creature had determined upon suicide on the spot where

her faithless lover had fallen? He was
reassured in another moment by the rustle
of skirts in the undergrowth.

"I was becoming quite alarmed," he
said, aloud.

"You have reason to be," returned a hurried voice. He started. It was Miss Porter, who stepped swiftly out of the cover.
"Look," she said, "look at that man down
the road. He has been tracking you two
ever since you left the cabin. Do you
know who he is?"

"No!"

"Then listen. It is three-fingered
Dick, one of the escaped road agents. I
know him!"

"Let us go and warn her," said Cass,
eagerly.

Miss Porter laid her hand upon his
shoulder.

"I don't think she'll thank you," she
said, dryly. "Perhaps you'd better see
what she's doing, first."

Utterly bewildered, yet with a strong
sense of the masterfulness of his companion, he followed her. She crept like a cat
through the thicket. Suddenly she paused.
"Look!" she whispered, viciously, "look at

the tender vigils of your heart-broken May!"

Cass saw the woman who had left him a moment before on her knees on the grass, with long thin fingers digging like a ghoul in the earth. He had scarce time to notice her eager face and eyes, cast now and then back toward the spot where she had left him, before there was a crash in the bushes, and a man,—the stranger of the road, — leaped to her side. "Run," he said; "run for it now. You're watched!"

"Oh! that man, Beard!" she said, contemptuously.

"No, another in a wagon. Quick. Fool, you know the place now,—you can come later; run!" And half-dragging, half-lifting her, he bore her through the bushes. Scarcely had they closed behind the pair than Miss Porter ran to the spot vacated by the woman. "Look!" she cried, triumphantly, "look!"

Cass looked, and sank on his knees beside her.

"It *was* worth a thousand dollars, wasn't it?" she repeated, maliciously, "wasn't it? But you ought to return it! *Really* you ought."

Cass could scarcely articulate. "But how did *you* know it?" he finally gasped.

"Oh, I suspected something; there was a woman, and you know you're *such* a fool!"

Cass rose, stiffly.

"Don't be a greater fool now, but go and bring my horse and wagon from the hill, and don't say anything to the driver."

"Then you did not come alone?"

"No; it would have been bold and improper."

"Please!"

"And to think it *was* the ring, after all, that pointed to this," she said.

"The ring that *you* returned to me."

"What did you say?"

"Nothing."

"Don't, please, the wagon is coming."

. . . .

In the next morning's edition of the "Red Chief Chronicle" appeared the following startling intelligence:—

EXTRAORDINARY DISCOVERY

FINDING OF THE STOLEN TREASURE OF WELLS, FARGO & CO. OVER $300,000 RECOVERED

Our readers will remember the notorious robbery of Wells, Fargo & Co.'s treasure from the Sacramento and Red Chief Pioneer Coach on the night of September 1. Although most of the gang were arrested, it is known that two escaped, who, it was presumed, *cached* the treasure, amounting to nearly $500,000 in gold, drafts, and jewelry, as no trace of the property was found. Yesterday our esteemed fellow citizen, Mr. Cass Beard, long and favorably known in this county, succeeded in exhuming the treasure in a copse of hazel near the Red Chief turnpike,—adjacent to the spot where an unknown body was lately discovered. This body is now strongly suspected to be that of one Henry Cass, a disreputable character, who has since been ascertained to have been one of the road agents who escaped. The matter is now under legal investigation. The successful result of the search is due to a systematic plan evolved from the genius of Mr. Beard, who has devoted over a year to this labor. It was first suggested to him by the finding of a ring, now definitely identified as part of the treasure which was supposed to have been dropped from Wells, Fargo & Co's boxes by the robbers in their midnight flight through Blazing Star.

In the same journal appeared the no less important intelligence, which explains, while it completes this veracious chronicle:—

"It is rumored that a marriage is shortly to take place between the hero of the late treasure discovery and a young lady of Red Chief, whose devoted aid and assistance to this important work is well known to this community."